RAVAGE MC #1

RAVAGE
me

WALL STREET JOURNAL & USA TODAY BESTSELLING AUTHOR

RYAN MICHELE

Fourth Edition Published: October 13, 2019
ISBN-13: 978-1-951708-00-9
ISBN-10: 1-951708-00-8
ASIN: B00I9EG472

Previous Edition Information:
First Edition Published: February 4, 2013
Second Edition Published: February 14, 2014
Third Edition Published: November 17, 2017
ISBN-10: 149484172X
ISBN-13: 978-1494841720
ASIN: B00I9EG472

CONTENTS

RAVAGE MC FAMILY TREE

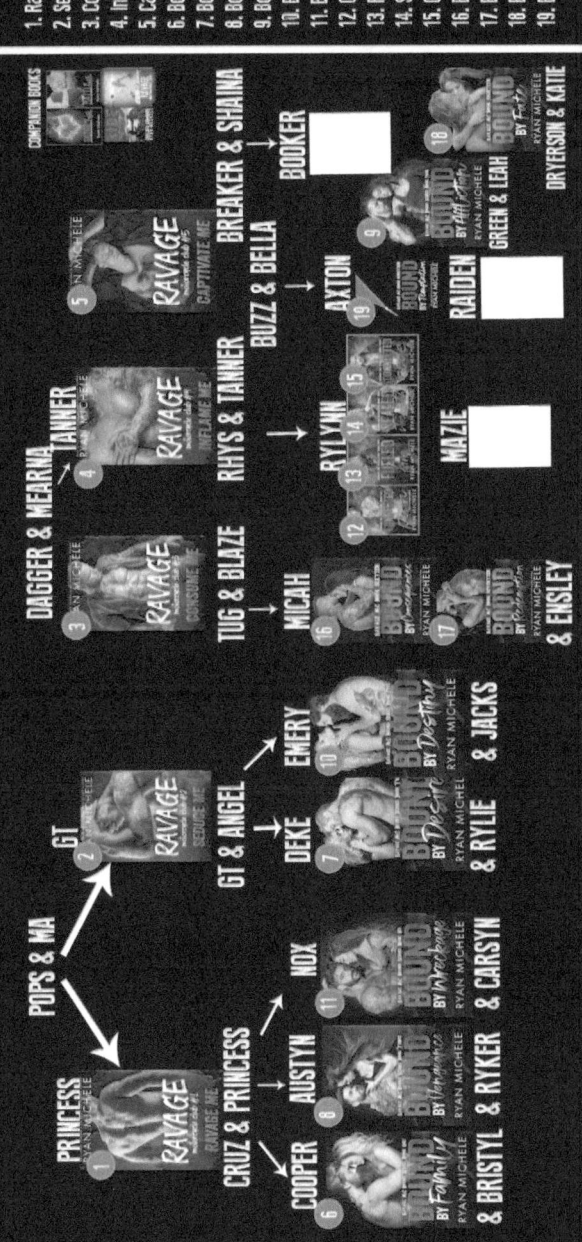

1. Ravage Me
2. Seduce Me
3. Consume Me
4. Inflame Me
5. Captivate Me
6. Bound by Family
7. Bound by Desire
8. Bound by Vengeance
9. Bound by Affliction
10. Bound by Destiny
11. Bound by Wreckage
12. Connected in Pain
13. Fueled in Fire
14. Sealed in Strength
15. Connected in Code
16. Bound by Consequences
17. Bound by Redemption
18. Bound by Fate
19. Bound by Temptation

POPS & MIA

PRINCESS — 1

GT — 2

DAGGER & MEARNA
TANNER — 4

TANNER — 3 (Ravage: Consume Me)

BREAKER & SHAINA
BOOKER — 18

BUZZ & BELLA
AXTON — 19

CRUZ & PRINCESS

GT & ANGEL
DEKE — 7
EMERY — 10

TUG & BLAZE
MICAH — 16, 17 & ENSLEY

RHYS & TANNER
RYLYNN — 12, 13, 14, 15

MAZIE

GREEN & LEAH
RAIDEN — 9

DRYERSON & KATIE

COOPER — 6 & BRISTYL
AUSTYN — 8 & RYKER
NOX — 11 & CARSYN

& RYLIE & JACKS

BLURB

Revenge always comes at a price—

Harlow aka **Princess** spent the last two years **locked up for a crime she didn't commit.**

Revenge has consumed her thoughts vowing payback for those who put her behind bars. Now, she's out, going home to her family—the Ravage MC. **Retribution** is coming.

Former **Marine, Cruz** knows what it means to lose it all. What this **single dad** found in the **Ravage Motorcycle Club** is a home, a **family** for him and his son.

He **protects** them at all costs.

When these two **head strong** people meet in the club's garage, he's caught off guard. She's there on a **mission**.

Anger and **challenge combust** around them, the push and pull only **igniting the flames brighter, hotter.**

Princess **refuses** to give into the lust.

Cruz **demands** to have her.

Each **not giving** in to the other. There is **no stopping** a **motorcycle man** when he knows what he wants. Not even a **strong, independent self-assured woman** can stop him.

Danger threatens everything they stand for, **ripping through** what they've each built with the **Ravage MC.** **Tables are turned** and the person who framed Princess is out for **blood.** Not just hers, but those **Princess cares about.**

Innocent lives are at stake. One **wrong move** from either of them means **death** in the **Ravage MC family.** One they will **never** come back from.

It could cost them everything.

Come and join the ride with the Ravage MC!

To my mom—Thank you.

PROLOGUE
Harlow

THIS WAS THE LIFE I WAS BORN INTO, AND BLOODSHED somehow always played a prominent part in it. Today, everything was coming to a combustible head. With the gun being held at my temple, all I could think about was *him*... getting him out of here alive. The bitch had put so much time and energy into coming after me, I knew it was coming. Now she had the most precious thing in my life. I never knew how empty my life was or how love could be so deep that it cuts you like a knife. I would do anything to get him out of here alive. The gunshots began, and my eyes locked with his. I prayed for survival.

CHAPTER ONE
Harlow

2 YEARS... I MONTH... 5 DAYS...

I had been living the perpetual monotony of my life for exactly two years, one month, and five days. It's like my life was the epitome of Groundhog's Day, repeating over and over again, eating away at my soul.

I hated white. I couldn't stand the fucking color. Everywhere I looked was the same cold, damp, sterility trying to suffocate me, forcing me to give up—to give in. But that wasn't gonna happen.

For seven hundred and sixty five days of my life, I've stared at the solid block walls and cold prison bars, only to be let outside for an hour a day. I knew it was for my own safety, but I missed lying outside in the sun, feeling it melt my skin, and wash everything away. In here, there was no relaxation... ever.

I'm not gonna bitch. I've been extremely lucky, and I

damn well knew it. Without my Pops' connections to guards and powerful people on the outside, life in this place could have been a hell of a lot worse. Having my own room has proved to be the best gig because, in there, those bitches couldn't get to me. They wanted me. I knew it. They all knew who I was and what I represented. Payback hits on me would give them status in their families and I wasn't willing to give anyone that.

Am I hiding? Hell no. I'd be more than happy to take these bitches on, but not here. The shit these women snuck in when no one was looking was deadly, and my goal was to do my time and get out alive. I knew what these bitches were capable of, and they knew my capabilities, too.

I've had my own incidents in here. They were all club related, and getting help from inside made them happen smoothly. It was help that I had to pay for, but I did what needed to be done and didn't regret a damn thing. I did it for my family.

I may have a pussy, but I ain't one. I've got bigger balls than most guys out there. Even though I'll never be a member of the club, because it's not possible, I always hold my head up high. I learned at a very young age that bitches didn't ever get patched in, and I accepted that, but I'd be damned if I acted like some pussy motorcycle club princess.

Growing up with the Ravage MC's hasn't been easy. The life, the world, was different than civilian life and I learned from the best. Ever since I was a baby, my life was the club. Pops has been a patched member since before I was born, and Ma's always been by his side. Even though

I was shielded as much as possible, I've seen my share of death, guns, drugs, sex, and blood in my twenty-five years than most people could tolerate. This was my normal. This was my reality. I accepted that a long time ago.

I missed my life, and I've always known my place in it. Being the Vice President's daughter hasn't given me any idealizations that I'm anything more than exactly that. I never get special privileges because, the bottom line, I'm not, nor will I ever be, a patched member. I've earned the respect I received from the brothers by learning what they have taken the time to teach me. I thrived on that and couldn't wait to get it back.

I was ready to escape this hell-hole and finally go back to my family. Back to a life that was taken away from me for two years, back to right some wrongs. I couldn't fucking wait.

WALKING DOWN THE LONG CORRIDOR, the sunlight cascaded through the small rectangular window. I began blinking my eyes, getting ready for the adjustment when the door opened. I've never liked surprises—they get you killed, quickly. I hoped my outside instincts kicked back in after all this time. It's the one thing I've been afraid of losing. I've learned to keep myself sharp inside to stay alive, but being free was a different kind of survival.

"Here." The cold tone of the guard, something I'll never miss, ordered me forward. Some of these assholes were utterly worthless individuals who preyed on women daily. Luckily, I've only had two encounters with said assholes. When I broke the first one's nose, he decided I wasn't worth the hassle. It got me locked in solitary for a few days and a few bruises, but I actually liked it there. I was left alone. I thought about doing it again, maybe get an extended stay, but my mind always reverted to survival, and getting the hell out of here the easiest way possible.

The other, I've tried to block out of my head. As soon as my feet step outside this door, I would forget what he did, and not a single soul would ever know.

I watched as the guard's hand extended from his body, holding a clear plastic bag. Reaching for it, not much was inside. The clothes I was wearing when I got in this hell-hole were ripped when I didn't move as quickly as the officer said, so only a few items remained. Inside the bag was the cross necklace I wore that night, my ID, and a few dollars in cash. The cash actually surprised me; I was sure that would have disappeared by now with all the crooked-ass people inside.

"Gavelson!" I didn't want to turn toward the voice, not with the exit so close. But I knew they still owned me until I stepped out that door. Until then, I needed to mind myself.

"Yes, sir," I said, slowly turning around to see the warden coming closer. His stocky build with his oversized stomach hanging over his uniform pants was nothing to get wet about, but he proved a good ally while I was inside. Warden Dunn was on Pops's payroll and set me up with my nice surroundings. He even passed certain things along from Pops during my stay. So I respected him as much as a person could while locked up. Did I trust him? No. The moment you trusted someone in here, you ended up dead.

Looking directly into my eyes, I saw a splash of concern come across his as he tilted his head slowly to the side. His voice reminded me of a whiny teenager, even though he was nowhere near his teenage years. His voice sounded raspy as if he was going through *the change* all over again. "You don't come back here, girl."

"I'll do my best," I answered, immediately knowing there were never any guarantees in this life, and your word was your only bond. If you didn't have that, you had nothing. I wasn't about to make him a promise; I didn't know for sure I could keep. I would definitely do my damnedest never to step foot in here again, though.

"Take care, Princess," the warden whispered while patting my shoulder gently. My blood boiled when I turned to walk back towards the door. I've spent my entire life trying to prove to everyone that I was no damn princess, but that name kept following me around like shit stuck to my shoe. Many women in my world would love that title. To me, though, it represented weakness. I couldn't afford to be associated with weakness.

When the guard opened the door, the bright light blinded me. I blinked quickly to get my bearings. Shielding my eyes with my hand, I looked around until I spotted the familiar, red '56 Chevy with the white flames painted on the front hood. More importantly, I spotted the woman standing next to it, Casey.

"Well don't you have a shit-eating grin on your face." Casey's smile was one of the most beautiful I'd ever seen on a woman. With her golden locks and flawless figure, she could get anyone she wanted, whenever she wanted, but damn if she used it to her advantage. Casey and I have been friends since we were kids, growing up at the club, right alongside each other. Her dad, Bam, was a patched member, who died a few years ago.

We've experienced everything together. She was my ultimate partner in crime and damn did I miss her. Grabbing her face between my hands, I stared into her emerald eyes before kissing her full on the lips. They tasted like cherries, reminding me of the little things that I've missed. Then I moved and kissed her once on each cheek.

"Well, hello to you too, girl." She laughed at my gesture and wrapped her arms tightly around me squeezing the ever-loving shit out of me.

Stepping back, "I just missed ya, babe. Get me the hell out of here." Throwing open the car door; I hopped into the beautiful piece of machinery. The sleek car was the ultimate ride, a classic. In our world, it was called a cage, since anything that isn't a motorcycle was considered just that.

Casey's father helped her fix it up at the shop, spending hours and hours perfecting it. He taught her everything that she'd ever have to know about fixing cars and bikes. When her father died, this car was the only connection to him she had. She treasured it more than anything on this planet and took care of it like she was loving her child.

Casey worked at the shop, Banner Automotive, attached to the Club. She may be beautiful and girly, but give her a wrench and an engine, and she was all over it. Not to mention, I've been told the guys really like the tight-ass jeans she wears. Men are so damn predictable.

"Sure thing, you ready to get that mop tamed?" Casey's eyes travelled over my ugly, stringy, brassy brown hair. I knew I looked like shit, which was why it was the first order of business.

"Absolutely."

After three hours in the chair, chatting it up with Cam while she worked her magic on my hair, I felt like a new woman. My dark brown hair was back in place with the bright streaks of red, just like I liked it. Instead of stringy, it was soft and silky. The natural wave was always a plus. Keeping it long in jail was a feat I never wanted to repeat. Just because my Pops had guys on the payroll, didn't mean that things were handed to me. I had to earn it, and damn it if I didn't. Not that I ever wanted to relive any of that again.

The drive to our place was quick, and I couldn't wait to get the hell out of these prison clothes. I needed to get the stench of that place off of me. Wrapping my hair up, I jumped in the shower letting the water wash away the two previous years of hell. After turning into a prune, I exited getting myself together quickly. I found my favorite pair of jeans with the thousands of holes in all the right places and my tight, black Harley t-shirt. After a bit of makeup, I was ready to go see my family.

Walking into the living room, Casey was flopped on the couch with the remote in her hand, thumbing endlessly through the channels. "Where is she?" I asked, wanting my girl back.

"Come on." Casey got up and headed towards her room, with me following closely behind. She dug through her closet, pulling out a locked box. Casey walked the box over to her dresser and placed it softly on the top. She rummaged through her top drawer, pulling out keys and unlocking the box.

Sitting inside was my girl. 9mm's of power that fit the palm of my hand perfectly. I learned how to shoot with this gun. My dad gave it to me when I was fourteen, and I never leave home without her.

Feeling the weight in my hand, I thumbed the beautiful piece of metal, feeling happy and at peace. I always felt protected when this was with me. It's one of the things that kept me alive for this long. Not only am I fast, but I am a great shot. Two years was a long time with no practice, though. I needed to get to the firing range and shoot off some rounds.

Checking my gun, I made sure the bullet chamber was fully loaded. I locked the safety, gave it a soft kiss, and placed it underneath my shirt in a small holster on my back.

Casey wrapped her arms around me, hugging me tightly, which I returned. "I'm so glad you're back," she whispered softly in my ear.

"Me too. Let's go see the boys."

I pulled away staring into her eyes. She was the one person that I knew would always have my back no matter what. "Let's go." She smiled, pulling my arm through the door.

Driving through the streets of Sumner, Georgia, everything seemed exactly the same as before I left. The same shops and banks lined the center of town with people walking through the streets without a care in the world. They were free, just like I was, and how I was going to stay.

Good people lived here. They were honest people; well, for the most part. When the outsiders came in, that's when we had problems.

Unfortunately, I've been kept in the dark about most of what was going on with the club. When Ma came to visit, she never discussed the brothers, and I never asked. People were always listening to us, and neither of us could risk it. I didn't know the good or the bad of what was going on, and I felt quite lost. Ma would only say that my family loved me. I knew that.

What I didn't know was what I would walk into once I got to the shop and the club. It was a bit unnerving, but I couldn't let that show. I'd never show any weakness... ever.

Pulling up to the locked gates with barbed wire lacing the top, the smile that was plastered on my face was irreversible. I was finally home.

A man I'd never seen before, wearing a Prospect rag, came to the side of the window. "Hey, Casey. You working today?"

Smiling widely at him, she reached over and grabbed my hand, squeezing it tightly. He was pretty hot for a newbie Prospect. His dark hair hung low covering his ears, but not quite down to his shoulders. His brown eyes were the color of chocolate, matching the smoothness of his voice. His nose looked like it had taken one too many beatings over the years and hadn't been set quite right. He had a very hot, dangerous persona.

Squeezing Casey's hand back to let her know I understood his hotness, she finally spoke. "Hey, Tug. I brought Harlow home."

Tug looked me up and down, eyeing me. "Get a good look there, Bud," I said with my signature smirk that I knew would make him putty in my hands.

"Sure thing, Sweetheart. So you're the famous Princess, huh?" Rolling my eyes, I turned to face the windshield already done with the conversation. Spending your entire life trying to prove something wrong was exhausting, and I knew everyone here would be calling me that word.

"Let's go," I said, snapping my fingers in front of me, pointing to the gate.

"Your Pops is real excited to see ya, but they're in church. They'll be out soon." Tug turned to the gate, throwing the switch to unlock the steel doors. They began to move, opening wide.

When the gates spread, I took in the view. To the left was the shop, Banner Automotive. This was one of the businesses the Ravage MC owned that did really well, not to mention they all needed some place to work on their bikes. My mom worked there doing the books and handling all the clients that came in and out through another entrance, opposite of where all the guys come in. She'd been doing it since I was a kid. I spent a lot of time in that office with Ma. My eyes scanned to the members and Prospect only parking to the right. One parking spot after the other and I could name the owners of almost every one of them. That's how I knew there were five new guys, either patched in or Prospects.

Casey parked the car in front of the shop doors and killed the engine. Walking in, it actually felt eerie. I didn't recognize anyone, but they all said hi to Casey. I should have expected a new crew of workers; they rotated quite often. Club business was kept separate from the shop. I could feel their eyes boring into me, but I kept my eyes trained on the back door. I wanted to see my man.

"Ma'am, you can't go back there!" one of the guys called out.

"The hell I can't." I began marching towards the door, knowing that my own personal heaven was on the other side. I had to see him. I had to feel him between my thighs. One of the guys grabbed my arm, turning me to look at him square in the eyes. He was pretty cute, in that rough-mechanic-having-my-hands-dirty-all-the-time, kind of a way. His blonde hair was cut very short, and his green eyes were the color of leaves.

If I wasn't so pissed that he actually put his hands on me, I might have been really attracted to him, but right now, I was livid.

"I said you're not going back there. Why the hell did you bring this slut around?" he accused Casey. This guy went from cute to an ass in about two seconds. Before Casey could say anything, I wrenched my arm out of his grasp and swung, my fist crashing into the guy's nose, squirting blood everywhere. "You bitch! Call Diamond!" he barked at the guys turning and coming towards me. *Bring it fucker.*

I'm known for my speed, and this guy coming after

me was going to be a challenge, but I needed it. I needed to feel alive again.

"Don't!" I heard Casey yell, but totally ignored her. I knew I could take him if I was smart.

He swung with this right hand, but missed, sending him off balance. Taking advantage, I laced my fingers together creating a large fist. Pulling back, I swung hard, hitting him directly in the back, making him fall to the ground on his knees. He grunted, and I was pleased with my skill. Swinging my right leg, my boot slammed his face hard, sending blood flying through the air. He fell with a thud.

Looking around the shop, I noticed the other guys were starting to come at me. I smiled. I loved this shit. It was so different fighting on my own turf than in jail.

"Please stop," Casey said, looking at her nails as if she were bored out of her mind.

"You could help me out here; ya know," I said, laughing.

Her eyes met mine. "You got this, and I just got a manicure while you were getting your hair done. I never get my nails done. I want to keep them nice, and I have to work with them." Casey smiled that beautiful smile.

Hearing boot steps behind me, I glanced quickly to see another man trying to sneak up on me. I loved the ones that thought they could one up me. When the guy approached, I turned quickly, kicking my leg up high and swung hard, hitting him directly in the face.

My joy was quickly tarnished when a gun was pressed into the back of my head and cocked. Shit. Well, this was how we were gonna play this, huh?

"Sugar, you just stirred up a shit storm." The southern drawl to his voice mixed with the smell of leather, cigarettes, and radiating testosterone would have made my pussy clench, but he ruined that by pressing a damn gun to my head.

"Low, don't." I ignored Casey just as I always did. Quickly, I turned my body. As my arm reached back to knock the gun out of his hand, I instantly froze. The three patch rag falling on his chest was a red light flashing in my eyes. Immediately, I stopped, putting my hands in front of me. I would never touch a brother, outside of the ring that is.

The man standing in front of me caught my breath and short-circuited my senses. His broad shoulders were covered with a skin-tight; black t-shirt and leather rag adorned with several patches that fit him like a glove. His bulging arms were covered in tattoos from the wrist up. They were flexed; one pointed the gun with precision, and the other was fisted at his side. His light caramel hair was cut short on the sides, but longer on the top, begging for a woman's fingers to run through it. His beard was cut very short to his skin making my mouth water, wondering what it would feel like between my thighs. His sapphire eyes narrowed at me as I stared effortlessly into them, becoming entranced unable to speak.

"What the fuck is going on here?" Breaking from this man's stare, I focused on the familiar voice I've missed for too long. Pops eyes swept the room quickly, and when his eyes landed on mine, the anger in them instantly faded. "What the hell's going on?" He eyed the man with the gun pointed directly at my head, and he clenched his hands into fists.

"Hey, Pops," I said, turning my eyes back to the beautiful specimen in front of me, wanting him to know that I wasn't afraid. If I needed a bullet in my head, so be it. I wouldn't shy away.

"You know this bitch?" the hot asshole in front of me clipped, and my lip curled slowly. If he wasn't wearing that rag, I'd show him how much of a bitch I could be.

"Put the damn gun down, Cruz," Pops said jokingly. The anger dripping off this man's face in front of me told me he didn't see anything funny about this. He began to take a step closer. "Cruz. Stop!" Pops barked loudly as the other guys started walking up behind him. Cruz instantly stopped but kept the gun on me. "Cruz, this is my daughter, Princess."

"Shit. Are you fucking kidding me?" Cruz's anger was actually pretty funny, and I had to stifle the small laugh that wanted to escape. I had too much respect to let it fly. But the shocked look on his face was pretty priceless coming from a tattooed hot-ass. I probably should have told him that sooner, but what can I say... I was born a bitch.

"No, I'm not fucking kidding you. Get the fuck away from her, and put the goddamn gun down." Turning my head towards Pops, I could see he was fuming. Whenever Pops was mad, his forehead turned bright red, and the lines throughout it became more prominent along with the vein in his neck that ticked with his heartbeat. It's a look I always hated growing up; it used to scare the ever-loving shit out of me.

My eyes flicked back while Cruz took one more look at me. "If you're still pissed later, we can meet in the ring." I smiled my damnedest. I could see the smoke threatening to come out of his ears. Confusion laced his eyes, but I wasn't about to explain right now. I held out my hand to Cruz, "Nice to meet ya. I'm Harlow." He stared me down as if he was hoping he could make me combust into a million pieces. Sorry Buddy, your super powers, won't work. I've been here too long to let that get me.

He tentatively lowered the gun, putting it behind his back, bringing his hand to mine. My hand slipped into his warm, rough, strong grip, a shock raced through my body, beginning at our connected hands and racing all the way through to my feet setting my body on fire. "Cruz." Snapping myself out, I pulled out of his grasp quickly not wanting him to feel the same. Breaking away from his intense eyes, I winked, brushing past him, I jumped in my Pops' arms. He picked me up and hugged me tight.

"Hi Daddy," I whispered in his ear, so he was the only one who could hear. I hadn't called him that in public since I was a kid. He's Pops to everyone around here, including me.

"Hey, Baby Girl. About time you got back here." He squeezed me and set me down on my feet. Looking up at him, his long black beard had a lot of gray growing through it, making it look salt and pepperish. The hair on his head looked the same, but with even grayer hairs sprinkled throughout. The eyes I stared into were the most beautiful powder blue. They were the eyes that held safety for me through all of these years. Sporting a lot more lines around his eyes, I wondered how he's been feeling.

"You okay, Pops?" I asked, tilting my head to the side and raising my eyebrows. My hands rested on his chest.

"I am now." His beard tried to hide his smile, but I saw it there, his silver front tooth flashing at me, the smile warmed me like no other. My Pops may not lead a conventional life, but one thing was an absolute; he loved his family and would do anything for us.

"You come back, and I get nothing?" Turning towards the low voice, I launched myself into my brother's arms, wrapping my arms around him as tight as I possibly could, squeezing the shit out of him. My brother... and this one was by blood. Growing up, we knew he'd be a member of the club as soon as he could be patched in. We were raised here together. Ma kept me further away than G.T., but that was for obvious reasons. G.T. patched in when he turned eighteen. I was so damn proud of him.

"Hi, G.T.," I said, burrowing myself in his strong chest.

"Hey, girl. You doin' all right?" He was utterly handsome. His short beard covered his face, while his blonde-brown hair hung low to his shoulders. He had the exact same navy eyes that I had, and every time I looked into them, I felt that same deep connection we've had since we were kids. I would do anything for him, and I knew he would for me. His tatted up arms were rock solid, and the shirt he was wearing was tight around the sleeves, showing every ripple. His small nose and strong jaw complete the package. Not that I was attracted to him, but the hordes of women that came and went for him definitely were.

"Yeah, Baby Brother. I'm good." I smiled up at him, turning to see all the men that I've known my entire life. Pride and joy melted through my heart. After hugging Dagger, Rhys, Zed, and Becs, I looked for him. Our President. I know I'm not a member, but I am in this family, and Diamond was our head man.

"Where's Diamond?" I asked Pops, looking behind him at the strong men I've grown up caring about. Yes, they were menacing, and no one would want to piss them off, but to me, they were my family. I loved each of them in their own way.

"He's inside. We wanted to check out everything before having him come out." Diamond was king around here. We all respected him and accepted his words as law. He took over as President after my Gramps passed away with Pops as his Vice President. He was sharp as a tack and knew his shit. He's a very smart business man and rode with the guys regularly. You'd never know he was pushing seventy.

"I'll see him in a minute. I need to see Sting." I needed him more than I needed to breathe at the moment.

"Come on." G.T. put his arm around my shoulders squeezing me as he led me to the back room.

Blocking the path in front of us was the garage man from earlier. "I'm so sorry. I was just trying to protect him." His voice was shaky, but who could blame him, I dislocated his nose.

"I appreciate that. Thanks." I smiled sweetly. I knew he was just doing his job. I just didn't care, 'cause no one keeps me away from my man. Could I have handled it differently, sure, but shit happens.

G.T. opened the door, and sitting inside was my man. In the middle of the room, my '97 Ultra Groundpounder Hardtail stood proudly. His chrome body hard and the beautiful red and black paint graced him like a glove. He was the ultimate man. He felt great between my legs, never let me down, and was always there when I was in need. Warmth and love flowed through my body.

"Anyone been taking him out?" I asked to the roomful of men that piled in behind us.

"I have. He's in good shape." Pops' voice came from behind. I knew could count on him.

"Thanks, Pops," I said straddling my beast between my thighs. Reaching for the handlebars, I fired him up. The roar of the engine and the rough vibrations had my panties growing instantly wet. They didn't call this machine a Milwaukee vibrator for nothing.

"Umm... You okay, Princess?" G.T. asked eyeing me, a wide grin spread across my face. "I'm not gonna sit here and watch you get off."

Looking up at him, I responded, "Then you better get the hell out of here quick." My body was burning for release. It'd been way too long, and the vibrations were just too damn good hitting my clit just perfectly.

"I'll watch." Dagger cut through, crossing his arms across his chest.

"Dagger, you'd stop to watch two dogs fuck," I said, wiggling my eyebrows suggestively.

"Damn right, and the only thing better than watching you come would be my dick making you do it." Dagger's been in the club for years and was a monumental whore who fucked anything that had a hole, female of course, and made no qualms about it, even to his ol' lady. Dagger's a very rugged man. His leathery skin was masked by his long blond hair that's braided down his back with his red, white and blue bandana covering across his forehead. He's made no secret over the years that he'd love to take me for a ride. Too bad for him, I stay far away from brothers.

"You're not watching my girl. Get the fuck out!" Pops barked at the men, but none of them seemed to move, surprising me. G.T. and Pops made a quick exit. I shook my head, swallowing my laughter.

Getting back to the task at hand, I felt my body almost there. My hips rubbed back and forth on the seat, feeling my strong man taking care of me. Closing my eyes, the hot rush of feelings took over while I continued rocking back and forth. I didn't give two shits if the guys were there. I've seen them do more garbage in that clubhouse than I'd care to mention.

Sparks flew through my body, and my breath became sparse. Throwing my head back, I enjoyed the feelings racing through my body. Damn, I loved my man. Opening my eyes, every eye in the room was staring at me, and I couldn't help the amusement coursing through me. I shut down Sting and pulled myself off of him, feeling my damp panties rubbing against my jeans, making me smile. I needed to take him out for a ride very soon.

"Damn girl." My eyes landed on Zed's wide grin. My eyes traveled down his body appraisingly. I could see a very large bulge trying to bust through his leathers. I loved that I had this effect on the guys. I may not sleep with them, but teasing never hurt anyone.

Nodding to his dick, "You may need to have that taken care of."

"You wanna do it?" He took a step closer to me grabbing his dick. His hair was the color of muddy water, cut short in a buzz and eyes as dark as midnight penetrated me. His solid build was intimidating to most, but not me.

"In your dreams," my voice said sternly, brushing past him, making sure my arm grazed him just enough to get a reaction out of him.

And sure enough, "Damn, Babe," he growled making me smile.

"All right, I'm better. Let's go see Diamond." Looking over to the side of the room, Cruz was eyeing me. "What's wrong Big Boy? Can't handle it?"

"Hell yeah. Just wonder if *you* could." As his stare penetrated me, I asked myself that same question, but didn't need to answer it. My heart rate picked up giving me an answer that scared the shit out of me. But I wouldn't let it show. Ever.

"Sure, take it out and stroke it." I wanted to see if this man was just blowing smoke up my ass, or if he was a sure thing. Torturing myself was always fun and I knew I'd never act. Never make the mistake of sleeping with a brother.

The corner of his mouth curled up into a sexy grin as he reached down and started unbuckling his belt. "All right, everyone out. Now." Pops barked from outside the door not bothering to take a step inside.

"Come on, Pops, Cruz and I have some unfinished

business here," I said, my eyes not leaving Cruz as he unbuttoned his pants and pulled his zipper down.

"You are not doing this shit." Pops voice grew angry as he walked in the room, coming up next to me. His eyes solely focused on me.

Turning to Pops, I searched the depths of his eyes knowing he was protecting me. "Pops, you know my rule." I reached up and patted his chest reassuringly.

"Fine, but you're playing with fire with this one." Pops stormed out of the room with the guys following behind him. Walking to the door and closing it, I listened to the snap of the handle.

I turned slowly around; Cruz held his hard thick dick in his hand stroking himself up and down methodically. Watching him had my body heating up again, catching on fire actually and my mouth watering. "You like this, Baby?" God, that deep southern twang to his voice could make me shatter into a million pieces alone.

"Oh yeah. It's been two years too long. Maybe you could help a girl out." I dropped my voice to a quiet, seductive purr and did that stupid girl batting eyelash thing. Guys always loved that shit.

He stepped closer. My mouth began watering as the scent of him assaulted me. I wanted him. Badly. Reaching up, I ran my nails over his chest, feeling the hard defined pecks underneath his shirt while my fingers bounced along. Before I could move away, Cruz grabbed the back of my head hard, crashing his lips to mine. The kiss was rough and seriously intense, sucking every bit of breath out of my body. My body was telling me I needed this.

But, my brain kicked in, and I knew I needed to break

away. One thing I didn't do was sleep with brothers. It caused too much tension, and I didn't want to deal with that shit. Mustering every bit of energy I could, I pulled away from him trying to catch my non-existent breath. I stared into his penetrating blue eyes, and I for once wished my brain would shut the hell up. I wanted this man.

Licking my lips, I walked to the door reaching for the door handle. "Too bad for you, I don't fuck the brothers." I didn't give him a chance to respond. I turned quickly strolling out of the shop towards the clubhouse leaving him with his dick in his hand.

My body was ignited from the taste of his lips. I wondered what that body of his could do to mine. After our brief exchange, I knew he'd turn me inside out. Sad part was; I wanted to know how his touch would feel... how he would make me scream because there was no way a man like him wouldn't make me scream... repeatedly.

G.T. was waiting in the common area. Sitting out on the park bench, his eyes were not on me. His focus was on the hot blonde bending over the engine in the shop, Casey, which really didn't surprise me. She's a very beautiful woman, and my brother, God love him, loved women. "You think I can't handle myself, Brother?" I said climbing up sitting next to him on the bench, trying to calm my raging body down, and catching his attention away from Casey.

G.T. held out his pack of smokes, and I reached for one. Placing it between my lips, he lit, and I inhaled slowly, feeling the burn. While inside, I wasn't allowed to

smoke, new rules, some shit about fire codes, whatever. I
sat there actually feeling a little head rush from the nico-
tine, which made me suck harder.

"I know you can take care of yourself. How are you?"
We stared out across the courtyard watching the action
around the shop, people coming and going, mechanics
working on cars and bikes. Everyone going on about their
lives without a care in the world.

"I'm good, now that I'm out." I hadn't felt this good in
a long damn time. Being locked in a cell was something
one should never have to do, especially if you're in there
for something you didn't fucking do. Blackmail, yeah,
right. If I'd actually did that shit they accused me of, I
wouldn't have been so stupid to leave so much evidence
around. "I'm so sorry you were in there. I should have
done something," he said shaking his head back and
forth. I knew he felt guilty just like the other brothers, but
there was nothing that any of them could have done. The
lawyer said so.

Placing my arm on his back, I began rubbing it up
and down. "There was nothing you could do. I was set up,
and somehow she had her shit together. That's no one's
fault, but hers." And mine for not trusting my gut.

"You gonna take care of it now?" G.T.'s eyes wandered
back to Casey, who was talking animatedly with her
hands to one of the mechanics.

"Hell yeah. Those bitches won't know what hit 'em."
Spending the last two years planning their demise, I went
from fast and furious to slow and painful. It would all
depend on my mood that day on how it'll all play out. It
took a year of being locked up to figure out it was even

Babs that did the set-up. I didn't want to tell Ma because I knew she'd tell the brothers, and I wanted that bitch. But I did anyway, knowing they deserved to know what happened. But Babs disappeared off the radar for a while. I didn't know if that was a good thing or a bad thing. "But, I need to think and get my shit together first."

"You need to be smart. I don't want you back there... ever." His eyes bore into mine at the seriousness of his statement. I took it deep to heart.

"I'm not going back. I made a mistake trusting the wrong person. I should have known better. It won't happen again." Stomping out the smoke on the table, I leaned back feeling the heat of the sun warming my skin.

"Love you." G.T.'s hand landed on my leg and squeezed. My heart warmed instantly.

"Love you, too." Sitting there in silence for quite a while, we let the everyday noises of the garage fill the void. It was nice having the sun on my skin and not having to move for anyone. If I wanted to stay all damn day, I would. Yeah... never going back. "So, what's new around here? Ma couldn't tell me much when she came up."

"Sorry, I couldn't come." None of the club members had been up to see me the entire two years. Part of me felt deserted by them, but deep down, I knew they were doing it to protect the club. One wrong word and they could all go down. I couldn't live with that.

"No worries. Tell me."

Blowing out a deep breath, G.T. began laying out the new shit going down and even some old shit. I knew he couldn't tell me club business, so he just kept to the basics and more about the people and families than anything.

"What about my studio?" Two years before I went in, I started Studio X. The club owned the business, but it was mine. I built it from the ground up, making it the number one strip joint in Sumner. Every town needed one, and people came from miles around to partake, mostly married men who needed a little escape. I'm not one for cheating, but in my world, it happened all the time. As for me, I'd never tolerate it.

I took really good care of my girls and paid them exceptionally well. The club provided me with security that I was too busy to handle, and I handled the girls and money. The manager, Liv, handled all the scheduling, and whatever the girls needed she brought to me. Or that was how it was before I went inside.

The strip club was a legal way for the club to make money, and I was glad to help. Not to mention, the paychecks I received allowed me to live very comfortably. Win... win. But while I was gone, who knows what the hell happened. I knew I was ready to get back to it, though.

"X is doing great. Liv's been running the show, keeping everything in line. Any issues we've taken care of. Nothing too much. Couple of the girls got roughed up. Money's good." G.T. said blowing out the smoke from his cigarette and paused. "You going back to work?"

"Yep. I'm gonna check in on everything tomorrow. Tonight is about partying." Standing up, I brushed the ass of my jeans getting whatever dirt off. "I've gotta go say hi to Diamond."

Out of the corner of my eye, Cruz walked out of the shop, putting his sunglasses on and making that already sexy body even sexier. Was that even possible? When his head turned, and he met my stare, he shook his head and kept walking. "What's his story?"

"Patched in about a year ago, completely trust him. Came out of the Marines, and he's an honorable man. He's proven himself over and over again." My mind flashed to Cruz in uniform, and I liked what I saw.

I spotted a man in the corner of the garage wearing a Prospect rag sweeping the blacktop and nodded his way. "What about him?" The man's straight long hair covered his face, but his dark beard was long enough to see beyond the ends. His body was lean and lanky, but his movements were fluid and knowing. G.T.'s eyes followed mine.

"That's Rocky. Pretty quiet, but talks when it's important. He's only about six months in." I tilted my head to the side trying to get a better look at him. Something about him seemed familiar, but nothing I could pinpoint.

I turned to G.T. "I missed you," I said, pulling my baby brother into a tight hug, which he reciprocated effortlessly. Ever since we were kids, he's always acted like my big brother instead of younger. He taught me more than any one man in the club. He's been in the ring with me, at the shooting range, and by my side throughout all these years coaching me to be the woman I am today. G.T., also known as Gage Thomas by birth certificate only, was the rock that I would fight for till my dying breath.

"I missed you too, Princess."

Nodding, I began heading in the direction of the clubhouse with Cruz a few feet in front of me. "I know you're there, girl." I could get lost in that deep drawl of his voice. I didn't slow my pace, but I did answer.

"I'm going to see Diamond."

Cruz turned around suddenly, halting me in mid-step, "We will talk about this later."

"We will, huh? You think this is how it works?" Leaning in close to him, my lips almost touched his ear. "I don't fuck brothers. It's not gonna change."

He challenged me back, leaning into my ear, the smell of him and leather assaulting my senses. "Everything changes."

I tapped down the shiver that ran through my body. I was not giving in. I couldn't. I've seen so many mommas come in and out of the club, that's what the guys called whores, club mommas. The names were interchangeable with them. I would never become one of them.

It's one thing to find a guy outside the club, have a good time, and get away. Here... you never get away. I was not one to be passed around by the guys and deal with all the drama of seeing them with another woman. I was strong, but some things, I knew were too much.

Pulling away from him, I stepped through the club-house doors. The smell of stale beer and cigarettes lingered everywhere. Adjusting my eyes to the darkness, I took in everything in the room. Dark paneling encased the entire room. One was a wall of pictures, those who we have loved and lost. The other wall was the bar. Mirrors lined the walls with beer signs shining brightly. Liquor and glasses encompassed the shelves. The L-shaped bar had tons of nicks and dents, representing years of men drinking and becoming brothers.

A man about my age wearing a Prospect rag was behind the bar. "Hey, Sweetheart, can I get ya something?"

"Oh, Honey. What I want, you can't give me," I purred, cozying up to the bar, leaning on my elbows, giving him a good show of my tits. Yep flirting.

"I'm sure I can." His eyes lingered on what I've just put out in front of him, and he licked his top lip.

A hand slammed down hard on the bar next to me, catching me off guard and causing me to jump a bit. Cruz stood next to me, eyeing the Prospect. "She yours?" he asked Cruz.

"Yeah. Hands off," Cruz growled.

My temper flared. There was no way in hell this guy was going to lay claim to me. I knew how this shit worked. Once a brother claimed a woman, she was untouchable to anyone. I shouldn't care since I wouldn't get with anyone in the club, but my independence took over. This was so not happening. "Fuck off. I'm not yours. I'm not anyone's. Let's get that shit straight right now." The Prospect actually looked nervous which pissed me off more. "Grow some balls," I murmured, staring at him.

"Who the fuck do you think you are?" The Prospect glared intently at me. Respect goes a long fucking way, and if these shits didn't show it now... they'd never make it.

Before I could let the asshole know how I felt, Cruz stepped in. "Shut the fuck up. You don't fucking talk to her like that. You hear me?" His eyes fell as he went back to cleaning the bar.

"I don't need to be rescued. I can damn well do it myself." I gripped the side of the bar tight enough to turn my knuckles white.

"Maybe that's the problem. You need a man instead of the pussies who let you get away with that shit." Cruz said grabbing the beer bottle from the bar taking a long swig. Watching his Adam's apple bob as he swallowed, I held back the moan that wanted to escape my dry lips turning my insides to mush.

"You know what I need?" I leaned in close to him breathing him in, but mustering my strength. "I need a dick. One that has no association with this club, and I'll get it tonight. After that, I'll be just fine. Don't worry your little heart about that." Hearing Cruz's breathing pick up, I turned back to the bar smiling.

"Princess?" Turning towards the church doors, Diamond stood there tall and proud. Man, these two years since I had seen him last had aged him. He was still as handsome as always, however, with his short gray hair and green sparkling eyes; it was obvious that time was wearing on him. I could sense the power radiating off of him though.

Before I was able to walk to him, Cruz reached out and gripped my arm. "We're not done here."

Nodding and pulling away from Cruz, I leaned into Diamond's arms. "You all right, Old Man?"

"Never better now that you're home." Diamond wrapped his arms around me tightly, kissing me on the cheek. "They let you do that red shit to your hair in the joint?" His own question made him laugh. He has always given me shit about my *wild* hair ways. Back in the day, I'd have three or four colors at a time. He just liked to give me shit.

"Yep, some bitch named Berta. Made me eat her pussy first."

His deep laugh was music to my ears. "Glad to know your smart ass mouth came home, too."

He squeezed me tighter. "Thanks, Di."

CHAPTER TWO
Harlow

DIAMOND LED ME PAST THE LARGE ROOM WHERE THE brothers held church, towards his office. Sitting in the large space, he grabbed both my hands. "Princess, I'm so sorry you had to deal with that shithole."

"I'm good, Diamond. I'm out now." Ma told me the brothers were chomping at the bit not having any control over my fate. They hired the best lawyers, and we fought, but in the end the evil bitch won. At the time, I didn't know it was Babs. That bitch did a bang-up job with all the evidence against me. I could feel the tension in my body starting to rise just thinking about her. This wasn't the time for a blow up.

As he squeezed my hand, I tried to get a grasp on my anger. "First, I wanted to thank you for handling that shit for us. I know we asked quite a bit."

Looking him right in the eye, all anger left my face.

"I'd do anything for this club. You know that. Those bitches deserved what they got." He smiled, not acknowledging it again. I knew this was his way. The things they've had to do were secret, and I couldn't help the bit of pride I felt that I was privileged to do my part. The fact I was let in just a sliver was enough to fuel me to do what needed to be done, which I did. Taking out those bitches that wronged the club was an honor.

"For right now, you'll have a brother with you at all times." I looked at him confused, wondering what was going on. I've been taking care of myself for years before I got locked up and never needed anyone's help, not even the brothers.

Fire ran through my body, sending it on a course of explosion, but I controlled it and took a deep, heaving breath. I spoke as calmly as I could. "With all due respect, I don't need a babysitter. I can take care of myself."

Diamond's happy nature disappeared, and I knew I had overstepped my bounds. Shit. His face turned tight, and every muscle in it pulsated. His eyes turned menacing, and no longer belonged to the warm, fun-loving guy that just hugged me a few minutes ago causing a sliver of fear to creep through my body. "This is not up for discussion, young lady. You will have a brother at all times."

I dropped my head in shame. Disappointing Diamond sent an ache throughout my body that I could spend an eternity not feeling again. "Sorry, Diamond."

He leaned back in his chair lacing his fingers together and placing them behind his head, reclining. "I hear you had a little run-in with some mechanics."

Of course, he would know already. Nothing gets past

this man. "Yes, Sir."

"You know you can't go beating up the workers." His eyes were serious, but his warmth returned and emanated from his words.

"I'm know. I'm sorry."

"Damn right you are. You will apologize." Diamond and Pops were the only two that could rein me in. I was not scared of them. Well, I guess I kinda was, but for a good reason. I respected them with every fiber of my being. I trusted them and knew they had my back always.

"We have a party planned tonight for you." A smile graced my face at this knowledge. I just knew they wouldn't let my homecoming pass without something. I was almost disappointed when I arrived, and the welcome wagon wasn't in full force. But I didn't let it show.

Diamond leaned in close, stilling my hands of their rhythmic movements that I didn't even know they were making. "We'd do anything for you. You know that, right?"

"I know."

"You need to keep your eyes and ears open all the time." I wondered who the hell he was warning me about, but knew I wouldn't get any answers even though I had to ask.

"Are you gonna tell me who I'm looking out for?"

He eyed me, his expression impassive. "Everyone. Now get out of here and see your Ma." He nodded towards the door. I knew my dismissal and took it. As I reached the door, Diamond wasn't done. "Also, you apologize to Cruz."

My body stood frozen; it was as if all the blood left instantly. The hand that clutched the handle on the door gripped it so tightly I thought for sure it would bust off in my hand. Not looking back, I asked, "This my punishment?"

He laughed but didn't say a word. I knew the answer. One thing I had a hell of a hard time doing was showing weakness to the brothers. As a woman, I was already considered weak. I've spent my entire life trying to prove that wrong. From fighting to shooting to riding... I did everything I could come up with to make the brothers see me as strong. This was going to be a bitch.

The bar was illuminated, like always. The Prospect behind it and Cruz were the only two men in the room, but what caught my eye was the long brown-haired vixen, with small scraps of fabric barely covering her essentials, standing next to Cruz. She was definitely a club momma. They all seemed to look the same, no clothes and an eagerness about them that screamed slut. I've seen a lot of them throughout my time here. Did I like it? No. But they were part of it, and I ignored them. They were free pussy for the guys, all of the guys, something I refused ever to be.

The woman's hand began snaking up and down Cruz's bulging arm as she pushed her body up against his side, her fake tits rubbing on him relentlessly. Normally, my eyes would roll at the situation, and I'd turn and walk away, but this time, I felt rooted in my spot. The men took club mommas all the time using them for their holes and nothing more. But with this woman touching Cruz, I couldn't help the desire to go over to her and beat the fucking shit out of her.

I knew I wouldn't. He was not mine, and I didn't want him to be. *Right?* Shaking off my thoughts, I approached the bar. Blowing out a breath, I knew I had to tackle this damn apology first, but I didn't want to do it with her hanging all over him. I really needed to get on Sting and clear my head, which would definitely be my next order of business.

Pushing my shoulders back, strengthening my spine with all I could muster, the Prospect's eyes widened as I approached. "I'm sorry. I didn't know you were Princess." Cruz must have filled him in on a bit of my history. What I didn't know was why, considering Cruz didn't know shit about me.

I smiled softly. "No problem. Nice to meet ya."

"How'd it go?" Cruz asked, cutting in while taking a pull from his beer. The sound of his throat swallowing filled my ears and my eyes wanted desperately to watch his Adams apple move, but I tore them away.

"Fine. Can I talk to you for a minute?" I asked siding up on the stool next to him.

"You can talk to me anytime you want, Baby." His voice melted me like butter, and I wanted to kick my ass for it. I needed to keep my head on straight around this man but feared it wouldn't be an easy task. He turned to the woman at his side, "Get lost."

Her high-pitched whine had me rolling my eyes in disgust. "But, Cruz. I'm horny." Seriously? Why these women did this shit, I'd never know. It's one thing that Casey and I vowed together never to be. We would never start sleeping with the brothers and turn into this woman standing by Cruz.

"I am, too." His eyes found mine as the words flowed from this mouth. The woman grabbed his arm tighter, but my thoughts drifted to the intense kiss that he gave me just a while ago, and my face flushed.

"Good. Let's go back and fix that," she purred loud enough for everyone to hear, but I was sure it was a show for me.

"We'll see. I've gotta see if someone else will help, first." His eyes never left mine as the woman huffed. She turned and glared at me. I laughed right at her. I couldn't stop myself. I knew it was bitchy and catty, but fuck if she wanted to put herself out there like that, this was the shit that happens.

"Take a hike," he told the Prospect as he scurried off into the club. "What's so fucking funny?" he asked, turning his body to me in the stool.

"You." Shaking my head, I reached for the beer the Prospect left for me before his hasty retreat.

"*Me*? You're the cock tease." His voice had a bit of humor to it but was also laced with his frustration.

I smiled 'cause I knew I was. I was surprised he wasn't pissed as shit and most men would be with my little game out in the shop. Needing to get this over with, I blew out a deep breath. Pulling from every bit of strength I could muster, I started strumming my fingers on the bar and suddenly it felt like the room was a thousand degrees, and I was burning alive. I just needed to get this out. "Look, sorry about earlier." I looked down at the bar, not wanting to make eye contact.

After a few beats with him not saying a word, I turned to him, looking at a very remarkable man with a strong jaw and rough beard. It made my pussy clench, and I squeezed my thighs together trying to relieve some of the pressure. His hand grazed my chin, sending an electrical current through my body. As he pulled my head completely up, we were eye to eye. My breath caught as I stared into the most beautiful blue eyes.

He smirked as if he knew what I was thinking deep inside, making my insides flutter. Then he shocked me. "That was the hottest fucking thing I've ever seen." My eyes widened. I expected him to give me shit, yell at me... something. Those words were not what I thought would come out. I kept my mouth shut.

He leaned in close, his lips a hairs breath away from mine. His arms wrapped around my waist, and before I could catch my breath, he pulled me close, slamming his lips down on mine for the second time. The taste of beer, smoke, and desire invaded my mouth, sending every part of me into convulsive shivers. My arms wrapped around his neck, and I instinctively pulled him closer to me. It had been way too long, if ever, since I felt this kind of passion from a man, and I was lost in it.

We began tearing at each other's lips, nipping, sucking and exploring. His tongue pushed its way inside my mouth, and we dueled for power. His hands tightened around my body pulling me tight against him. His rock-hard erection pressed against my body, making my pussy ache. I wanted it... needed it.

I started rubbing myself against him like a cat in heat, trying to get the smallest amount of friction. I badly needed to come, and since my brain had decided to take a vacation, I was relishing in the feel of him.

"Sis!" G.T.'s voice boomed from across the room. I jumped quickly trying to get out of Cruz's arms. Feeling like a teenager getting caught doing something was not a feeling I liked. "What the fuck is going on here?" my brother barked.

"Nothing," I said, wiping my lips with the back of my hand, actually feeling a bit embarrassed. Of course, he's caught me in compromising positions before, but never with a brother. I really didn't like this gutting feeling at all.

"The hell it's nothing." Cruz wrapped his arms around my waist pulling me to his body tightly. I could feel his bulge resting in the crack of my ass, making my legs quiver, wanting him that much more. Shutting my eyes, I hoped my brain kicked in soon.

"Cruz, back the fuck off. She hasn't had a dick in over two years. She doesn't fuck brothers. Ever. She's not a club momma." G.T. crossed his arms over his broad chest standing as my protector, even though I didn't need one; it was still a sweet gesture.

Cruz's body stiffened at his words. I didn't know if he thought maybe I'd turn into a whore for him, or if he knew I was different. I hoped the latter. He didn't say anything, but "things change," his voice booming in my ear.

"This shit doesn't change. Stay the fuck away from her." G.T. began to move closer to us, just then my brain decided to join the party.

Grabbing Cruz's arms, I pulled them from my body,

stepping away. "If you boys are done with your pissing contest, I'm going to see Ma."

"Princess, don't. You need to get your head on straight," G.T. barked.

Placing my hands on my brother's chest, I grabbed his shirt with both hands pulling him to me focusing on his eyes. "My head has been fucked up since that bitch set me up. I already have a Pops; I don't need another. I don't say a fucking word about all the mommas going in and out of your room. Don't you dare start with me."

G.T. placed his hands on my shoulders and began rubbing them up and down. "I'm sorry you went through all that. You know I have your back." He turned to look at Cruz. "In everything."

"I'm good, Bro. I just need to ride. I'll be back later." Letting go of G.T.'s shirt, I smoothed it straight, moving my hands up and down.

"Princess!" Diamond's voice reverberated from the office.

Turning to the sound, "Yes," I answered politely.

"Cruz rides with you," he ordered, not skipping a beat.

"I'll ride with her," G.T. stated firmly.

"No. Cruz goes. End of discussion." With those words, the issue was dropped, and I knew it would be Cruz next to me.

"I'm fine. No worries. Cruz will protect me from all the bad people out there," I said, rolling my eyes.

"You watch out for her," G.T. said while seeming to have a silent, private conversation with Cruz over my shoulder.

Pulling myself together, I knew I needed to get on Sting. "I'll meet you out front," I called back to Cruz as my pulse picked up at the thought of riding my man.

FEELING the wind in my hair and the vibration between my thighs was the ultimate high. It was better than any drug or even sex. This was the only time that I felt truly free. Even when I left those prison gates, I didn't fully feel it. This... I feel it. Having Cruz right beside me was an extra bonus, one I wasn't expecting. Astride his bike, he stayed in sync with me, or maybe it was me staying in sync with him. I really didn't know, but it was beautiful.

I pulled up to Ma's house, loving my first home. I loved the small, yellow, one-story, ranch style home. I'd grown up here, and it held so many wonderful memories for me. All along the front of the large white wraparound porch were all different kinds of flowers, which Ma loved. She's told me repeatedly what they were, but hell if I could remember. All I knew was they were pink, purple, yellow and white, and she took exceptional care of them. Me? I killed anything green I touched. Give me a motor or a carburetor, though, and I could rebuild it like a champ.

Ma must have heard Sting's rumble because she ran out of the house with a broad smile across her beautiful face. As she embraced me, I felt whole.

CHAPTER THREE
Cruz

HARLOW, THE PRINCESS. FUCK ME. I'VE HEARD ABOUT HER since I became a Prospect two years ago. She was all any of the brothers could think about for the longest time. They were sick to death that she had to spend time in the joint. There was nothing the lawyer could do. The bitch involved really used her head and had an air-tight case against Princess, claiming she was blackmailing the mayor because he came to the studio, threatening to tell the town. Like she'd fucking say a word about shit like that. I've known her for a few hours and can see the way she was with the guys. She'd do anything for them... and them for her.

Pops and G.T. were beside themselves those first few months she was in lockdown. They were chomping at the bit, to find out if she was okay. I was just a Prospect at the time and wasn't privileged to know everything, at first. I just watched, and you'd be amazed at what one could see.

I know life in the joint was rough, and when you have a MC like Ravage at your back, shit gets a little more difficult. All it took was one disgruntled woman who's pissed we offed her man to make Princess's life a living hell.

Diamond and Pops pulled some serious strings and mega cash to make sure she was safe inside. She doesn't know what they had to do fully, but I knew they'd do it again in a heartbeat. Looking at her hugging her mom, I could totally see why.

She was everything I never knew I wanted in a woman. She was strong, fierce, smart-assed, loving. And I got all that in the course of a couple hours. When the hell did I turn into a fucking pussy?

"I'll hang out on the porch." I was here to guard and protect. That's exactly, what I planned on doing.

"You want a beer?" Ma asked. We all called her Ma. She was the official mother of the club. She doesn't take shit and tells people like it is, but she knows her place in the club and we respect her for that. Her daughter has learned a lot from her. I could tell, by the way, she was with Diamond.

"Yes, ma'am."

"Damn you, Cruz. Don't call me that. Makes me feel old." She smiled. She was anything but old. She was blonde, with long legs, and had a hot body. At forty-three, she was smokin'. It was no wonder Pops never strayed.

"Sorry," Respect. It's all about respect, and it ran both ways. I had the utmost for Ma. She grabbed me a beer, and I made myself comfortable in the chair. It was unbelievably peaceful out here. Not too many cars drove by, and those that did, knew who lived here and that it was off limits. Everyone knew in this town that we were not to be fucked with.

The Ravage MC has been in order since 1953, thanks to Pops's dad, Striker. Striker was the president and had a real knack for business. He began branching out and taking on new chapters right away. Now, we have a strong name and presence with many other chapters across the country. People don't mess with us. We kill first and think about it later. If you're a threat, you were treated as such. Our threats became more numerous as others wanted what we had. Money. It all boiled down to money. But for the most part, we all stayed to ourselves.

Our runs were becoming longer, and more frequent. But the cash flow was nice, keeping us all very comfortable. We always made sure to do our charitable runs, too. We love our community and protect it with everything we have. That's why most people who live here leave us be and stay out of our business. They get our protection and their happy lives, and we get ours. Win... win.

For me, getting into the club was my lifeline. After spending too much time overseas in a shithole fighting for this country, I came back to a very sick mom who only lasted about a month. Breast cancer. It spread like wild fire, and there was no treatment that could help her. Unfortunately, she didn't have medical insurance, and instead of spending the money, she waited... way too long. This was one of the reasons I opted for early release from the military. I loved every minute I spent with her, but her death tore me up inside. As the once beautiful

Clara Cruz died in my arms, part of me died right along with her.

My old man left when I was a kid, never to be seen from or heard from again. I couldn't even tell you what the hell he looked like. Mom said he looked a lot like me, but I hope she's wrong. I didn't want to be anything like him. Supposedly, he had a piece on the side that he left Mom and me for. It gutted Mom to the bone, but she was always so strong never letting it get her down.

Mom worked her ass off, working two jobs as a waitress, one at a diner, the other at a bar to keep a roof over our heads and food on the table. When I was old enough, I busted my ass mowing grass, cleaning shit, and just about anything else I could come up with to make money. It killed me seeing her come home every night to pass out on the couch from exhaustion. She'd usually take a small nap, then get right back up, and switch into mom mode, making sure homework was done, and dinner was made. She always did the best she could.

As soon as I turned eighteen, I joined the Marines, trying to make to something of my life. Working my ass off to take care of mom was really all I knew. I thought joining would give her a little reprieve from busting her ass so hard. I could send her money without being another burden, and maybe I could go to school later. The school part was lost in the wind when I held my mom in my arms.

My anger got the best of me after mom passed. I went back into fight mode from being overseas to being pissed all the time, which got me locked up for a bit. I was out soon enough, only six months for aggravated assault. The bastard deserved it though. Fucker tried to cheat me out of some cash. I bet he never pulls that shit again... at least not on me.

I had a buddy, Steeler, who was a hang-around to the Ravage MC and didn't think much of it at the time. I was too lost, and really my only salvation was riding. When Steeler talked to me about coming and hanging out with them, I scoffed at the idea. But as I hung around with him, I got to know the guys, and got further in. What I liked best was that these men didn't take shit from anyone. They followed their own rules and had their own way of life. They answered to no one. That was exactly how I felt at the time. With the pussy, always around, it was an extra fucking bonus. Prospecting was fucking hell. Cleaning the guys shit up, cleaning their barf after parties... trust me, it wasn't glamorous. But I did my time. And when they voted to patch me in, I was on fucking cloud nine. I couldn't imagine my life without the club.

I wondered how much Princess knew about what happens in the club. I was sure she knew more than any of the other women around, considering the shit we all voted on for her to help out with while in the joint. The one bitch we had her take care of went through my personal shit after I fucked her and passed out. Apparently she found my book. It's where I keep important information about the club. There wasn't much documentation, just mostly numbers. When I found out she had the info, she was already locked up on drug charges.

That's where Princess stepped in. She did it quietly, and everyone inside turned a blind eye.

I can't say our first meeting was pleasant. I could

sense by her stance in the garage that she was planning on taking my gun from me, but the fact her arm stopped so abruptly when she saw my rag, was astonishing. Respect. She totally had it.

Then her fucking ass challenges me to the ring. I don't hit women, not my style. I've heard stories from the guys of Princess completely holding her own in the ring, even banging up Dagger pretty good, and I do admit I'd love to see her kicking ass in there. Just thinking about it makes my dick hard.

When she climbed on her bike and fucked it in front of all of us brothers, I almost came in my damn pants. That was the hottest fucking thing I'd ever seen, her long dark hair cascading around her curvy body. I knew her tits had to be real, by the way; they hung in her shirt, heavy and full. Those damn ripped jeans leaving little to the imagination, and her tight Harley shirt showed off a small bit of ink through the sleeve. I knew then that I had to be inside her. She threw out some bullshit excuse about not sleeping with brothers, but that wasn't going to deter me in the slightest. Truth be told; I liked the fact my brothers hadn't had her.

She would truly be mine. And she would be underneath me.

Those lips of hers are unbelievably soft. I could still taste that fucking berry shit from her lips on my tongue. The way her tongue dueled mine had me wanting to throw her up on the bar and fuck her raw. I couldn't wait to get between her legs. When she came on her bike, she was so damn quiet. Not when I'm done with her. She'll be screaming my fucking name.

Pop... pop... pop... Gunfire rang out as a black cage drove past with its side door wide open. Grabbing my gun, I fired back in quick reaction and dropped behind the porch post. The front door flew open as Princess stormed out, gun pointed and firing with great aim, hitting the cage repeatedly. The shots kept coming, and Princess didn't flinch or shy away. She ducked a few times, but kept moving.

We were both in a dead sprint to our bikes firing them up and taking off after the cage. Weaving in and out of traffic, we kept on its tail, firing shots back and forth. I couldn't help the hard-on I got watching Princess shoot while still maneuvering her bike effortlessly. *Not the time for that shit.*

Pulling up besides the cage, I began shooting rapidly, hitting one of the guys. Princess's shots hit another who fell out, causing her to stop her bike abruptly, unable to swerve out of the way. Shooting again, I aimed for the tires, but fucking missed as it spun off. There was no way I was leaving her alone out here.

Turning back around, I reached Princess, who was down on the ground checking out the shooter. "Dead?"

"Yeah..." Grabbing my phone, I called Dagger giving him our current location and advising clean up. I knew it would only take about five minutes before the cavalry came in.

"You all right?" Looking at her, I could see she seemed fine, no blood anywhere, but being a woman you never know how they react to this shit.

"I'm good." She smiled. "Home, sweet home. You know this guy?"

"Looks like one of Rabbit's crew." Damn it. Rabbit's known for running drugs throughout the state and we have dealings with him. This can't be good.

"I take it he's one of *the everyone* that Diamond wants me to be careful of, huh?" She looked as if she was studying the body before her, lifting up the shirt, taking in all the ink and marks on it totally unfazed she was looking at a dead body.

"Somethin' like that." The roar of bikes in the distance snapped me into action. "Get your ass on your bike and go back to Ma's house. I'll send some guys over."

If looks could kill, I'd be lying dead next to the man on the road. "I'm just as much a part of this as you are," she growled out. It was sexy as hell, but her trying to control shit was gonna stop quick.

"I'm not gonna say it again. Fucking go. Now." I ordered.

"If you remember, it was my fucking shot that killed the bastard." She stood up heading towards her bike. I could see in her face it was killing her to have to leave the scene, but she listened and headed back the way we came. I held in my chuckle. Damn woman.

"Pops and G.T. are at the house. What the fuck happened?" Dagger clipped, looking at the dead body at my feet.

"Drive-by. Black cage. Four guys inside. Two in the back were shot; this one fell out. Cage drove off." I relayed.

"Shit. It's one of Rabbit's guys," Zed said, kneeling down to see where the wounds were. "She shot him, didn't she?" He eyed me suspiciously.

"Yeah. She came out guns blazing, and I didn't have time to fight with her about staying back. She got him; I got the other." I pressed my hands deep in my pockets.

"I'm sure you got the other," Rhys said, laughing. Fuck. I didn't need this shit.

"You got this? I wanna make sure the house is all right."

"Go. We got this." As Dagger, Guns, Zed, and Tug began their work, I rode quickly to the house.

"THEY FUCKING SHOT HER, POPS!" Princess's voice was enraged, the anger dripping off every word coming out of her mouth. I noticed a splattering of blood on one of the walls, as I walked into the house. Ma was holding her shoulder and appeared to be in a tremendous amount of pain, but didn't utter a complaint. "Get Doc here now!" she barked out.

Princess began ripping away the clothes on Ma's body, finding the entrance of the bullet. Turning her softly, she also appeared to find the exit wound.

"I'll find them. Don't you fucking worry about that," G.T. ground out, rushing out of the room.

"What do you need?" I asked, since standing there watching was not helping anyone.

"I need towels and duct tape," Princess ordered.

"Here." G.T. was one step ahead, handing both items to her. Watching Princess work like a well-oiled machine was beautiful. She didn't shy away from the blood or do that prissy shit that most women do. She dug in and got the job done. I was in a bit of awe. Every fucking move this woman made, made me want to stick my dick in her. *Shit*.

Pops stopped my admiration. "Cruz, you get Princess and Ma back to the clubhouse. Call Breaker and Buzz to bring the cage. Call Doc and get him to the clubhouse now." I nodded as he turned to G.T. "You and me ride."

THE CLUBHOUSE WAS BUZZING while Doc worked on Ma. She appeared to be just fine, but one woman was not. Princess hadn't stopped pacing since Doc started working on Ma. Every so often she paused to have a shot of Jack and then continued to pace.

Everyone left her alone not wanting to be on the end of her rage, I assumed, but I couldn't care less if I pissed her off. Walking up in front of her, I gently grabbed her shoulders.

"Don't," she barked at me.

"Come on." She looked at her Ma laying on the pool table getting stitched up and shook her head. "It'll just take a minute. Trust me." She looked up into my eyes as if she was battling some inner turmoil then sighed.

She nodded, "All right. A few minutes, then I gotta get back."

Smiling, I led her outside the clubhouse to the back gym. I'd been in her shoes before, seeing someone I love shot and not being able to do a damn thing about it.

When Steeler was shot outside of the club, I didn't know what the fuck to do. The brothers swooped in and took care of it, and at that exact moment, I knew this life was for me.

"The ring?" she questioned, looking at the large square in the center of the gym, her eyes wide.

"Yep. Get taped up."

She smiled. "You wanna fight me?" I could see her wheels turning.

"I'm not going to fight you. You're just gonna get some of your frustration out." There was no way I wanted to hit this woman, whether she accepted it or not, I'd protect her till my dying breath. God, I knew this fucking woman a day, and she was already so fucking far under my damn skin.

"Oh, come on. You're just going to let me hit you like some pansy ass bitch, huh?" The devil gleaming in her eyes had me utterly intrigued.

"I'll tape up, but I'm not swinging."

"Pussy."

After helping each other tape up and removing our boots, we climbed into the ring. She pulled her hair into some kind of bun thing on her head as she moved her neck from side to side. Hearing stories about Princess' ability in the ring, I admit I was intrigued. The guys supposedly taught her to fight, and she always held her head up high even if she ended up bloody, or so I was told. Now I'd get a personal view.

As we squared off, my pulse began to pick up. I dodged swing after swing until she nailed me right in the mouth, sending blood flying. Wiping it from my face, we began a fighting dance. I never once swung, only blocked.

"Come on. Fight me damn it!" she growled at me, swinging hard, kicking me in the gut.

"No," I said as I regained my composure, standing tall. I didn't hear the door to the gym open, only the whoops and hollers of all my brothers and Ma coming into the gym. Shit.

"Hey, boys. This pussy here won't fight back," she goaded me. I knew what I had to do. I didn't want to, but I knew I had to. No fucking way I'd let the brothers see me not fight back.

She blocked several of my swings, but I made contact with the right hook to her cheek and she stumbled back. I stopped what I was doing and rushed to her. She smiled giving me a right hook of her own sending me staggering back a bit.

This went on for what seemed like forever. Blood was gushing down both of our faces. The bell on the side started going off as Dagger banged on it, hard. We knew it was over. Fuck if this bitch didn't have the biggest balls I've ever seen.

I stalked towards her, and her eyes widened. I'm not sure what my face looked like, but all I could feel was my throbbing dick needing a home and fast. Grabbing her, I slammed my lips to hers; just taking everything I possibly could from her. As her body melted into mine, I kept going, not giving two shits about the crowd below us. Tasting the sweat and blood throughout my mouth spurred me on.

Princess pulled away, wincing. As I looked at her lip, I

could see it was split wide open. "Doc still here?" I called out.

"In the clubhouse!" Rhys called out.

"Get checked out," I said, staring at her lip, not believing I just did that to her, a bit ashamed with myself, in fact.

"I'm fine," she uttered and patted her lip with her hand.

"I didn't ask. Go," I ordered. Getting right in her face, "Get your fucking ass in there and get checked out. Now." My voice was dead calm and utterly serious, and when her eyes flashed acceptance, I knew I'd gotten her.

Princess took off out of the ring, and I climbed out. "You sure you want that, Brother?" Dagger asked. He's always in protection mode. I didn't think he had any other switch.

"Hell yeah," I said, wiping the blood from my face with a towel.

G.T. stepped in front of me. "You fucking hurt her; I'll put a bullet in your fucking head."

"Wouldn't expect anything less." And I wouldn't. She's his blood. You protect blood and family at all costs. I respected that about G.T.

"I'm fucking serious. She's not free pussy." The anger radiating off my brother was tangible. I understood it, but it was fucking pissing me off.

Going toe-to-toe with G.T, I never thought I would want to rip someone's head off so much. "You don't think I fucking know that?"

"I'm starting to wonder. You forget I see the pussy coming out of your room."

"And I see what comes out of yours," I fire back knowing he didn't want his business being known by his sister.

"Just don't fuck her over." G.T. shoulder-checked me, blowing past me towards the clubhouse. Fuck that shit. As I walked towards him to show him what I thought with my fists, Dagger's words stopped me in my tracks.

"Cruz. You need to get your kid here. We're on lockdown." Fuck. Those words sent everything spiraling. I knew if Cooper came here, his bitch of a mother would make it a point to come, too. Shit if this wasn't gonna be fucked up.

CHAPTER FOUR
Harlow

THE SHOTS OF JACK HELPED NUMB THE PAIN COURSING through my body. I didn't know how Cruz knew what I needed, but damn he did. Feeling lost and broken wasn't easy. I wanted to rip those assholes apart for shooting at Ma. Throwing blow for blow was such a relief, and I didn't know if he knew, but he brought back some awesome memories. I learned so much in that very ring, mostly from G.T., but the other brothers, as well.

Casey left earlier in the day and was due back any time. With us now on lockdown, everyone who was involved with the club was making his or her way inside. Casey went to our place to grab our stuff, and I desperately wanted her to get back here.

Pops was nice enough to let me crash in his room for a bit after the fight. I needed to rest, and being on lockdown, I didn't want to be out in the main part of the clubhouse or in the bunks with all the kids running around. I needed a bit of peace.

Taking another swig of Jack from the bottle, I placed it on the small nightstand by the bed. Falling down, I spread out on the blood-red comforter and pillows that I'm sure Ma picked out 'cause Pops could give two shits what the place looked like. My face was hurting like a bitch, and I bet it looked just as bad.

After the Doc patched me up, I showered and called Casey giving her a list of the stuff I wanted. Lord knows how long we'd be on lockdown. No one was saying shit about the guy who shot Ma. When I asked, I was told it was *club business.*

Bang... Bang... Bang... I jumped up feeling a horrible head rush from moving way too fast. I hoped I didn't have a concussion from the hard ass blow Cruz gave me. "Hang on," I groaned pulling myself out of bed. Opening the door, Casey stood there. Her beautiful smile instantly fell at the sight of me. "Looks that bad, huh?" I laughed.

"Holy shit, girl. You weren't kidding about the fight." Casey took in my face as she stepped in, locking the door behind her. When she reached to touch it, I shied away, heading back over to the bottle of Jack, taking another deep swig.

"That shit helping at all?" she asked throwing our bags in the corner. If we were on lockdown, she was on lockdown, too. Her dad, Bam, died three years ago during a run. We never got the details, but Bam was all that Casey had. Her whore of a mom left her when she was a baby. Bam raised her here, in this world. She was tough, but not a fighter, like me. She was more inclined to use her brains to get what she wanted instead of her fists. But since she was the kid of a patched member, even though passed, she was protected, too.

"A little." Sitting on the edge of the bed, I sighed.

"What's up?" she asked, sitting next to me and wrapping her arm around my shoulder.

"Case, I haven't been home twenty-four hours yet, and I've kicked a shop guy's ass, got shot at, patched up my Ma, and got into a knock down drag out fight with a brother."

"Welcome home," she said smiling.

Laughing, "Yeah, welcome home." I paused, thinking. "I haven't had shit going on for two years. I missed this."

"I missed you," she said, squeezing me. "Come on. This is your party. Let's get out there and enjoy it."

After Casey worked her magic on fixing my face, we headed out to the bar. She wasn't shitting when she said the place was packed. There was wall to wall people, and I had no idea where they would all sleep, and why I cared I had no idea. I guessed the bunks. I couldn't remember the last time I was part of a lockdown.

As we walked through the crowd of people, I began seeing more and more people that I knew. Hugging each one of them, I made my way to the bar, getting a shot of Jack from Buzz or Breaker. I couldn't tell who was who. They took being identical twins to the ultimate level. Maybe I could talk them into some ink on their hands so I could tell them apart. I laughed at the idea, yeah, right.

Legs, Bubbles, and Flash were there with open arms, hugging me repeatedly. These ol' ladies have been around since I was a kid and were my Ma's best friends.

They proudly wore their 'Property of' patches, and while some hung tight to their guys, others like Flash didn't stay close, at all. She free-floated, and Dagger never seemed to say a word as he was doing the same.

Even seeing the other ol' ladies I didn't know so well and watching their little kids run around the clubhouse felt comforting. The guys added on a room off of the gym for all the kids to go and play. It also had tons of bunk beds, so they could all have a big sleepover. Pops said they had to since so many of the brothers had families that need protection.

Scanning the room, my eyes landed on an adorable little boy. His hair was a light brown and his eyes shined a beautiful blue. He had adorable carpenter jeans on with a 'Support Your Local Ravage MC' t-shirt on. "Cooper!" I heard Cruz's voice boom my eyes shot up in his direction. He scooped the little boy up and began tickling him up in the air. The little boy laughing uncontrollably. He had to be Cruz's son. Damn.

Standing next to Cruz was a beautiful, long-haired, blonde with very short shorts on, making her legs look like they went on for miles, along with a tank top that showed most of her tits off except for her nipples. Her body kicked ass. Her huge boobs and curvy hips made her stand out in the sea of people, and she carried herself like she knew it. Hell, I knew it. As the woman touched Cruz's arm, he turned and smiled at her. My heart dropped. She must be his ol' lady, and I kissed him a few hours ago, in front of all the guys. *Shit. Shit. Shit.*

"Is he the one you fought?" Casey asked, following my line of sight.

"What gave it away? The black and blue eye or the busted lip?" My sarcasm hiding my true feelings inside.

"Ha. Ha. So what do you think? His ol' lady?" she asked, and I didn't want to answer. I just wanted to drink. A lot. This was the exact reason I never got involved with brothers. Now I'm on lockdown with them and had to watch them be one big happy fucking family. I couldn't stand this shit. This was the exact reason rules were in fucking place, even if they're self-imposed.

"Looks like it. I need a drink," I said, turning back towards the bar. "B.Boys!" I called slamming my hand to the bar but not knowing who was who and using the first name that came to mind. "I need Jack and beer. Please." I downed the Jack and began on the beer. I needed to forget what a dumbass I was.

"Princess?" Cruz's deep voice behind me sent shivers up my spine, and I wanted to kick myself in the ass. Turning slowly, I came face to face with an adorable little boy who looked like an exact replica of Cruz, and if I had to guess was around two and a half years old, not that I was a child expert. But the smile radiating off of him was contagious.

"Hey, little guy," I said, smiling at the boy. "You look just like your daddy."

"Cooper, say hi to Princess." Cooper gave me his sparkling megawatt smile and giggled.

"Pin... ess, owie," Cooper's adorable voice tried to say, making my smile grow wide.

"It's nice to meet you, Bud. I'm okay. The owie doesn't hurt." Yeah right. As the beautiful blonde approached Cruz's side, I felt my body stiffen. Then, seeing Cooper cling to his daddy's arm set several warning bells off in my head, but it wasn't my business.

The blonde ran her fake nails down Cruz's arm, and damn if part of me wanted to tear her fucking arm off. But I kept myself in check, taking another swig of my almost empty beer; I watched the scene unfold in front of me. I should have known that Cruz would have an ol' lady. "Who's this?" her way too high pitched voice questioned.

He addressed me and not her. "Princess, this is Mel, Cooper's mom." I eyed him, waiting for the other part of the introduction, but it never came.

"Harlow," I said, nodding. "I got shit to do." Looking at Casey, I chin nodded to the door, but she shook her head.

"I'm not going out there," she said, taking a shot of Jack.

"Why?"

"I'm just not. Go on. I'll be fine." She nodded to the door. I pulled myself away from their happy little family, needing some air. Grabbing another beer and leaving Casey in the bar, I headed out to the courtyard. The guys made a separate space right off the clubhouse that was protected all the way around by tall, elaborate gates. In the center was a huge fire pit that was roaring to life.

Pops and Ma were sitting around it, along with many of the brothers. As I scanned the area, G.T. was leaning up against the fence talking to some brunette who looked like a club momma judging from her nonexistent clothes. That was another reason why I hated lockdowns, having the whores and ol' ladies in one area was always a bad idea. One slip and chaos could erupt sending everything spiraling into oblivion.

Making my way to Ma, I asked her "You feeling okay?" and sat down next to her.

"Yeah. I'm good. Nothing, a few drinks, can't fix," Ma said, smiling. She's always been so damn strong. I envied her. I never said that I wanted to be her when I grew up, for the mere fact that I didn't allow myself to get close enough to one of the brothers to become an ol' lady. But I learned from her strength and the way she held herself and took that to heart.

"You know who this was?" I asked, knowing that my Pops was going to interject, but I had to keep trying.

As if on cue, "It's club business, Princess, let it go." It was Pops' way of giving me a direct order without me flying off the handle. I loved that he knew me so well.

"Pops, why didn't you tell me that Cruz has an ol' lady?" No offense, but the brothers knew me and knew that I didn't mess around with them. To have not one of them tell me that Cruz had an ol' lady pissed me off considering most of them were there in the ringside seat for the kiss.

"He doesn't. And it's not my business to tell," Pops stated firmly. I knew he wouldn't ever tell another brother's business when it came to women, but I had hoped being his daughter it'd be different. Once again, I was wrong.

"I just met her, Pops. Mel and Cooper," I said, gazing into the fire, pulling from the bottle in my hand, trying to tap down emotions I had no right to have.

"That's just his kid's mom. She's been trying to get

back with him for years. He doesn't want her. She's a whore." I didn't respond. There was no use. I knew what I saw, and she was staking a claim on him. Fine. Whatever. Time to get over it.

"So, how's it feel to be out, girl?" Dagger's voice came from behind me. Dagger has been my uncle, which I use the term loosely because he's always trying to fuck me, for as long as I could remember. He got his name because, I hear, he's very good with his knife. Not that I've ever seen him in action. A light beard and mustache lined his face, falling down to his chest. His hair was tucked under his stocking cap with the Ravage MC skull with flames symbol on the front. He sat next to me, and I turned to face him.

"Like coming home," I answered honestly.

"Well, we're glad to have our Princess back in the fold. We missed your smart little ass around here."

I rolled my eyes. Some loved my mouth, while others still didn't get me. "Hey, someone's gotta keep you boys in line."

"We're damn glad you're back to do it, girl." Dagger wrapped his arm around my shoulders, pulling me tight into him. Resting my head on his shoulder, I smelled the familiar smell of leather and smoke making being home real. Closing my eyes, I let the warmth of the fire and Dagger flush through my body.

Dagger was known as a ladies' man. His ol' lady, Flash and him, have some sort of arrangement, or so it's been said. All I knew for sure was I've seen Dagger with many club mommas in and out of this place, and Flash never bats an eyelash. Flash was a huge flirt with all the guys, but I have no idea if she hits any of it. It's really not my business.

"What the fuck?" Cruz's growl had my eyes popping open, but I didn't move out of Dagger's arms. I had no need to. In one arm, he was carrying Cooper, and not too far behind him was his woman.

"Problem?" I asked, faking boredom with the question.

"Why the fuck are you curled up with my brother?" his voice turned dangerously angry, sending pin-pricks up the back of my neck. I didn't know him, but from being in the ring with him and the concern shone in his eyes after he hit me, I didn't think he'd ever physically hurt me.

I couldn't take it. "He's welcoming me home." Yeah. I was egging him on, sue me.

Cruz stalked closer, handing off Cooper to Pops. I watched closely, staying still. I could hear Dagger's slight chuckle, but he didn't say a word. "You think I'm fucking kidding when I tell you all she's my girl?" His question was directed at Dagger, and not me.

"I'm not your girl," I clipped, but my words were ignored.

"I'm just providing *our* girl with a little comfort." Dagger was baiting him; that much was clear, but why? For shits and giggles?

"If she needs comfort, I'll fucking provide it. Get off of her." My anger was growing, but I tapped it down. Dagger released his arm as I sat back in my chair, crossing my arms over my chest, pushing my breasts up higher in my shirt.

Cruz grabbed my arms roughly and pulled me up to him, so our bodies were flush against each other. He slammed his lips down on mine, and my body gave in. Gasping, I pulled away. "I'm not doing this. Especially in front of your ol' lady and your kid." I tore myself out of his grasp and walked towards the clubhouse.

Cruz didn't let me get far. Wrapping his arms around my waist, he pulled me flush to his body and I tried to pull away. He leaned to my ear. "You think that whore over there is my ol' lady? Fuck no. She's Cooper's mother. That's as far as it goes."

"I will not be someone's piece of ass. Not Ever."

"No, you definitely won't, but you will be under me tonight." His arrogance was annoying as shit, but the authority he gave off was making my panties wet. I needed space. His presence was just too much.

"Fuck no. Dream on." Fighting to get out of his grasp, I was at a disadvantage with all the alcohol coursing through my veins.

"Honey, what's going on?" Mel stood before us. I looked into her eyes, and I wanted to claw them out. I hated her just for breathing. Shit.

"Don't fucking 'honey' me. Get the fuck back in the club." She took a step back and walked towards the door.

"Wait!" I yelled as she turned, facing me, her eyes laced with ice. "You his ol' lady?" I wanted to hear it from her mouth.

She paused for a moment as I waited for the words to come across her lips. Her face looked pained to say them, "No. I'm not."

"But you want to be," I said, not missing a beat.

"I *am* the mother of his child," she clipped, putting her hand on her hip.

"And that don't mean shit," came from Cruz's hard body behind me.

I turned in Cruz's arms facing him. "Look, I'm not big on all this drama. That's why I stay clear of the brothers." I gave him a soft peck on the lips. "Bye," I pulled out of his arms and flew back to the clubhouse.

Rushing through the crowds of people, I made my way to the bar. "B.Boy, I need a shot of Jack, please." He placed it on the bar, and I took it, quickly feeling the burn as it reached my stomach. There was no need to slow down, Pops' room was only a few feet away even if I had to crash on the floor or I could always bunk with Casey.

Speaking of which, where did she go?

Looking out over the sea of people, many of the brothers were already in the throes of getting laid. And it made my stomach clench. I wasn't supposed to be on lockdown. I was supposed to be out finding me a dick, but instead I get to sit back and watch. Fun times.

"Hey, Baby." An unfamiliar voice came from my side. Standing before me was a tall man, broad shoulders, blonde hair, and green eyes; attractive in his own way. His smile was bright before he put a smoke inside of it. He wasn't wearing a rag. He didn't look like a preppy boy but definitely not a biker, either. Promising.

"Hey. Who are you?"

"Buzz and Breaker's brother, Nick. They told me I needed to come down here. I'm hanging around... thinking of patching in."

I eyed him. "But you're not a Prospect yet?"

"Nope. But I will be soon." This couldn't be more fucking perfect.

"I'm Harlow. Nice to meet ya." I smiled my most seductive smile knowing he'd be putty in my hands. I reached out, grazing my hand on his chest, turning the heat up a few notches.

"Wanna tell me what happened to you?" he asked, looking at the black and blue on my face, but not seeming to be put off by it in the slightest.

"Minor squabble." I shrugged.

"You're still hot as hell," he said stepping closer into my space. I grabbed the Jack, downing another gulp.

"Really? Wanna show me how much?" I asked, not beating around the bush. There was no point. As of that moment, this man had no affiliation with the club, and it would just be a one night thing. The chances of him actually becoming a Prospect were slim, judging by his demeanor. He was too soft for this life; nothing like his brothers seemed to be.

"Absolutely," he said, stubbing his smoke out and standing. "Can I borrow your room?" He asked the B.Boys.

"No!" they yelled in unison. "You're not fucking her," one of them said adamantly.

"Now... now boys." I said, letting my words drip like sweet honey. "It's all right. We'll make due," I said, grabbing his hand.

"Dude. You wanna get patched in... this is not one to touch," one of the B.Boys said.

"Come on." I pulled his arm before he had a chance to think. No one needed to know. It'd be a quick fuck and done. I raced to the hallway because I needed his dick inside me now.

Reaching the bathroom, I slammed the door and locked it, pushing Nick against the door and kissing his neck while tearing at his clothes. His chest was defined, and his stomach had a small pouch to it, but I didn't give a flying shit. Ripping his pants off, I got to work.

CHAPTER FIVE
Cruz

AFTER SETTLING COOPER IN HIS CRIB IN MY ROOM, I searched for Princess, but everywhere I looked she didn't turn up. I knew she had to be here somewhere. No one would dare let her leave the property.

Finding Breaker and Buzz, they pushed me a beer across the bar. "You seen Princess?" They both eyed each other as if they were talking between themselves with their eyes. It was pissing me off. What the fuck was going on?

"I asked you a fucking question. Where is she?" I growled, slamming my hand down on the bar causing everything on it to shake.

"We had our brother come here for lockdown," Buzz said, visibly nervous as he should fucking be.

"She's fucking him?" Fury raced through my body as

they ignored my question. I was gonna crush this little asshole and then spank her fucking ass. "Where?"

"Bathroom, I think," Breaker mumbled.

"I'll deal with you two later." Stalking off down the hall, there was no way to keep my temper in check. It was full bore. She wanted to fuck... I'll give her a fuck. I turned the door handle; it was locked. "Open the fucking door, Princess!" I said banging on the door hard, shaking the walls. "Now!"

"Go away!" she yelled through the door.

"Open it or I'm busting it the fuck down!" Fuck it. Using my boot, I kicked the door as hard as I could, sending pieces of it flying in every direction. Princess didn't move from the countertop, but the prick that was on his knees in front of her jumped as far back as he could crashing into the bath tub. What a pussy.

Stalking over to the guy, I picked his naked ass up off the ground, throwing him out the broken door, slamming him against the back wall along with his clothes right behind him. "Don't let me see you later." I snarled in warning.

"What the fuck is wrong with you?" Princess clipped. She sat there in her black lacy bra with her jeans unbuttoned. She looked like a beautiful goddess, and if I weren't so damn pissed at her; I would want to treat her like one. But right now I was too fucking pissed.

"Wrong with me? I'll tell you; you're with me, and you go and fuck some asshole?" Moving in between her legs, I looked at all the curves of her body making my mouth dry and my throat catch. The tats on her upper shoulder and arm were works of art... skulls, flames with intricate flowers mixed in, no doubt a tribute to the club.

"I'm not yours. You can't claim someone who doesn't want to be claimed." She crossed her arms, pushing those beautiful tits higher as her nipples peeked from under her bra.

"Bullshit. You've been here long enough to know how this shit works. No other guy here is to touch you. No guy period is to touch you. Ever. Except me."

"You fucking wish," she said, trying to pull away from me like that was gonna fucking happen.

"I don't wish shit. I take it." Grabbing her legs, I pulled her down to the edge of the counter. She tried to squirm away, but I locked her down with my arm. "Don't, you know you want this."

Pulling her zipper and pants down, she was commando and damn if that didn't cause my dick to throb. "I can't," she said quietly.

"Fuck yeah, you can." She acted as if she was fighting with herself. She wasn't fighting what I was doing, but she wasn't participating, either. Something in her snapped as she tore at my clothes. In a matter of seconds... we were both naked. Her lips crashed into mine as she tried to take control, but I wouldn't allow it. This was my show.

Princess's breathing picked up rapidly. Reaching down between our bodies, my hand grazed her sopping wet pussy. Sliding my fingers in her hot flesh, her pussy gripped them, tightly pulling them further into her body greedily. "You like that?" Princess made some sort of strangled sound deep in her throat urging me on.

"Answer me." I growled. "Always answer me."

"Yes." She whispered.

She was way too fucking quiet. There was no fucking way she wasn't going to be screaming my name. Her quick panting noises were driving me crazy, but I wanted the scream. Reaching into my jeans on the floor, I grabbed a condom, sheathing myself in record time. I needed to feel her pussy around my dick. Pulling her legs up and bending them at the knees, so her feet were resting on the counter, and she was open wide to me, I placed my arms on either side of her body trapping her. "This isn't gonna be gentle," I said before crashing my lips down feeling her soft flesh.

Punching my cock inside her, I wasn't surprised that she was tight as shit. The knowledge that no one had been inside of her for two years had me pushing harder. I wanted to claim this woman, and as soon as this shit gets sorted out, I'll have her fucking bareback. She screamed as I rammed the last little bit of my cock inside of her. "You're so fucking tight, Baby."

"God, that feels so good," she said as her head rolled back. Lifting up, I pumped in and out of her hard, loving her vice grip pussy. The room was sweltering, and sweat dripped down my body mixing with hers creating an erotic aroma my dick couldn't get enough of.

"Time to come, Princess." Taking my thumb, I rubbed her clit roughly, sending her off into her explosion. She screamed my name loud, just as I said she would. My dick throbbed as she milked every last drop of cum out of me. Collapsing onto her, our bodies trembling as we tried to catch our breath, I didn't want to disconnect from her yet, the connection was too much.

Claps coming from the doorway had both of our heads snapping to the sound. Shit. The fucking door. "Get out!" I shouted.

Dagger and Rhys were standing in the doorway with shit-eating grins plastered on their faces. "Fucking awesome show. Now I need to get laid." Dagger took off, and Rhys just stood in place.

"Get one of the Prospects to find a door out back!" I growled as he eyed Princess's body. Not that he could see much, but I didn't fucking like it. He chuckled, shaking his head walking off.

"Get off," Princess said, trying to push me off.

"No." Her damn brain was taking over again.

"Now!" she yelled her anger rising.

"No. Stop whatever it is that you're thinking." I could only imagine the shit that was racing through that thick skull of hers. She seemed to like to conjure up shit for the fun of it.

"This is why I don't fuck brothers. It won't happen again." She tried to push me off of her, but I wouldn't budge.

"Listen to me. That's enough of this fucking bullshit. My dick in you right now says that no one touches you, but me. Got it?"

Her eyes showed a small bit of vulnerability that I hadn't seen before. She's always so damn strong and hard to read. "What about her?" Her voice was barely a whisper.

"She's nothing. She's only here because she wouldn't leave Cooper. But that shit's about to change."

"How?"

"You're gonna be my ol' lady. You're gonna be part of Cooper's life. I'm not having her hanging around."

"You want me to be his mom? We just fucking met! Are you fucking crazy? And ol' lady?" Her eyes lit up in panic as her breathing picked up.

"I'm not playing games. Not my style. You're mine, and you will be at my side." Her body relaxed a bit, and she melted back into me, but the trepidation was still there. I needed to find some way to get rid of that shit.

"You have no idea what you are doing," she said, shaking her head.

"From what I saw already, I probably don't." Smiling at her, I brushed my lips against hers as she arched her body, taking the kiss to another level completely. My dick grew inside of her, and my hips began pumping. Her moans and mews kept me going.

As we both stood there breathless, for the second time, I edged out of her, needing to get the condom off before it exploded.

Movement at the door caught my eye as Princess tried to cover her body haphazardly with her hands.

"Cruz?" Tug's voice came from the doorway.

Grabbing the door from his hand, I snapped, "Thanks."

"You need help?" He eyed Princess, which pissed me off.

Looking down at my naked body, I growled, "What'd you think?"

"Later."

Instead of attaching the door to the hinges, I rested it against the frame to block out all the fucking eyes that were everywhere. Princess hopped down from the counter grabbing her clothes, quickly throwing them on. "I'm gonna head to bed," she said not looking at me. To hell if she was gonna be embarrassed.

"You're in my bed," I said grabbing her arm and pulling her to me staring into the beautiful blue eyes of hers.

"I can't," she whispered as her head sunk into my chest.

"Why the fuck not?"

"I have a roll in Pops' room. I'm just gonna crash there." Her head shook slightly on my chest.

Placing my hand under her chin, I forced her eyes to meet mine. "You didn't hear me right. Get your ass in my room and lock the fucking door. Coop's sleeping in the side room. I've got shit to take care of. You'd better be in there when I get back. If you're not, I'll come find you." My eyes didn't leave her until she nodded. I moved the two doors getting out of the tight space.

I needed to get shit sorted out with Mel. I was tired of that bitch. I swear to God I think she poked holes in the condom when I fucked her. How the hell else would she get knocked up? And Coop looked just like me so I couldn't fucking deny him, not that I wanted to. Since she told me she was pregnant, she's been trying to get in with me. Sure, I've fucked her a couple of times, why the hell not, it was free pussy. I didn't want shit from her. I was only grateful she gave me my boy.

Stalking over to the couch in the main room of the clubhouse, she sat snorting powder haphazardly draped over the guy next to her; I couldn't believe I was stuck with this woman in my life forever. She looked up at me, eyes dilated, completely high.

"Hey, Honey." She smiled as much as she could and tried to get her bearings.

"Don't come to my room. Stay the fuck out here and away from me."

"I wanna see my boy," she whined, but it didn't mean shit to me. I was done with this bitch.

"No, you can see him tomorrow. Till then, stay the fuck away." Turning away, Mel said a few words that I didn't catch, nor did I fucking care. I had a Princess that needed attention.

Walking into my room, I couldn't help but smile seeing Princess lying in my bed covered from head to toe with my blankets, making me hard a-fucking-gain. I needed to be inside of her, but I had beaten the shit out her and fucked her good already. She needed to sleep.

Checking in on Cooper, I was glad to see that he was sound asleep. Coop has always been a great sleeper; not much could wake the boy up. That was good considering God knows what happened at his mom's place.

After locking the door and stripping, I climbed into bed, pulling this beautiful woman into my body. As she melted into me, I knew I'd made the right decision to hang on to this one.

BANG... BANG... BANG "WHAT THE FUCK?" Princess groaned from underneath me. Somehow during the night she laid on her back, with my body draped across hers. Having this little interruption when I could have my dick inside her again was not making me happy.

"Hang on, Baby." Scooting out of bed, I threw my jeans on, not bothering to button them.

Pulling the door open, I was confronted immediately with a very angry G.T. "What the fuck is going on here?" he said, as he barged in the room, his eyes landing on the woman clutching the sheet around her naked body in my bed.

"G.T., calm down, you're gonna wake up my boy."

Princess sat up in bed, her eyes growing wide as a strangled gasp came from her lips, but remaining quiet. She was a grown fucking adult and had no reason to feel embarrassed.

"Princess, what the hell is going on here?" G.T. moved to her side of the bed kneeling down to the floor, his eyes turning soft for his sister.

Princess stared at her brother attempting to open her mouth, but nothing came out. As her eyes found mine, they flickered, not telling me much of anything, but as she looked back at her brother the words fell from her lips. "Get me out of here."

Moving away from the door; I'd be damned if she was pushing me away. "Princess, you're not going anywhere." I stood at the end of the bed staring down at her. Her head bowed low to her chest.

"Yes. I am." Her voice was a quiet whisper. This was not the Princess that I met yesterday. This one was timid, lost, and I didn't fucking like it one bit. This was not the fierce bombshell I knew.

"Baby ..." my words were cut off abruptly when G.T. stood toe-to-toe with me, so close I could smell the stale beer on his breath from the night before.

"Don't!" G.T.'s voice boomed as Princess jumped. "I'm getting her out of here and so help me fucking God, I will pound your ass if you try to stop me."

"Stop," Princess's voice croaked out over the testosterone thickening the air. Both our eyes snapped to hers. "Cruz. It was a mistake. I have to go." Princess scooted off the edge of the bed as G.T. stood in front of her, his back to her and fierce eyes on me.

"It wasn't a fucking mistake. You're damn head's overthinking again," I growled, my anger coming through me full bore.

As Princess began grabbing her clothes, she quickly put them on, not once showing her brother or me any skin. Her movements were methodical and fast. It was like Princess took a bit of a vacation and this other woman decided to visit. What the fuck? What got me the most was she didn't respond to my comment about her head. Nothing, no smart ass comment. No snarky comeback... nothing... dead... cold...

G.T.'s eyes were focused on me, but I could give two shits. He wasn't my priority.

"Princess, stop this shit." I knew I was talking to

her like when I scolded Cooper, but I didn't care. She was not walking out on me like this. Not happening.

Princess stepped around G.T., who tried to put his arm up to block her from me, but she pushed it out of the way. Her eyes met mine, and inside them I saw a swirl of emotions that I couldn't place. Normally she wore her heart on her sleeve, but this, this wasn't getting me anywhere.

Her hand reached up as she cupped the left side of my face, her fingers moving through my scruff. I loved her soft fucking hands on me, just that one touch, and I was hers. "Cruz. I'm sorry. I can't do this. I know you don't understand, but I can't."

"The fuck you can't," I snarled as she shut her eyes only to open them right back.

"You don't know me. This isn't me. I don't just fuck one of you and go on my merry way."

"Damn right. You only fuck me, Babe." Her shoulders sagged almost in defeat. This couldn't be. Couldn't.

"I'd appreciate you keeping this just between us." Her words shocked me to my core. She didn't fucking want anyone to know. Fuck that.

"Honey, I'll tell every fucking guy in this place. No one is touching you."

It was as if my words flipped a light switch inside her. Her sagging body instantly snapped straight as if her spine got its hardness back. Her face came eye to eye with mine and the fire that was inside before began to burn bright. "You do what you gotta do. But this," her finger motioned pointing to her and then me, "is done. Won't happen again. I fucked up last night. It won't happen again."

Princess's legs began moving, but I wasn't letting her fucking go. Grabbing her arm, she pulled as hard as she could, but I kept my grasp.

"I guaran-fucking-tee this will happen again. I'll let you leave for now, but this shit is far from over." She whipped her arm quickly, this time breaking free and she walked out of the door.

"I fucking told you not to do this shit. It's the one thing she always said she'd never fucking do. You don't think she knows what it looks like to be a whore around this club? And now... you open your fucking mouth... all these guys will know."

"Dagger and Rhys saw us. I'm sure everyone already knows, and even if they didn't, it will be known that Princess is mine."

"Great, just fucking great." G.T. began shaking his head in disbelief as he walked to the door.

"You know I'm not done with her."

"I didn't think you were," was all he said as he continued out the door slamming it shut.

"Fuck," I uttered to myself as I laid on the bed staring at the ceiling. This was not how I wanted to spend my fucking morning... I was supposed to be balls deep in Princess. Fuck!

WATCHING Princess sit at the bar joking with Buzz and Breaker has been getting under my skin the past hour, but I was supposed to be listening to Dagger and Rhys talk with the other chapter members, so I tried not letting it show. Too bad I was having a fuck of a time focusing on shit.

"I wanna see my boy!" Mel stomped her foot like a fucking little kid not getting her way as she approached me. It was fucking noon, and she was just rolling out of whoever's bed she was in last night. I was tired of this fucking bitch. Growing up with just a mom, I knew how important she was in Cooper's life. That's why I let some shit slide. I knew I shouldn't, but my mom's words always rang in my head: *a boy always needs his momma*. I couldn't forget that, even if she was a junkie.

"Cooper!" I called from the main room. Ma had him back in the kitchen helping her make sandwiches for everyone. He loved helping.

Cooper ran out of the kitchen, but instead of running to Mel or me, he veered towards Princess sitting at the bar laughing. "Pin... ess!" he screamed, holding his hands up in the air for her to pick him up, which she did without hesitation.

"Hey, Bud. How's it going?" Her beautiful smile illuminated the entire fucking room, and it looked like Cooper was entranced with her.

"Good. I cookin'!"

"You are? Whatcha makin'?" she asked, just as their conversation was rudely interrupted by a very pissed off Mel. Personally, I had forgotten she was even in the fucking room.

Mel stormed over to where Princess was holding Cooper. "Give me my boy!"

Cooper clung to Princess, holding on as if she was his lifeline, and it was scaring the shit out of me. I'd known things weren't perfect with Mel by any means, but seeing this really made me think.

Approaching them, I demanded, "What the fuck is going on?" Holding out my arms, I expected Cooper to jump into them, but he seemed to like where he was. I couldn't blame him a damn bit.

"This woman won't give me my boy." Mel huffed, but honestly I thought she was more pissed off about the scene in front of everyone than Coop not wanting her.

"He doesn't want you, if you can't tell," Princess clipped as she clutched Cooper tightly, this setting Mel off even more.

"You bitch. Give me my fucking kid, now!" Mel grabbed Cooper's arm and began pulling him as he screamed. Wrapping my hand around Mel's throat, I pulled her away from my boy and Princess. Her gasps for air didn't register through the anger radiating through me.

"You never fucking touch him like that," I barked out, my hands wanting to teach this fucking woman a lesson. But one thing I didn't do, what most of us guys here at the club didn't do, was hit women, but this needed to be hands on. "You leave here, now. Don't fucking think of coming back."

"I will not leave my boy here," she had the audacity to argue.

I involuntarily began gripping her throat harder,

pulling her against the wall. Her eyes widened; my voice turned menacing with the anger dripping off of me. "You will stay the fuck away from him, and if you don't I'll fucking kill you myself." I needed her to understand that I wouldn't tolerate her hands on my boy another minute.

Her words were lost. She couldn't speak and when she did, all thoughts of not beating the shit out of her intensified. "What about the money you send me?" What the fuck? Money?

"Are you fucking kidding me right now, you stupid bitch? You're worried about the fucking money!" My other fist made contact with the wall, crushing the drywall next to Mel's head, causing her to gasp. "Get the fuck out of here! Now!"

Letting go of her throat, she began rubbing it over and over again, but didn't say a word as she walked out the door. I never wanted to take Cooper away from his momma, and I sure as shit knew he'd never know the pain of not having a daddy around. But fuck it, she was toxic, and I'd be damned if I ever saw her lay a hand on my boy again.

Anger pulsated through me. I really needed to fucking punch something.

"Cruz?" Princess's voice fell over me as I continued heaving.

"Yeah..." I clipped at her knowing it wasn't her fault, but it was just a really bad time.

"I'm gonna take Cooper to the playroom, yeah?" Looking at Cooper curled up with Princess, my damn heart fell as the anger subsided a small bit. Shit. I didn't want him to see me like this.

"Yeah, thanks." I stalked off to the gym needing a release.

THE AFTERNOON WENT by quickly with more guys, and their families coming in and out of the clubhouse. Diamond set up the basement into several small rooms about a year and a half ago to accommodate all the people that came in and out. He also created a kid's play-room. Thank God for that; at least everyone would be comfortable during this lockdown.

"Church!" Diamond yelled out with his arms crossed standing by the chapel doors.

As we took our seats, and the door shut, it was standing room only for all the chapter men that came. The large, rectangular oak table in the middle of the room housed several chairs where we spent many hours talking about business. Diamond sat at the head with the gavel. Pops was to his left, Dagger to his right. G.T. and Becs sat next to Pops, and Rhys and Zed next to Dagger. My spot was at the other end of the table facing Diamond.

One wall was covered in pictures of the brothers; anything from party shots to mug shots lined the wall. The other was the Ravage MC name with our symbol, a skull with fire coming out of the top, which was also on the back of each of our rags.

Diamond slammed the gavel down on the table. "Look. We know that it was Rabbit who shot up Pops place, and we just found out why." Diamond's stare turned deadly, "Princess."

The words made my blood run cold even though my anger spiked. "What about her?" I asked, as all eyes around the table turned to me. "What? She's mine, and I will protect her."

"Not what she said this morning," G.T.'s deep grumbled voice spat at me, but before I could answer, Diamond did.

"Son, she's all of ours," Diamond said, eyeing me. "Apparently, Rabbit has taken a liking to Babs. For those of you who don't know, Babs was instrumental in getting our Princess locked up. She disappeared off the radar about a year ago and now has popped back up, with protection this time. They were sending us a message."

"I've got a fucking message for them; I'll fucking kill 'em." My pulse was racing to the point where I thought steam would come out of my ears. No one would take this woman away from me. Ever.

"There're no worries there son; he's already dead for hitting up Pops' place. But his crew has grown over the years, and it won't be pretty. We also have an issue with runs through his territory. We'll need to find a different route for the time being."

"We can't let him dictate where we go!" I yelled, not even trying to control it.

"Calm your ass down," Pops said, slamming his hand on the table catching everyone off guard. He's normally the calm one when situations arise. This one must cut too close to home. "He's not. We need to think about this short term and long term. Right now, no one else is in danger but Princess. She's gonna be pissed, and we all know what she's like when she's pissed." Groans echoed throughout the room.

Diamond cut in. "We're gonna go on soft lockdown for everyone except for Ma and Princess. They must stay here unless escorted by a brother."

"She's gonna be pissed," G.T. said, rubbing his face up and down.

"Yep. But she's a good woman. She'll do what's right." Diamond eyed me. "She your girl?"

"Yes, sir," I said not skipping a beat. But G.T had more to say.

"She ain't your fucking girl!" G.T. jumped up from his seat sending it flying to the floor behind him.

Standing from my seat, I met him stare for stare, his outrage dripping off his body. I've never wanted to punch my brother more than this moment. I wanted to beat the living shit out of him. "Shut the fuck up!"

"Stop it, now!" Diamond's stern voice had us both sitting back in our seats. "Then... you keep her here. If she goes out, you make sure someone is with her. She's your responsibility." He smiled as the rest of the room chuckled. Damn, I knew I had my work cut out for me, and I sure as shit didn't need any lip from my brothers.

"She ain't gonna let you five feet in front of her. Good fucking luck!" Irritation seeped through my pores, but I knew it wouldn't help a damn thing right now to react. And I knew I had my work cut out for me. G.T. was probably right, not that I'd let that stop me.

Ma banged on the church doors in a panic screaming, "Pops get out here, now! Princess!"

Jumping out of my seat, I rushed to the clubhouse taking in the scene, in front of me. Princess swung a pool stick at a blonde-haired woman's face, hitting her hard against her nose sending blood flying everywhere as she screamed. Danny, a patch member from the Clayton chapter, was getting ready to charge Princess when my voice boomed. "Danny, stop!"

Danny looked at me, "You gonna let this bitch beat up my ol' lady?"

Narrowing my eyes, I thundered, "This bitch is my ol' lady. There must be a fucking reason she wants to rip your girl's head off right now." Moving closer to her I called out, "Princess, you okay?"

"I'm fucking fine. And I'm not your fucking ol' lady." Her voice was cold, icy, and detached, not really something I enjoyed.

"Danny back off!" Pops boomed. "Princess, what's going on out here?" His voice calmed as he talked to her, the gentleness of a father taking over.

"You remember that whole two year in jail thing," she said sarcastically, gripping the pole in her hand so tight you could see the wood bend. "Well, this bitch here... is part of Babs's, crew. She was part of it."

"Shit," was heard collectively throughout the room.

"Brother, I suggest you get her out of here if you want her whole," Pops clipped to Danny.

"Oh, Pops," Princess's sarcasm coming back, "I think this bitch needs a lesson before she goes."

"Not here. Not under this roof," Pops growled as Princess turned to him, her hands clenched into fists. Nodding her head, she backed away from them, throwing down the pole crashing it to the floor, but the fury was emanating off of her body.

"Brother, she doesn't hang out with her anymore. Babs is part of Rabbit's crew." Shit. Damn Danny, you just couldn't keep your fucking mouth shut.

Princess stopped in her tracks, coming around to stand beside me, not quite making it to Pops. "What?" she asked, covering her mouth as if she didn't mean to say the words aloud.

"Mindy's not part of Babs's crew anymore. Babs is Rabbit's ol' lady."

"You've gotta be fucking kidding me," Princess growled under her breath walking over to Pops. "That's who shot Ma. I'm the reason why." Damn this girl was smart and caught on way too quick for her own good. And dammit, it made my dick hard as steel.

Pops rested his hands on her shoulders, "Princess, the club will handle it."

From the stiffness in Princess's body, I knew she wanted to argue, but all she did was nod and walk away. She didn't stop to look at me. She brushed past me as quick as she could, heading towards the hallway. Shit.

CHAPTER SIX

Shit. Shit. Shit. What the fuck was I thinking going out to the main room. Not only was that bitch Mindy there, but fucking Cruz. Why in the hell does he have this magnetic force about him that just pulls me to him, making him hard to resist.

I couldn't have him. It'd just turn into the same shit I've seen a thousand times over and over again in here. A brother starts seeing a woman, fucks her a thousand ways to Sunday, gets tired of her, and then passes her on to the brothers. I won't be that girl. I may spread my legs, but not to these guys... at least until Cruz. What the fuck was I thinking?

I knew... I was horny. Plain and fucking simple. Why does he have to be... well, Cruz? Power just emanates off of him, beckoning me, engulfing me. I swear that man short circuits every brain cell in my head just by his smell. Then, being in the same fucking room with him, my body throbbed craving his. This didn't happen with the brothers, never. It had to be just because of my two year dry spell.

If it weren't for this fucking lockdown, I'd get the hell out of here and wipe my memories of Cruz... or at least I would try to.

Fuck. Throwing open the door to Pops' room; I found Casey sitting on the bed. "Where the fuck have you been?" I barked. She didn't look at me but fidgeted with her hands.

"I slept in the spare room downstairs." Casey turned towards me. "So one night and you're someone's ol' lady. What the hell happened?"

Sitting on the bed, I explained, "I'm not..." Running my fingers through my long dark hair, I shook my head. The last day had been a rollercoaster ride. I knew coming back to this life would make things interesting; I just didn't realize how much.

"Thought we didn't fuck brothers," she said twirling her hands in her lap.

"I know. He's just so damn overwhelming, and I couldn't say no, I didn't want to say no."

"Is this an 'I needed a dick thing,' or is it real?" she asked, puzzled.

"For me... a dick thing. He says it's the real thing, but he's a brother. I'm not stupid. Anyway, even if I thought it was real, and it didn't work out; I'd be fucked." Knowing if I left him, I'd be out, out of the club, out of the life, yet another reason to be scared shitless about him. It didn't matter that I was the VPs daughter or a sister to a member. Once I was an ol' lady, my status with the club would change forever, and there'd be nothing I could do about it. Club rules. This has been my family, my entire life. I was not ready to give it up.

"I think Cruz is a good fit for you." Her voice was low but serious.

I stared at her as if she grew three heads, not recognizing the woman sitting next to me. Of all the people, I would have never thought those words would come from her. We've always talked about the women of the club and how each had their places. And one of those places was the club momma. These women get passed around from brother to brother as free pussy, and for some reason they loved it. It's the one role that we vowed always to steer clear of.

And more recently, there were reasons that Casey, nor anyone, for that matter, knew. They were reasons that I locked down deep, and they would fucking stay there.

"What?"

"Cruz is a good guy for the most part," she said, smiling. We all knew that none of these men were angels, far from it. "He's great with his kid. That bitch of a baby momma is a pain in the ass, from what I hear, but other than that, he doesn't have a lot of drama." She turned facing me. "And he can hold his own against you." She smiled, and I returned it, shaking my head.

"I can't. I won't be a whore around here, who the brothers think they can pass around. I can't. I won't." Casey flinched.

"No one's saying that."

"Why the hell are you all the sudden okay with me fucking a brother? Wasn't it you that sat there and made a pact that we never would. Even doing that stupid cut your finger open blood shit." She laughed her beautiful laugh.

"Yeah. I was there. We were also thirteen. Things change," she said blowing out a huff of air.

Breathing in deep, I stared at Casey. She's been my best friend for so long. If I could talk to anyone about this, it'd be her. "There's something there. I've seen more guys in and out of this damn place than I can count. Not one has done what Cruz has. He sparks something inside of me, something I haven't felt before. But it was one night, and it will be the last."

"You don't have to rush into shit."

A knock on the door stopped her thoughts. Opening the door, I was surprised to see Diamond standing there. "Yes?"

"Need a minute." His arms crossed over his chest as if power didn't already radiate off of him.

"I'll go," Casey, knowing protocol, called as I stepped aside letting her out. Whenever the President wanted to talk, we knew the others needed to leave immediately.

"What's going on?" I asked trying to be calm, but inside my nerves were a bit on edge from this impromptu visit.

Diamond eyed me intently. "We're going on soft lock-down, except for you and Ma. You two are not to leave this clubhouse. If there's somewhere you have to be, you take a brother. No discussions..." My anger began boiling over. This was all because of Babs and fuck if I didn't want to kill the bitch. But I locked my lips as he kept going. "I know you're pissed Princess, but this is a club decision. It's what's best for the club. You want what's best for us, right?"

Hanging my head, "Of course." In all my years, in this club, I'd always wanted to make the brothers proud, now would be no exception, even if I hated it.

"Look, Princess, we have dealings with Rabbit and his crew. We need to keep those in mind while we deal with this situation."

Swallowing my pride, "I understand."

"Good."

"I need to go to Studio X and check on shit."

"Then you take a brother with you... and your gun," he said as he walked out of the room not looking back.

CRUZ FOLLOWED right beside me the entire way to X. After arguing about who was riding with me, Cruz won the pissing contest when Diamond stepped in, again, ordering him to go. I wasn't happy, but it was what it was. Ma said she'd watch Cooper, so I'm sure he's getting spoiled rotten.

Pulling up to X, I was happy to see that the building looked exactly the same as I left it two years ago. The blackened bulletproof windows had the sun's light reflecting off them. The large X hung above the door, but with it being closed, the bright red light wasn't shining.

Parking my bike near the back entrance, Cruz followed closely. I kept my eyes out but didn't see a damn thing.

Walking in, the place was eerily quiet. The black walls had red drapery that hung all around the room. There was a large bar on one end and the stage with poles on the other. The black tables and chairs were placed exactly where they should be, filling me with pride. I began this place to help the club bring in clean money, and it has profited greatly.

"Harlow?" Liv called from the office as she ran towards me smiling. "Oh, my God!" She squealed. Liv had been running the place for me this entire time, and from the looks of things, she was doing a kick ass job.

Her arms wrapped around me. "Hey, girl. How's it going?"

She pulled away, "Great. We've tripled our profits, and I brought in five new girls. You'll love them; they're hot." She eyed Cruz up and down, and her sharp intake of breath told me she liked the assessment. "Hey, Cruz." She gave him a very seductive smile, and damn if it didn't piss me off, not that I had any right to that feeling.

"You two know each other?" I didn't want to know the answer, but I loved punishing myself, and if I couldn't be with him, may as well put salt in the wound.

Liv stepped closer to him running her hands up his chest. It took every bit of strength in my body to keep still in one spot. "Cruz and I..." her words trailed off as Cruz cut in.

"I fucked her a couple of times." His voice was completely unapologetic.

I didn't give him the satisfaction of a sound escaping my lips even though my stomach fell to my feet, and the air rushed out of my body. I didn't want to feel this way, but fuck if him screwing Liv didn't make me want to rip her eyes out. Shit. *He's not yours, Harlow*.

"Wait a minute. Am I missing something?" Liv turned to me, questioning.

Eyeing Cruz, I turned back to Liv. "Nah, we're good."

Cruz came up wrapping his arms around my waist as I tried to push away from him. "She's my ol' lady. Doesn't want to claim it yet, so I'm claiming it for her."

Liv's eyes grew wide. "I thought you didn't date brothers? And you've only been out for what... a day?"

"I don't, and I'm not his ol' lady. And yeah, a day. Let's get down to business. Let me see the profit and loss sheets and the files on the new girls," I said, pulling out of Cruz's grasp as he chuckled.

After going over the paperwork and hugging the girls as they came in, we headed back to the club. I didn't want to stay all night, and Cruz needed to get back to Cooper.

The clubhouse was pretty quiet, but after last night that was understandable. The guys were drinking at the bar, and Ma was playing with Cooper coloring at the table. A couple of women sat on the far couches but didn't say a word. The club mommas. I rolled my eyes ignoring them.

"There she is!" Dagger yelled, running up to me wrapping his arms around me.

"Here I am... what's up?" I walked up close to him breathing in the booze and cigarettes, his familiar scent.

"Things have gotten more interesting with you back, Babe." His words made me laugh.

"Yeah. I'm sure you had enough going on without me interfering in it."

Zed came up kissing my cheek. "Princess, this is the most fun we've had in a while."

"What? Watching me beat shit up?" I said rolling my eyes.

They laughed. "Something like that."

Cruz strolled in. "Get you're fucking hands off of her." I didn't move. He had no rights to me, and he needed to fucking learn that quickly.

"Dude, calm the fuck down. We've known her since she was a kid." Part of me was a little giddy at the whole alpha thing Cruz had going on. I'd really never had that before with a man. Damn these fucking feelings. I. Don't. Want. Him.

"Pin... ess!" Cooper screamed from across the room. My eyes smiled at the little man running towards me and jumping into my arms.

"You have fun with Ma?" I asked, brushing his hair out of his eyes.

"Yep. Me's got cookies." I began to tickle his belly as he laughed uncontrollably.

"Where's mine?" He pointed to his tummy. Lifting his little body up, I began to pretend to eat his tummy, making weird eating noises as he laughed and laughed.

Looking up at Cruz, he had a puzzled look on his face. "What?" I asked.

He lit his cigarette and shook his head. "It just amazes

me that the woman who met me blow for blow can turn it off and be what I just saw."

"What is that?"

"A loving, caring mom." His words made me freeze, making it difficult to breathe. I slowly walked Cooper over to Ma handing him off, not ready to hear this shit coming out of his mouth and wanting to get away from the audience in the room.

"I've gotta go lay down." Turning, I didn't stop when my name was repeated over and over; instead I locked myself in Pops' room. Climbing into my roll on the floor, I laid my head on the scruff pillow as my mind tried to take on the tornado of thoughts bombarding me.

Mom. Are you fucking kidding me? I've known this man all of a day, and now he's talking about me being a mom to his kid? I didn't know the first fucking thing about kids. Never thought I'd have any. Why does the damn thought excite me? Why does being with Cruz ignite me?

Emotions, I fucking hated them. They always turned me into a blubbering idiot, which was exactly why I've stayed away from any type of *relationship*. Made my head feel heavy and crazy. I'd much rather stick to my hard shell and not feel.

A hard knock on the door had me covering my head with the blankets, trying to escape from everything and everyone, but its persistence made me get my sorry ass up. Opening the door, the oxygen left my body at the sight of Cruz standing in front of me. His tight black shirt fit his body like a glove, showing off every curve of his

100 | RYAN MICHELE

muscles. His hair was its normal disheveled self, and his eyes were on fire with lust.

My pulse picked up as blood began racing through my body. My heart was about ready to burst out of my chest as the air around us became electrified. Remembering the night before, and the intensity that came from Cruz, I knew I needed him. Dammit.

The sexy smirk gracing his face told me he knew exactly what I was thinking. Shaking myself out, "Whatcha need?" My tone had a small bit of its punch back. When G.T. found us together, I didn't know what happened to me. I knew I sounded like a sullen child, but in a way, I was. I embarrassed myself, and I didn't like that feeling. Too many memories started flooding my mind that I wanted to keep locked up, and I needed to get away from him. Time to snap my shit back.

"Talk," was the only word he uttered, confusing me. I raised my eyebrow and crossed my arms over my chest.

"About?" The defiance came back fully.

"Stop the fucking bullshit. What the hell was that this morning?" His sexy voice washed over me, remembering the words he grunted in my ears over the course of the night while he thought I was sleeping. That voice alone can cause a woman's panties to fly, so forceful, deep and sexy.

"Nothing to talk about. It was a mistake." Normally, men would be happy with a one night fuck and leave me the hell alone. But not Cruz for some fucking reason.

"The fuck it was a mistake. You didn't feel that way when my dick was pushing in and out of that tight pussy of yours." Wetness seeped out of me from his gruff words. I couldn't help but get hot as hell when he talked this way. It made every part of me tingle something no man has ever fully done before.

"I'm not one of those women out on the couch. I can't be." I steeled my voice, not letting the vulnerability come through. I'd already given him enough of that shit this morning.

"Why the fuck you are so hung up on this shit I don't know. But you need to deal with it and get the fuck over it. Now. Do you want me to treat you like a whore? I can arrange that. But I don't fucking want to. That's the damn difference."

"What happens when you're done? I know the rules. I'll be banned. This is the only life I've ever known." Damn if this man didn't bring out all my weaknesses even when I tried to hide it. Family. I didn't want to lose my family.

"First, I ain't gonna be done. Second, any of these men touch you, I'll pound their asses down." He stepped closer closing the door behind him. The room instantly became electrified with a current so strong it was pulling me under. "Third, I didn't say you were my momma. I said you were my girl, my woman, my ol' lady. End of discussion." He grabbed my shoulders and pulled me to him. I didn't want to resist. My body was in such a tornado it was making my head spin.

"You don't even know me."

Looking up into his blue eyes, they warmed me, and my insides melted. Dammit. "Let's go over what I know.

You're strong; you met me blow for blow, stood up to me when no other female would even dare, you've got balls of fucking steel, and know how to take care of yourself. And you're good with my kid, who's already taking quite a liking to you. Fast. Yeah. But that's how I live my life. I see it. I take it. I'm taking you."

Uncertainty ran through me, but my body was craving this man's touch, craving those magical lips to send me over the edge. Everything around me was swirling out of control. Why the hell was this happening? I'm so damn sure of myself all the damn time, one day with this man, and I'm questioning everything.

Fuck it.

Gripping Cruz's shirt, I pulled him hard, down to my lips as I took what I needed from him, and he gave, punishing me in return. "I'm glad you see things my way," he murmured, before cupping my ass and lifting me up as I wrapped my legs around his body and my back crashed against the door. Our lips and hands attacked each other in a frenzy of lust.

Everything happened so damn fast that before I could process what was going on, my pants were removed; Cruz was sleeved and balls deep inside of me. His body hammering into mine so hard and so fast that I forgot where I was, much less... who I was. My body became one huge nerve ending that was on the verge of imploding.

Cruz's name escaped my lips as he gasped my name giving two more thrusts and slowly stilling as we came together. Our breathing was unbelievably labored, and I rested my head on his shoulder trying to regain myself.

I shook my head at the realization that this would happen. If for nothing else, his dick was becoming a drug, and I wanted more. Hopefully, he'd prove to be worth the risk.

TWO DAYS LATER

MY LEGS SPREAD WIDE as I gathered myself in my stance. It'd been so long since I've done this, practice. I was damn well gonna hit that fucking target over and over.

Raising my arms, I cupped my girl in my hands, loving the weight of her. As I squeezed the trigger over and over, the familiar lulling sound of each shot going off made me smile. Keeping my eye on the target, I kept firing.

As I pushed the button that brought my target close, I was ecstatic to see that I'd hit my mark repeatedly. Bitch has still got it.

"Great shot," Cruz's smooth voice came from behind me. Turning, I smiled and stared into those gorgeous blue eyes of his. These past two days have been a whirlwind. Not only was I trying to learn the ins and outs since being locked up, I was learning about this strong man behind me. And damn if he didn't send my entire life into a spiral, good or bad was still up for debate.

"Look," I pulled down my target sheet handing it to him as I added another.

"You killed him; that's for sure."

"Her..."

"What?" Cruz eyed me as if he heard wrong.

"You said I killed him... when it's actually, I killed *her*."

"Babs?" I nodded, pushing the button to send my target back through the chute.

"I'm firing!" I yelled out seconds before I began blasting the target again, thinking of Babs bleeding on the ground, gurgling her last breath. It only fueled me up as I kept shooting, adding another clip, going for it again, not stopping until the paper was dangling off the grip.

Placing my gun in my holster, I turned around to see Cruz staring at me. "What?"

"I know the brothers taught you to shoot, but damn babe." His body moved closer to mine as his hands filtered through my hair, pulling it, so his eyes met mine. "Fucking hot."

His lips smothered mine in his signature, sexy way as my body instantly reacted. Over the last couple of days, my body had tuned itself with Cruz's, wanting him more than I ever thought possible. Not that I would tell him that, but my body couldn't lie.

The clearing of a throat brought our deep kiss to a stop as we looked over to see Rocky standing at the doorway to the range.

"What's up man?" Cruz asked as he wrapped his arm around my shoulders.

"Came to shoot," Rocky's voice was so quiet, I felt like if I could squint my ears to hear better I would. But what got me was his voice. There was something about it. Something familiar, but I couldn't place it.

"You done?" Cruz asked, looking down at me while I smiled, nodding. "All yours man."

"Thanks..." Cruz slapped Rocky's shoulder as he walked by. When he breezed past me, my body went on alert, full-blown red alert. Something. I didn't know what the hell it was, but something with him was setting me off, and not in a good way.

Turning, I stared at him. His long hair, beard, and lanky body were nothing that I'd ever seen before. Racking my brain, I tried to place him, but came up blank. As we walked out of the range, Cruz must have sensed something off. "What's wrong?"

Not one to shy away, I said, "Rocky. Was he around before I went in prison?"

"No, why?"

"I don't know. I get the sense I've met him before."

"Like where?" he questioned, seeming interested.

"Not sure. I could be totally full of shit."

"Far as I know, he's never been near the club. But I'll have it checked out." Cruz pulled me close, "Let's go for a ride." I smiled up at him, nodding my head.

BEING on the back of Cruz's bike was an exhilarating experience. I've always loved riding, but something about my thighs pressed against this rock hard man was making this one of the best rides ever. His smell of leather and testosterone combined with the roar of the bike was making my body pulsate, throb, and ache. Pressing my pussy as close to his ass as I could, I began slightly rubbing just to give myself a small amount of friction to go along with the rumble of the bike.

Cruz's hand squeezed my thigh as if he knew what I was doing, before placing it back on the throttle. As he revved the bike, I got just enough friction that my body shuddered. It wasn't an all-consuming orgasm by any means, but it felt good and briefly cured the ache.

As my hands released the clutching grip I seemed to have placed on Cruz's abs, his body began to move as if he was chuckling. With my body very relaxed, I held on, enjoying my first ride with him.

Cruz pulled the bike into a small diner, Sam's, just outside of Sumner. I'd missed this place while being inside. The smell of grease and fries surged into my nostrils as my stomach took notice and growled. They had the best burgers and fries, and I couldn't wait to sink my teeth in them.

After getting off his bike, Cruz wrapped his arms around my body pulling me flush to his. "You owe me," he whispered onto my lips.

"What?" I said; my breath barely leaving my body.

He shook his head slowly. "Getting yourself off and not letting me watch. Not. Happening. Again." His lips crashed down on mine, and I felt lost in all that was Cruz. It amazed me how this man seemed to have some sort of spell that mesmerized my body instantly.

Pulling away, "I might let you watch next time." I smirked patting his broad chest as I turned to the door.

It didn't take but a minute for Cruz to be seen in the diner. Many guys coming up to him, shaking his hand and doing that man hug thing. He didn't introduce me, which either meant he didn't want anyone to know who I was, or I was insignificant. I was hoping it wasn't the latter.

Instead of Cruz taking his seat across from me in the booth, he pulled himself right in beside me, pushing me all the way against the wall with his broad body. "You know you can sit on the other side," I said, wiggling to make room.

"Then I couldn't do this…" Cruz leaned down placing the sweetest, softest kiss on my lips causing my insides to flutter.

"What can I getcha?" I heard the waitress's voice, but couldn't pull myself out of the shock of the gentleness that I just witnessed. This rough man, who has shown me this hard, demanding side of him, has an unbelievably soft side too, who'd have known.

A sharp squeeze of my hand sent pain through my arm causing me to snap out of it. "What?"

Cruz chuckled, "What do you want to eat, Baby?"

Shit. Shaking my head, I smiled at the waitress, but it instantly fell. Her eyes were totally focused on Cruz sending a surge of fire throughout me. As if sensing it, Cruz's hand came up under my chin, pulling me towards his face. My eyes locked on his just as he placed another kiss on my lips.

"Order what ya want." He winked.

Without looking back at her, I ordered, as did Cruz, sending her away. "You don't like her looking at me, Babe?"

I didn't give him the satisfaction of an answer, because I didn't fully understand it myself. "So, you were in the Marines?"

His body stiffened, "Yep."

"You don't like talking about it?" I asked as the waitress placed our drinks on the table, and I reached for mine.

"Nah..."

I knew better than anyone about not wanting to talk about shit. So I changed the subject. "Why'd you join Ravage?"

A smirk claimed the corner of his mouth. "I realized this is where I belong. This is my family."

His answer was utterly diplomatic and really didn't give me a lot to go on, but deep down I understood. The brotherhood wasn't something that most men talked about. Even if I grew up here and knew the life, he steered away.

"Do you have a family outside of Ravage?"

"Nah, Mom died when I got out of the service. She was all I had."

"Didn't know your dad?" I instantly regretted the question when his voice spoke.

"He left when I was young. Loved some other woman; crushed my mom. It wasn't pretty."

My insides churned for this man. I couldn't imagine Pops ever leaving me, abandoning me. He's taught me so much throughout the years. Reaching over, I clasped his hand and squeezed as his eyes locked on mine. As I tried to release him, he held tighter, and I began to relax into him. He absently began rubbing circles with this thumb, sending shocks throughout my body with each swipe. "Sorry."

"Don't be. It's who I am, but enough about me. What about you?" I didn't know what to say. These past two years, all I did was survive. What do I say to that question? He must have sensed my apprehension. "Growing up."

"This has been my life. Hanging out at the clubhouse, and the brothers are really all I've known. They've taught me how to be me."

"Must have been weird growing up around all those guys."

"No. Not actually. They were all Pops' brothers, and they treated me very well. I always respected them, and they did me." Not saying they didn't try to fuck me as I got older, but I thought I'd leave that part out.

"You ever want to get away from here?"

His question caught me off guard, but I answered immediately. "No. This is my home. You wanna tell me about Mel?" I asked, really not wanting to know, but thinking I should.

"No. She's inconsequential." There were questions there, but I could tell the subject was closed. "You wanna tell me about your time inside?"

No. I didn't, but I would. "Boring. Same shit different day. I kept to myself as much as possible. My only goal was to get out alive."

"Understandable. Heard you had your own space."

"Yeah. Pops and Diamond worked something out, and I owe them." I did. I knew it. That's why when they asked me to take care of a couple of things for them I didn't balk one bit.

He didn't respond. As I looked around the diner, eyes were focused on us. It was the same as it was when I was out with Pops and G.T. The Ravage patch held great honor and respect around here, not to mention curiosity. They all probably wanted to know everything that was Cruz's life. The thought made me snicker because no one would ask... not that they would be told anyway.

As our food came, and we settled into small conversation, I felt happy, something I hadn't felt in a long time.

FROM GOING to sleep on a mattress that felt like a board in prison, to being wrapped up in Cruz's arms in a soft bed, was a huge change. I've had to admit his arms were beginning to be one of my favorite places to be. Prison was so stark, and Cruz was colorful and bright... life.

"You gonna tell me your real name?" I asked him, running my fingers up and down his washboard abs to chest and back again.

"Cruz," he answered lying there with is arm resting over his eyes.

"Okay, Cruz what?"

Removing his arm, he looked down at me. "Donavan Cruz, but no one calls me that except for the cops. I love to ride, so Cruz stuck."

"Donavan, huh? I'm gonna start calling you that."

"Bull-fucking-shit you are. It's Cruz. That's it. Got it?" I nodded, hiding my smile. Since I grew up in the club, I never called any of the brothers by their real name. My brother G.T. has been called that since he was a baby. No one ever uses his real name, except when I'm really pissed. I might throw it out there a couple of times to get under his skin. It's the same as my name. No one calls me Harlow around here, even though I think it's a pretty kick ass name. I'm always Princess.

"Got it. How about Stud? Can I call you that?" I smirked, looking up into his blue eyes that engulf me every time; my head rested on his chest.

"Babe, you can call me that whenever you damn well want." I smiled, climbing up to him, kissing him on the lips.

Yawning, I mumbled, "I'm beat." I curled up alongside Cruz as he absently began rubbing circles on my shoulder as I drifted off to sleep.

No... I don't want to... it hurts. I wanted to whine, but I knew better. It wouldn't help what was about to happen. 'Shut the fuck up. You want this you dirty little whore.' He pushed my stomach down onto the hard bed as my arms tried to pull myself up; he pushed harder, his fat beer belly pushing the small of my back. 'I know you need what I've got. Lay there and take it... or fight. I don't give a shit which you choose.' Everything in me wanted to fight, wanted to put this asshole

on his ass, but I knew I couldn't do it. I knew I needed what he had for me. I had to do it for the brothers. As he tore into me, I cringed from the pain, biting down on my lip so hard I tasted blood. He was never gentle, but he always brought lube. I think it was more for him than for me. 'You fucking little whore. Doing this for daddy, huh?' Every time he came to me, he repeated those same fucking words. And the sad thing was they were true. My body was on fire as each time he thrust into me; it would tear me more and more... I couldn't breathe... I was suffocating...

"PRINCESS!" My name being called startled me awake. As I turned to the voice, Cruz was sitting up on the bed towering over me as if he'd been working really hard at something. "Are you okay?"

I rubbed my eyes trying to wake myself up. "Yeah. Why?"

He rubbed his hands over my face. I could feel the sweat as he glided his fingers across. Fuck. The dream. Everything came flooding back, but there was no way in hell I was talking to Cruz about it. Not for a single fucking second. "Really. I'm okay."

"You were mumbling and thrashing your arms around. It didn't feel like nothing."

"Really. I'm good. I just need sleep." I didn't know how, but by pure luck he let it go, wrapping me in his arms and kissing the top of my head. "I'm just really tired."

"You will tell me what that shit was about." His voice was firm and absolute, but I wouldn't be telling him. Ever.

"Cooper!" I called looking for the little guy. One thing I would fully admit was that little man warms my heart in ways I never thought possible. The more time I spent with him, the more I *wanted* to spend time with him.

"Pin... ess!" I hear before I saw him as he barreled down the hall, Ma following close behind.

"Hey, Buddy." Picking him up, I squeezed him in my arms. "You ready to go outside?"

"Yes!" He jumped in my arms excitedly.

"Hey Ma, he okay for ya?" When I needed to go to X, Ma would watch Cooper when Cruz couldn't, and lately, that's been quite a bit, club business and all. Ma's been a life-saver. I admit, becoming an instant caretaker, has been a bit of a challenge. But it's one that I actually didn't mind.

"Yeah. I gotta get back to the shop." Her brilliant smile appeared as she took off out the clubhouse doors.

"Thanks..." Squeezing Cooper, we went outside to enjoy the day. The guys built this whole playground contraption that would make old Ronald blush. It had slides, swings, monkey bars, a small clubhouse, teeter totter, rock climbing wall, tire swing, and so much more. It also had a huge sandbox with lots of big trucks and toy motorcycles, of course. This was Cooper's favorite place, and who could blame him, it was a toddler's dream.

"Pin... ess, come get me!" Cooper yelled as he took off running. He loved playing chase, and I found I did, too. I loved catching him, twirling him in the air, and hearing that wonderful laugh of his.

Cooper took off around the playground. "Shit!" My foot stumbled on one of the trucks I didn't see laying out, and I fell hard to the ground knocking my leg with a thump. Shooting pains raced up my leg quickly as the blood began flowing. The shorts I was wearing left no protection, but I could handle the pain. It was the blood I was gonna need to get cleaned up and make sure the cut was okay.

"Pin... ess!" Cooper screamed and started crying hysterically at the sight of my leg.

Wrapping my arms quickly around him, I began rocking him back and forth, his head buried in my chest. "I'm okay, Buddy. It's just a little blood. No biggie..."

"Hurt... owie," his muffled cries said in my shirt as my hands rubbed his back.

"Just a little owie, it's okay." I rubbed his back gently and kissed him on the top of his head. I surprised myself after I did it but quickly smiled.

Boot steps running our way had my eyes peering up into Rocky's. I still felt on edge with him, but since talking with Cruz it has lessened quite a bit. "Stay," was all he said as he looked at my leg and ran off. When he came back, he was holding a first aid kit and began doctoring me up without saying a word.

"Do I need stitches?" I asked with Cooper still clinging to me.

"Nah..." He reached into the kit to grab the liquid stitch; that stuff's like superglue and burns like shit going on. As he continued working on my leg, Cooper calmed down enough to begin watching what he was doing. He even smiled when Rocky put a Superman Band-Aid over the cut.

"Now I look like you," I teased Cooper, who giggled. "Thanks Rocky." I smile at him. He's more than proving my initial reaction wrong each time I'm around him.

Instead of responding, he grunted and took off. He was a man of few words. Kinda weird, but I actually liked that in a twisted sort of way. I mean, hell, a guy who doesn't give you any shit. What's not to like, right?

TWO WEEKS LATER

"Harder!" I yelled, feeling the wonderful pain-pleasure mix of Cruz slamming deep inside of me. Ma had Cooper for the day, and we were enjoying every minute of our time together. The guys had a run tomorrow and would be gone for a few days. It'd be our first time away from each other since we met.

Cruz and my need for each other was growing uncontrollably; I never thought I'd get enough of him. More than that, we've actually talked more. We went from not knowing a damn thing about each other, except for our lust-filled minds to learning so much in the course of two weeks.

He never mentioned club business, and I respected that. I didn't need to know anyway as everything was calm on the home front, neither Rabbit nor Babs had made any moves, causing me to relax a bit. The brothers wouldn't take me off lockdown, though. It was starting to wear on me. There's only so many times a girl can go to the shooting range or work out before she goes nuts.

Cruz began pounding me with everything he had. He picked me up, flipped me onto my stomach, and pushed my knees up and slammed deep inside of me causing a powerful orgasm. A scream escaped my lips. Cruz stilled behind me as he spilled inside of me. We were still using condoms. I had gotten the shot, but had to wait another week before it was completely effective. We both got tested and, thank God, came up clean.

We collapsed down to the bed, gasping for breath.

"Shit."

"Yeah... shit, Cruz."

"When I'm gone, you go nowhere without Buzz, Breaker, Rocky, or Tug. Got me?"

"Yeah, I got ya." My heart swelled with this man, and I knew I was in deep shit. Falling in love with a brother was never part of my plan, but damn it if it wasn't happening and I couldn't do anything to stop it. I wasn't sure I wanted to.

"You know that you sleeping around on me isn't gonna work." My mind spun back to Flash and Dagger's relationship; they could handle that shit; there's no way I could. Then it flashed to Cruz's mom and dad... I couldn't deal. I could deal with guns, drugs, killing... but my heart wasn't as strong. I knew that. I've also learned over the years that many of the brothers had their road whores, the women who took care of their needs on the road. As most of the runs were consistent, having a road whore in another city happened. I couldn't deal with that. If I wasn't woman enough for my man, he didn't need to be mine.

Cruz turned on his side, resting his head on his hand. "It's not, huh?"

"Look Cruz, I know how this works. I've seen it. I've seen the women around when the ol' ladies are gone. I'm not stupid. The only one I haven't seen it with is Pops and Ma. I can't do it. I'm not the woman that can handle my man being with someone else. If that's the case, then we need to end this. I couldn't take it."

Cruz brushed the hair from my face, "I couldn't either." He bent down kissing me softly.

THE GUYS HAVE BEEN GONE for two days and were expected back tomorrow night. Coop and I have been enjoying each other, and Casey has been around quite a bit. I have to say it's pretty shocking, considering I haven't seen her much since I got out. She kept making excuses about what she was doing. It's nice having her around, but something with her seems a bit off.

Living at the club hasn't been hard. Coop and I fell

into a great routine with Ma watching him while I went to X for a while each day. I listened to Cruz, and took a Prospect with me each time I left the clubhouse, with the strict instructions from him that *they'll help you with whatever you need.*

"Princess, you got a package." One of the B.Boys called from behind the door.

Taking the large envelope, I thanked him before closing and locking the door to Cruz's room. I'd been staying here now since that first night. Cooper was playing on the floor with some toys Tug went out and got for him, totally content with the world.

As I opened the envelope, I began to stare and read all of the papers inside. I'd been waiting for these to arrive since I got out, but it must not have been clear to send them to me until now. Inside was information on Babs, where she lived, worked, her family history, social security numbers, birth certificates, her crew, and recent photos of her and Rabbit parading around town. There was also a detailed description of how she spent the last week from the time she fell asleep to every step she took during the day.

While inside, I made some friends of my own, ones who have eyes and ears everywhere. While I gave Diamond my word not to get involved with club business, I would get my *personal* business with Babs taken care of.

My cell going off made me jump. Seeing it was Liv, I answered right away. "What's up?"

"Get over here, now. Some guys are in here tearing the place up. The girls are locked in the backroom, and I'm in the office." Liv's hushed voice came through the line. I began stuffing all the contents of the envelope back in and threw it in a drawer, shutting it quickly.

Hearing gun shots in the background, I scooped up Coop and ran to Ma's room. "I'm on my way. They say what they want?"

Banging on Ma's door, I yell, "Ma take care of Coop, gotta run to X." Ma nodded.

I began running down the hall. "They didn't say anything. Just asked if you were here, and when I said no they started tearing up the place."

"Shit. Stay locked up. Be there in a few." Crashing into Cruz's room, I grabbed my gun and placed it in the holster on my back, along with my two smaller ones to go in my boots. Rushing out into the clubhouse, I yelled at the B.Boys and Tug to hurry. I had to go. Rocky had left to spend time with his woman, whom I didn't know he had.

They didn't argue, just followed me to the bikes. "What the hell's going on?" Tug asked.

"X. There's gun fire, and my girls are in danger."

"Shit," Tug sent off a quick text; I'm assuming to the brothers, as we raced to X.

Weaving in and out of traffic on our bikes, we got there in about ten minutes. No cops were in sight, but that was just a matter of time. Parking the bikes, we moved to the back entrance of X. "Get behind us, Princess," one of the B.Boys said.

I didn't have time for this shit. "Don't treat me with fucking kid gloves. Let's go!" I barked, opening the door from the side. When no shots rang out immediately, I dipped my head slowly in and nodded for them to pass. I pointed B.Boy one to the left and B.Boy two to the right, then for Tug to follow behind me.

Gun shots began raining everywhere, and from the sound of it, we were walking right into the line of fire. "Stay down and only shoot when you have a clear shot," I whispered to Tug. He nodded. With our guns in front of us, we began creeping around the corner staying out of their line of sight. Three men wearing green and black rags were shooting the glass mirrors, destroying the room. Every liquor bottle was shattered with alcohol splashing everywhere.

Lining up my gun, I had a clear shot of Asshole One. Looking over at Tug, he was lined up, too. We nodded at each other and shot at the same time, each of us hitting our mark. Asshole Three came barreling towards the door blocking us, shooting as he came. Reaching my gun around, I began rapid firing low, not wanting to kill him just yet.

His grunts and groans as the bullets hit him sent a sense of euphoria through me. No drug could give anyone a high like this, not as good as riding, but up there. Peeking around the corner, Asshole Three was groaning, his gun about two feet away from his hand. Walking slowly towards him, Tug went to the gun, moving it out of his reach.

I walked over to the asshole bleeding all over my beautiful carpet; good thing it was blood red. Kicking him in the stomach, "Who sent you here?" I barked, pointing the gun at his head.

"You stupid puta!" I kicked him again. Asshole needed to learn respect, which he obviously didn't have, shooting up my place.

"Tug, check it out." Tug immediately took off.

"Listen, Fucker. You wanted me. Now you got me. What the fuck do you want here?" I barked, clutching my gun.

"Boss says you stay away from Babs, or this happens again." I laughed. It all comes back to that stupid bitch, and yet she hasn't had the fucking balls to show her damn face.

"This is because of that bitch?" I smacked his head with the butt of my gun, sending blood flying.

"Puta!" he yelled, holding his head.

"Tell me why she thinks I'm coming for her?"

"Fuck you."

Tug walked in the room, "Clear."

"Go let the girls out."

"My pleasure." He turned and walked toward the back.

"Again. Tell me why she thinks I'm coming for her?" Each word I emphasized with a kick. This fucker obviously thought I was a weak little thing. I needed to show him how wrong he was.

"Fuck," he groaned, trying to roll to his side.

"No, I don't want to fuck, but thanks for offering." I smiled, pointing my gun at his head. "I don't need you alive, I could care less if you live or die. That choice is up to you." The dead calm from my voice was even strange to me, but I've used it many times in my life.

"She put you in... doesn't want the brothers coming after her."

"It's not the brothers she needs to worry about, now is it? You think coming here and making a fucking mess is gonna get her in our good graces?" I paused, looking at Liv as she walked in the room. "Liv, make sure the girls don't come in here. Take them out the back."

She scurried across the floor to the backroom. "Now. What to do with you? We've already killed two of your men. So maybe I'll let you live to deliver a message." Taking the gun, I shot him once in each leg. His screams made me smile.

"Would you like that? Staying alive?" He shook his head like the pussy he was. "Okay, here's the message. Tell Babs, I love her."

He looked at me shocked. "What?"

"You heard me." Pausing, I looked at Tug across the room. "You might wanna look the other way." I smiled smugly, but he didn't turn away.

"Pull your dick out," I ordered to the asshole.

"No, puta," he growled at me.

Hitting him with the butt of my gun again, this time in the nose, sending more blood spattering, I ordered, "Do it. And if you fucking call me puta again, I will blow your fucking dick off." Looking at the asshole, I felt Tug by my side. "Tug since you're not looking away. Come hold the gun on him." He complied. "Wrap his hands with this." I handed Tug part of the drapery that had fallen to the ground.

With my gun in my right hand, I slowly grabbed the

asshole's dick. "Now, do you want your dick or your balls?"

"Wh… at?" He was visibly shaken by the question.

"Do you want use of your dick or your balls?" When he didn't answer, I made the decision for him. Wrapping my one hand around his balls, I pulled with all of my strength feeling the ligaments and flesh pulling away from his body. When he yelled, I pulled harder. I heard a small whimper from Tug but didn't look his way. Rewrapping my hand around him for a better grip, I pulled once more for good measure making sure the only way he'd use these bad boys again was with a lot of surgery. I didn't need him reproducing.

"Now you remember what the message is?" I asked, nonchalantly as if I didn't just rip a guy's balls off.

When he didn't answer, I grabbed his dick as he paused, fear laced in his eyes. "Ye…sss…"

"What is it?" My words dripping with honey.

"Tell Babs you love her," he stammered out.

"Good. Tug get him out of here. Ditch him far away." Tug nodded, picking up his phone, making the arrangements. "Where are the B.Boys?"

"Taking care of the girls… hey, Princess?" he asked.

"Yeah," I said looking around at the pit Studio X had just become.

"Remind me never to piss you off." I turned, smiling at him, not responding.

The B.Boys moved the bodies quickly, getting them the hell out of there. And by the time the cops came, there was only the mess to deal with. I told them that someone broke in and trashed the place, shooting guns off everywhere. By the time I got there, they were all gone.

The cops didn't ask any other questions. We've known the chief for years, and he kept our business... well, our business.

Liv came in, visibly shaken. "Girl, you okay?"

"Will be," she replied as her eyes searched the room, taking in all of the destruction.

"I'll ask Cruz if the Prospects can help clean up the mess and we'll get the girls to help. We'll be up and running soon." I hugged her, rubbing her back. "We'll need to be closed for a few days." She nodded.

"Princess, phone call." Tug held out his phone to me. "Cruz."

I figured and turned on the charm. "Hey, Baby. How's the trip?"

"Don't, what the fuck happened?" After explaining in detail what happened, he wasn't very happy with me. "Get your fucking ass to the clubhouse, now." He yelled loud enough; I had to pull it away from my ear.

"We're just about done here."

"No. Now."

I tried to swallow my frustration, but it was difficult. "I'm fine. Everyone is fine."

"You are not fine. You fucking shot two guys and ripped a guy's balls off. Not to mention the Studio is fucking trashed. Like I said, get your ass to the clubhouse, now. I'm on my way. Be there in two hours."

Blowing out a deep breath, I forced out, "Leaving now."

"Good. Lock yourself in my damn room with my boy, and don't fucking move."

Rolling my eyes, I responded, "Okay." I waited for him to hang up.

"Let's ride," I said to Tug, slipped my phone in my pocket, then turned to the boys. "B.Boys get Liv home, please, and lock this place up tight."

CHAPTER SEVEN
Cruz

WE HAD A PERFECT RUN, NO PROBLEMS OR complications... except for my girl. Dammit. I didn't get Tug's text until we pulled off for gas, and after that I drove like a bat out of hell. Hearing Tug replay the entire scene made my fucking blood boil. Not only was someone after Princess, she decided to take matters into her own hands. The two hour drive did nothing to cool me down. Pulling up to the clubhouse, my first stop was Tug.

"What the fuck happened?" I boomed, crossing my arms across my chest, trying to hold them back from ringing this fucker's neck. He should have never let her go.

"Your girl kicked some serious fucking ass," he replied, mimicking my pose.

"Why the fuck did you let her go?"

He laughed. "Have you met your girl? We weren't

gonna change her mind, thought it best to be there to protect her."

"Fuck," I rubbed my hands over my face. This was such a huge cluster-fuck. Nodding in understanding, I headed into the club.

"Hey, Cruz!" Buzz called from the bar.

"What?" I said walking by not wanting to hear shit from anyone.

"You serious about that girl?" His words halted me. Turning to stare at Buzz, my anger peaked.

"What the fuck do you care?" I said, narrowing my eyes at him.

Something flickered in his eyes, but he didn't back down. "Cause I saw what she can do. She's something."

"She's mine. Stay the fuck away." He held his hands up and stepped back.

"Got it."

"Don't you fucking forget it!" Striding towards my room, I couldn't help the small smirk that played on my lips. Not only does Princess have the adoration of all the ol' timers here, now she's got it from the Prospects, too. Damn.

Turning the handle, I found it was locked. My heart warmed that she actually fucking listened to me. Unlocking the door, I could see Princess's back stiffen as she was down on the floor playing Legos with Cooper. "Daddy!" Cooper ran into my arms as I knelt down to catch him in a full-out run.

"Hey, Buddy. How are ya?" I asked kissing the top of his head.

"Pin... ess pay boks." His smile was wide, and I could tell that he had fallen under her spell, also.

"She's playing blocks with you, huh?" He shook his head.

"And Ma gives mes cookies!"

"Sounds yummy. Let's go find Ma for minute. I gotta talk to Princess."

After dropping him off with Ma, I found Princess lying on her back with her arm covering her eyes. "I know you're there and pissed. I had to go and protect my girls. I'd do it again in a heartbeat," she said, looking up at the ceiling.

Kicking the door shut and locking it, I reached the end of the bed climbing between her spread thighs. Laying on top of her and removing her arm, I crashed my lips to hers, needing to feel her, taste her, and know she was alive with me.

Princess melted into me as I took what I wanted from her. Not wasting a single second, I ripped her shirt over her head, kissing, licking, and nipping her neck and the curve of her beautiful tits. Pulling her bra away from her body, I needed to devour her. I pulled her nipples in between my teeth giving them small bites and sucking hard.

As her breath caught and the moans became deeper, my dick became painfully hard and needed to be inside her tight pussy. Kissing my way to her jeans, I ripped them quickly away from her body. The scrap of fabric she had on as underwear tore easily in my hands.

Looking down at this beautiful woman underneath me,

I wanted to savor everything about her. Kissing down her body, my mouth latched on to her clit sucking hard. She set off like an explosion in my mouth, coating my tongue with her sweetness. Before she came fully down, I buried myself inside of her pumping and thrusting with everything I had.

"Condom," she choked out between pushes.

"No. You're mine. This pussy is mine." She didn't argue; instead her eyes rolled in the back of her head as her body arched up from the bed. As my dick slid in her wet heat, it took everything I had to wait to come. Screaming, she called out my name over and over again. I didn't show her any mercy, if anything, I pounded harder.

As she came a third time, I released deep inside her body. Every part of my body shook as I felt her deep in my soul. Collapsing on top of her, I slowly rolled to the side, taking her with me.

"So, you're pretty pissed, huh?" she asked, smiling, trying to catch her breath.

"Better now."

"Good." She squeezed me tight. I'd missed feeling her, shit; I've only been gone a couple of days.

I hated to break this up, "Diamond wants to see you."

"Shit. I swear I didn't start this shit." Her voice was laced with concern.

"He just wants to know what happened and what was said. We gotta get this shit taken care of."

Nodding, she rolled out of bed giving me an awesome look at her hot ass and making my dick hard again. We didn't have time; Diamond was waiting.

Walking out to the clubhouse, Princess was in front.

She gave chin lifts to the guys sitting around the bar. Dagger came up to her, "You okay?"

"Of course." She shrugged it off.

"Good, can't have your sweet ass getting shot." I tried to contain the growl that came out of my throat, but it was no use. It only made Dagger laugh. When Princess reached behind her, grabbing my hand, latching our fingers together, I couldn't help the smug grin.

"Princess. Get in here!" Diamond called from his office. "You too, Cruz."

Princess held my hand into the room. Not gonna lie, it excited me that she was acknowledging us to the club. Finally.

"Sit," Princess and I sat next to each other on the couch while Diamond sat in the chair by his desk.

"So, quite a shit storm you got going on, girl."

"Diamond, I didn't start this..." Princess began, shaking her head as she squeezed my hand. I reciprocated.

"I know. We gotta figure out what the fuck is going on. Tell me from the beginning." As Princess replayed the scene, she released my hand. Hearing step by step what happened and what was said, something was off with this whole situation.

"Why was the message that you love her?" Diamond stared at her.

"I promised you I wouldn't start shit. Figured it was a way of saying what I wanted to say without lying." She shrugged her shoulders as if it wasn't a big deal. But I knew it was. She followed Diamond's orders and damn if that didn't make my pride swell.

"You haven't contacted her at all?"

"No, Sir."

"So why is she coming after you?"

"Not quite sure. Preemptive strike? She knows I want her; it's no secret." Diamond eyed me secretly communicating that he agreed. Something was not right with this. "I did do one thing..." Princess let out a deep breath. "I didn't contact her, but I did have her looked into."

"Like how?" Diamond asked, lacing his fingers and setting them on the table.

Princess pulled out a folded manila envelope from inside her leather jacket. "A friend from inside, Deara, got this for me." Diamond opened the envelope, scattering the contents inside as he looked at each of them and pushed them towards me. "I just got them, and I haven't done anything with them."

"This friend, how the hell did she get them?" I asked, wondering how much deeper this shit went.

"She's part of the Lambalinis' group."

"You got involved with them?" My temper flared. There was no way I wanted her involved with those assholes. They'd cut her throat out and not think twice about it.

"It's fine. I helped Deara out inside; she owed me. It was just payback. There's no blowback."

"You're sure?" Diamond asked suspiciously.

"Positive. She even said she'd do whatever I needed to get this bitch taken care of. And I believe her."

"I'm taking you at your word."

She smiled. "Yes, Sir. What's the plan with Babs?"

"Club business," Diamond answered.

"With all due respect, the bitch had her boy toy goons shoot up my studio. It's my business, too."

Diamond stared at her, his eyes deadpanned. "You'll know what you need to know."

"What do you want me to do?" she asked sheepishly as she backed down from Diamond. I knew it was killing her not to be let into the loop of shit.

"Right now, clean up the studio and take care of the girls. You let us handle Rabbit's crew, and if that includes Babs, then so be it."

"When the time comes, do I get Babs?"

"She will pay for putting you in." When he didn't give her a definite answer, she sighed in defeat.

The door banged as it flew open. All of our eyes shot to Ma. "Get out here. Mel's here for Cooper."

"Oh, hell no!" Princess said, jumping up faster than both Diamond and I. Walking into the main room of the clubhouse, Mel stood with her hand on her hip, glaring at Princess as she got closer. "What the fuck are you doing here?" Princess's voice was cold as ice.

"I want my boy," Mel said, dismissing her and looking at me, which was the wrong move. Princess moved in front of her, going toe-to-toe.

"You want him. Get through me first," she growled.

"You're not keeping my son, Bitch." Mel didn't see the punch coming as Princess's fist landed right in her jaw, causing her to hold her face in agony. "You bitch!" Mel started to go after Princess, but I knew this shit had to be over.

"Enough!" I yelled causing Princess to flinch, but she brought herself in check as she came and stood behind me. I crossed my arms over my chest, trying to contain the rage flowing through me and the urge to wrap my hands back around this bitch's throat again. "Mel, you need to leave. Cooper's not going anywhere. The lawyers already drawn up the papers, and you are not to be on club property."

Mel's face dropped, turning white as a sheet. "What papers?"

"Custody. You'll get them tomorrow and sign them. Otherwise, I'll give the police all the pictures, and documentation I have regarding your drug use, and the bruises found on my boy."

Princess grabbed my arm, squeezing it tight, "She hit him..." she whispered. Putting my hand on hers, I gave it a gentle squeeze. Mel's eyes grew wide.

"If you think this bitch is a better mom to my boy than me, you are sadly mistaken."

"You call her a bitch again and I'll move the fuck out of her way and let her take care of you. Get out. Sign the damn papers or go to jail... you choose." I could see in her eyes that Mel wanted to fight. Mel turned and walked out the door. When the door shut, Princess let go of my arm turned and walked down the hallway without a word.

"Cruz, in here, now." Pops' voice came from behind me pointing to chapel.

Following Pops and Diamond to the table, they shut the door behind us, sitting in our respective places. "You serious about my daughter or you playing?"

I was actually surprised it took Pops this long to ask. "Serious."

"So she's your ol' lady?"

"Yes."

"She agree with that?" he asked, smirking.

"Working on it." Both Pops and Diamond full out laughed, causing me to do the same. "Pops, she's tough, but I'm not giving her up."

"Good. You got that bitch, Mel, under control?" Diamond asked.

"Burnzie's drew up the paperwork. She should be gone for good in a couple of days. And if, for some reason that doesn't work, I'll make her gone."

"Good. Shit's gonna get deep." I eyed Pops as he spoke. "Insider says that Babs is feeding Rabbit a bunch of shit about Princess threatening her."

"Shit," I groaned while lighting up a smoke.

"That's why the shit storm. I called for a meeting, but he hasn't responded. But there's more." He paused to look at Diamond. "There are whispers of another set-up going down to put Princess back inside."

Anger surged. "What the fuck?"

"And if Princess kills her, there will be a million dollar bounty on her head."

"You've got to be fucking kidding me. Babs's pussy that good to get Rabbit to fall for this shit?"

"Apparently." Diamond stretched back in his chair placing his hands behind his head as he eyed me.

"So, what's the plan?" I asked, rubbing my hands over my head.

"We're gonna go through all the info that Princess got, see what we can find and what clues we can come up with for this supposed set up. You need to keep a short leash on her. Which I know will be easy." Pops chuckled. "We wait to hear back from Rabbit and see if he's got any sense left. And you go find that bitch who came in here with Danny and get what you can out of her."

"What about her?" I asked, wanting to make sure that when I opened my mouth to her it wouldn't be the end of me.

"She knows what she needs to for now." Nodding my head, Diamond gave me the chin lift, which meant I was dismissed.

Princess was curled up on my corner recliner holding Cooper in her arms as he slept. As she brushed away the silent tears, our eyes met. The pain inside of them made my heart ache. Kneeling in front of them, I placed one hand on Coop and the other on her knee. "You okay, Baby?"

"No. I'm not," she whispered.

"Talk to me." Princess looked down at Cooper in her arms taking one hand and brushing the hair out of his face as she placed a kiss on his forehead.

"She can't have him. I won't allow it." Princess's tone went from gentle to fierce in seconds. "Cooper's mine. I won't allow him to be hurt. I'll kill her before she touches him again." A grin covered my face. "I'm not kidding, Cruz. I will end her if she touches him."

"I know Baby. It's not gonna happen. She'll be gone soon." My hand began rubbing up and down on her thigh trying to calm her, but damn if her fierce protectiveness for my boy didn't make me want to fuck her right here and now. Not to mention it filled my heart with more love, than I ever thought possible.

"Good. She shows her face here again it won't end well." She squeezed Cooper tightly. "I'm going to hold him while he sleeps for a bit."

"I got shit to do. I'll be back in a bit. Don't go anywhere." She didn't argue; she just nodded, pulling a blanket over the top of herself and Coop. I thought she was beautiful before, but seeing her with Coop did me in even more.

Kissing both her and Coop, I left, knowing that I needed to get shit handled.

FINDING MINDY WASN'T HARD. Heading to the Clayton chapter, Tug, Rocky and I rode fast. I had this urgent feeling that I needed to get back to Princess and my boy.

"Danny!" I barked as I took my lid off, and we parked at their clubhouse. "Guys, stay here." With our chapter being the mother, all the sub-chapters didn't say a word as I walked directly into their clubhouse. "Danny!" I barked again looking around their club, set up similar to ours.

"What's up brother?" Danny called from the hallway.

"I need to talk to Mindy."

"About?"

"None of your fucking business. Get her out here, now," I clipped. Fuck him if he thought for one second about protecting her ass. Sighing, he left and came back with a very scared Mindy.

"Tell me what you know." I stood crossing my arms

and standing to my full six foot two inch height. I knew my presence was menacing, and I didn't give a fuck.

"I... I don't know anything," she stammered out.

Moving closer to her, Danny stepped in front of Mindy, which pissed me off more. "Get the fuck out of my way," I said, my nose touching his.

"You're not gonna hurt her," he demanded, which sent my rage in fury.

"Get the fuck out of my goddamned way before I put a fucking bullet in your head."

"You'd shoot a brother in his own clubhouse?" he asked, puzzled.

"If the fucker keeps me from protecting my family, then he's not mine in the first place." My eyes stared him down. After a few beats, he moved out of the way of Mindy, as she shuddered.

"You will answer my questions and tell me what you know about Babs. Now."

"I... really don't know anything."

"Sit and talk," I said motioning to the couches to the side of us. I really didn't want to hurt the bitch, but if she didn't open her fucking trap soon, shit would fly.

Mindy looked at Danny for reassurance, and when he nodded his head she began talking. "Two years ago, Babs was pissed that Princess was, well, Princess. She had everything that Babs ever wanted. Princess had the club and all the guys at her beck and call. She's a badass on a bike, and she knew how to shoot and not miss. She also had power. Princess never flaunted it; that just wasn't who she was. But Babs didn't like it. She wanted it, and it was something she could never have." Mindy paused to think.

"Babs wanted to get rid of her once and for all, but didn't think things through the way she should have."

"What do you mean the way she should have?" Tapping down my anger was getting harder and harder with this bitch.

Blowing out a deep breath, she said, "She thought that if she got rid of Princess, she could move in on the guys at the club and take her spot. But when that didn't happen, her anger turned to fury, and it took over. She wanted to destroy Princess. It was stupid of her to think that the club would welcome her after sending their prized woman to jail."

"Yeah. Pretty stupid. What was your role?" Mindy's hand started to shake with nerves as she reached over to Danny. He didn't tell her or me to stop; he just squeezed it.

"The only thing I was asked to do was get Princess to Studio X. All I did was put in a phone call to her. I swear. I didn't have anything to do with the rest of it. I wouldn't say that Babs and Princess were ever friends, just respectful acquaintances. Babs did a little work for her regarding Studio X, but I would never say they were friends."

When Princess got locked up, they wanted to make an example of her like all the rest of us when we get locked up. She was convicted of blackmailing and cooking the books at Studio X. We all knew it was bullshit, but somehow that bitch Babs got into Princess's office and switched all her books. She even had pictures that looked like Princess was taking money from our very own prominent mayor, Stan Mason. He went up on the stand and lied through his teeth about Princess blackmailing him because he spent time at Studio X. When Pops shook him down, he stuck to his story. But the mayor didn't live to tell anything. Babs did a hell of a job with the *proof* she had, because our lawyer didn't see a way out of it. The kicker was that we didn't find any of this shit out till about a year after Princess was inside. I got all this information secondhand from Pops when I started prospecting for the club.

"So what's the deal now?"

"What do you mean?" she asked, puzzled.

"What's Babs up to now?"

"I... I don't know. I got away from her after that happened. I saw what she could do, and I didn't want any part of it." Mindy's voice cracked and stammered.

"So with what you know, she just let you leave?" Something here sounded rotten.

"No. I stayed about a year. Then when she hooked up with Rabbit and his crew, we just kinda fizzled out. She didn't come around much. I guess she got Princess's spot, just in a different club."

"Let me tell you what you're gonna do." Her eyes widened as I stared her dead in the eyes. "You're gonna call Babs and make nicey-nice with her. Get the low down on what she's doing to Princess right now and why."

"I don't want anything to do with Babs," she clipped, which pissed me off. Why the fuck she thought she had a say so in the matter was beyond me.

"I don't give a shit. You wanna be Danny's ol' lady and make this shit right?" She nodded. "Then you're gonna help us out. I want all information on Babs's plans and thoughts. You're going inside."

Her hands began to tremble uncontrollably. "But she'll kill me."

"It's a risk I'm willing to take," I said leaning back in the chair. "You get in there. Find everything out you can, and after this shit is done, you get out."

"It won't be that easy, and you damn well know it," Danny barked.

Cutting him off briskly. "If I wanted your opinion on the fucking thing, I'd ask."

"This shit is fucked up. You wouldn't ask anyone else's ol' lady to do this shit." Danny's anger spewed through his words.

"I'd move the fucking earth to protect Princess. Get that through your fucking head right now." I leveled my eyes at him, making him see inside of them. Then turning to Mindy, I demanded, "You have two days. Get in there and find something out."

"Two days. How the hell is she gonna get anything in two days?" Danny asked.

I cracked my knuckles as I stood from the couch. "Don't fucking care. Just get it."

Driving away from their clubhouse, I knew I needed to figure out how the hell this was all gonna work.

CHAPTER EIGHT
Harlow

PLAYING WITH COOPER HAS BEEN THE HIGHLIGHT OF MY day. I needed to go to Studio X, but I waited for Cruz. Lord knows what he had to do.

When the door opened, and Cruz walked through, he looked absolutely edible, his hair a mess from his lid as he ran his hands through it fiercely. His leather rag hung off of him with his black long sleeved t-shirt under it. His jeans hung low, and I knew that if I took his shirt off, I'd see the hottest V that led me down to his thick dick, along with his many gorgeous tats that lined his magnificent body. He was to die for. Smiling up at him from the floor, I turned Coop around so he could see his daddy. "Daddy!" he yelled, running into his arms.

"Hey, Buddy." Watching Cruz hold his little boy tightly in his arms made my heart flutter. Seeing him be such a great father to Coop was my undoing. This was my man. I loved him. Even though it's all been a whirlwind, there was no denying it. He was mine.

"Daddy, me's colorin'."

"I see that, Buddy. I need to talk to Princess for a bit, lets head to your room."

I sat in the recliner waiting for him to get Coop settled. "What's going on?"

"Coop's on lockdown here. He's not to leave for any reason. He'll be safe." His words were reassuring, but I needed to know what could happen.

"What if she doesn't sign the papers?"

"She will." I didn't know why he thought this was going to go so smoothly. If anything, these past couple weeks have proven that nothing goes smoothly in this world. "I know you can protect yourself, but until we get this shit sorted out, you gotta be extra careful."

I knew he was right, but having restrictions just reminded me of prison. But I knew I'd listen, because he's my man.

TWO DAYS LATER

"WHAT DO you mean she's fucking gone?" Cruz's rough voice bellowed through the clubhouse. Sitting on a barstool with Cooper letting him play with all the paper coasters as he lined them up repeatedly, I tried to distract him from his dad's yelling.

"She couldn't have just fucking disappeared, Danny!" I assumed he was talking about Mindy. I shook my head listening to the one-sided conversation Cruz was having on the phone, knowing I shouldn't be, but it didn't stop me.

"You know where she fucking is. Tell me!" Cooper didn't pay any attention to his dad, as he was too busy stacking the coasters just right.

"I will come over there and make you fucking tell me. You have twenty-four hours for her to show up. Then shit's gonna get real serious." Cruz hit end on his phone, slipping it inside his rag anger pouring off of him.

"What's going on?" Pops asked before I could.

Cruz stepped up to Pops saying something quietly in his ear, and Pops nodded.

Pops turned to me. "You okay?"

"I'm good."

"I need you to do something for me," Pops said, almost nervously, which wasn't his style.

"Sure, anything."

"I need you to contact that Deara and get any and all information on Mindy and Babs recently. You think you can get it quickly?"

"Yeah, I have an outside contact that can get to her. I'll see what I can do." I couldn't help the happiness that fell through my body knowing they trusted me to get the information.

LYING IN BED, I couldn't sleep for shit. My mind kept thinking of all the shit I've dealt with the past two weeks and two years. It was all because one bitch was jealous. She was flat out jealous of my life. I tried to shy away from this life and be manlier, like the guys, just to fit in with them. She was so jealous of a life in which I had to try relentlessly to escape from being called Princess, even though it grew on me. I loved this life. But I couldn't shake the feeling that there was more to it. There had to be.

Who the hell could hate me so fucking much that would work with her and help her destroy me... 'cause I knew there had to be more to this.

Thinking back two and a half years ago, my life was simple. I had my studio, the club, the brothers, and my family. We didn't want for anything. We were pretty well set. If I wanted to get laid, I'd find some unsuspecting fool at the bar, get my kicks, and never call again.

There wasn't anyone that I personally had any beefs with, at least any known beefs. I knew the club had tons of haters. That was a given, but I didn't stir up trouble. I just dealt with the trouble when it came.

I had to throw out a few guys from the studio because they got too rough with the girls, but nothing stood out. I just couldn't shake the feeling that Babs was working with someone, because considering Babs and I were not even classified as friends in my eyes, it had to be more.

My mind kept reeling trying to come up with some rhyme or reason to this madness, but came up blank.

Cruz left on club business a while ago leaving Coop and me to hang out. I really loved my time with him.

These damn dreams I kept having were killing me. Every time I closed my eyes, I saw him and felt him. I just wanted to take a scalding shower and let the water melt the skin off my body. I didn't want to close my eyes in fear of seeing the replay.

Having enough, I needed something to take my mind off all this shit. Walking into the clubhouse, Rhys, Becs, Breaker, and Buzz were all around the bar in some deep conversation, but immediately stopped when they saw me. Rolling my eyes, I slowly approached seeing the two women lying on the far couch. It's like they never left that fucking spot.

"Hey, Princess. How the hell are ya?" Becs asked as he strummed his fingers on the bar. His red hair made him stand out among all the other guys. It wasn't fire engine red, but a reddish-brown and with his piercing green eyes, he was a very attractive man. His nose had been in a couple of fights and not set quite right causing a large bump in the center, but to me it gave him character. He always acted like a second big brother to me throughout the years.

"I'm hanging in there," I said as I sidled up to the bar. "Can I have a Jack, please?" I asked one of the B.Boys. One of these days I'll be able to tell them apart, but tonight wasn't that night.

"You and Cruz, huh?" Becs asked as I shot down the Jack, feeling the burn down my throat, and slamming the glass to the bar. I needed another. I motioned to the B.Boys.

"Never thought I'd see the day when you finally gave in to a brother." He swigged his beer and shook his head.

I smiled. "Shocked the hell out of me, too."

"You do okay, inside?" Rhys's deep voice sent shivers down my back. There was always something about a deep baritone voice that had my body quivering. Rhys wasn't like the other guys to me. To me, he was far more dangerous, far scarier, but I never let that show to him. I'd heard stories that I wasn't supposed to hear growing up, of how he dealt with people who fucked with him. And shit if those didn't freak me out, I was ultimately glad that Rhys was on my side.

"The first few weeks were rough. I had to find my place, and it didn't come easy. But once that was over, it got a bit better. Then when Pops got the Warden to give me my own room, it got much better. Sleeping with one eye open is a lot harder than I thought. But I survived."

"You sure did girl. We're real proud of you. Not many women would have been as strong." Rhys wrapped his arm around my shoulders, and part of me wanted to cringe away, but I'd never be disrespectful to him.

"Thanks..."

"You get ahold of that chick for info?" Becs asked, taking a pull of his beer.

"Heard back a while ago. She's got her person on it. I don't know who that person is, but hopefully we'll have what we need in the morning." After the shit that I got for even using her, I was surprised I was asked to get more information from her.

"Good. I hate going into shit blind," Rhys added.

Shooting another shot of Jack, I felt eyes boring through me. Looking up, one of the B.Boys was eyeing me. "What?"

"You're the only chick I know that can take out two men and rip one's balls off without breaking a sweat." His admiration was funny, so I laughed.

"You'd be best to remember not to piss me off," the guys groaned. "Oh, come on, it's not like I did it to you."

"Oh, Honey, just the thought of it sends pains to my dick." Rhys grabbed his pants, adjusting himself.

"You are a pain in the dick," I said, smiling.

"You realize you and Ma are the only two chicks who can pull that shit, right?" There were no words that I could say to that because I knew it was totally true. Rhys didn't take shit from anyone.

"Got her!" Cruz's voice came through the clubhouse. Jumping out of my seat, I went to see exactly who he got. Walking in front of him was a very disheveled looking Mindy. Her hair was matted, and clothes torn. She was scratched up and black and blue.

Before I was able to ask any questions, Cruz said, "Come on, Baby. I'm beat."

I couldn't help myself and had to ask, "But what about her?"

Cruz leaned down to my ear, "Let them handle it." Each word he spoke sent shivers down my spine and made my panties wet.

Conflicting thoughts set in. I wanted to know what this woman had to say, but my body wanted Cruz. My body won. "Let's go." Cruz wrapped his arm around my shoulder leading me to his room. Looking in on Coop, we were glad to see he was sound asleep.

I needed something from Cruz. Something he'd yet to give me. We'd always had a passionate lust-filled no holds barred time in bed, but this time I needed something else.

Walking up to him as seductively as I could, I pushed him to the bed as he fell with a bounce. "Baby, whatcha doing?" He smirked up at me as I began to take my shirt off slowly, inching it up until I whipped it off my body. His hands started to touch my body, and I shook my head.

"Leave them on your thighs," I whispered as I turned around unbuttoning my jeans. Placing my thumbs inside my pants, I slowly pulled them down bending at the waist giving Cruz the ultimate view of my ass, only covered with a thong.

Cruz's breath hitched as I turned around staring into his beautiful eyes. Leaving my bra and underwear on, I slowly moved closer to the bed as my knees touched the edge. With my fingertips, I lightly grazed his chest starting at the neck and making my way down to the bottom hem. Those same fingertips reached under his hem, finding his thick chest waiting for me. As I moved my hands up, I took his shirt off feeling every contour of muscle he had on the way.

"Lift up," I whispered as he complied and stared into my eyes.

"You havin' fun?" I nodded my head, not uttering a sound. My hands found the side of his face feeling the scruff of his beard. Pulling his lips to mine, I kissed him passionately without being too rough. I didn't want rough this time. I sucked and nibbled his lips as his hands came up to my head. I instantly pulled away.

"Hands on your thighs," I ordered winking at him.

"So this is how we're gonna play tonight?"

"Yeah, Baby. Just lay back and enjoy." Kissing down his chest, I paid special attention to his nipples. He groaned as my tongue gave them one hell of a workout. Running my hands along the top of his chest were the words, Live and Let Live. I smiled kissing each word. I inched slowly lower until I reached the buckle of his belt.

As I kissed his abs, I methodically undid the belt and his pants. Reaching underneath both his pants and boxers, I pulled them down slowly, not allowing my mouth to touch anywhere near his dick. He'd have to wait for that, but my lips grazed every other part as I moved.

As I traveled back up his body, my tongue and teeth gave him slight nips and bites along his legs, thighs and chest. I was pretty proud he was able to keep his hands where I told him, even though he was clenching them repeatedly into fists making my body warm. At least he was trying. I knew it was hard for a man like Cruz to give up control fully, and I accepted the gift he had given me.

As I reached his dick, my hand wrapped around it as fully as I could, slowly stroking him up and down. My tongue reached out sweeping it from base to tip causing his entire body to jump. As my hand wrapped firmly around the base, I slowly began turning and pumping my hand rhythmically. He was fully erect and ready for me, but he was going to wait. I needed this. My hand moved back and forth ever so slowly, feeling the velvet of his dick move with it. Watching his fisted hands, his knuckles were turning white. I decided to give him a small reprieve.

Kissing the top of his dick, I licked the small amount of pre-cum that seeped out of the head moaning at his husky taste. Slowly I began sucking as I wrapped my lips around him leaving my hand at the base slowly pumping. Cruz had a beautiful dick; absolutely perfect in size and just like my pussy, my mouth fit it perfectly. I pulled him into my mouth as far as I could; his head touching the back of my throat repeatedly, but kept breathing out of my nose controlling my gag reflex.

Cruz's hips began moving in time with my sucks and the bobbing of my head, his hands itching to weave through my hair. "I'm gonna come if you keep this up," he groaned at me.

"Maybe that's the point." I knew he could get himself right back up. He's proven that numerous times, and I wanted the taste of him on my tongue. I wanted to feel him coat the inside of my throat.

"Fuck," was all the warning I received as his warm jets came rushing in my mouth. Rhythmically I swallowed as he continued to pump inside of me. After the last bit of his cum exits his body, I licked his entire cock, getting every bit off of him. "Damn, Baby," he said, breathing heavily.

My thong was completely soaked through, and I could smell my intense arousal, turning me on even more. "Now, stay right there," I told him. "You can use your hands in a minute."

Smiling at him, I stood, removed my panties and bra,

giving my tits a bit of a shake, as my eyes focused on his, the heat in them filling up the room. Climbing up his body, I needed his lips on my body. He was going to eat until I told him to stop, and love every fucking second of it. Straddling his head, I grabbed on to the headboard in front of me not saying a word. "What am I supposed to do with this?" he asked with a cocky tone.

"You don't know? I guess I can find someone who does," I shot back, looking down at his eyes that instantly turned to fire and began boring into my soul.

"No one touches this pussy, but me," he growled, grabbing my thighs pulling my pussy down to his mouth hard. His tongue worked its magic as he ate me like a starving man. His tongue moved in and out of my folds with utter precision. When he latched on to my clit and began to suck, I saw white spots form behind my eyelids as I came. I didn't dare scream in fear of waking up Coop. Instead, I pulled my hand to my mouth biting it hard, muffling the sound. "You like that, Baby?" I nodded breathlessly. "You think I don't know how to eat pussy?" I shook my head, no; this man definitely new how to eat a good meal.

When I finally caught my breath and came back down to earth, I climbed down his body crashing my lips to his, tasting myself which revved me up again instantly. Cruz's hands wrapped around my waist, as he flipped me over to my back.

"We did this your way, now we do it mine." Cruz didn't give me time to think or argue as he plunged inside of me in one long hard stroke. His hips became pistons plunging in and out of me with the force of a turbo jet.

Instead of screaming, I bit his shoulder hard muffling the sound. He jumped in surprise. "You bit me."

I smiled at his shock. "I can't scream; it's the only way."

"Then I better get ready for some vampire action, 'cause you'll want to scream." As Cruz began his punishing thrusts in and out of my body, he tilted my hips, giving him a better angle, making my head spin in a thousand different directions. His lips crashed down on mine just as he hit that one spot inside my body that set me off every damn time. Instead of biting, his kisses muffled my screams as my orgasm took over, sending my body into convulsive shakes.

Cruz grunted just as I felt his dick release warm spurts inside of me, filling me up completely. He collapsed on top of me, his weight pushing me into the bed. I didn't feel his weight at all; I felt loved, thoroughly, utterly loved. No man has ever made me come this hard before. I felt it all the way to my soul and back.

"I love you," I whispered so softly I didn't think he could hear me, not knowing what his reaction might be.

"Thank fuck, Baby." He lifted his body up, looking me in the eyes, the passion and love permeating through them. "I love you, too, Baby. Just you."

My heart filled more than I ever possibly thought. I wrapped my arms around his strong body, pulling him back down to my lips as I kissed him, pouring everything I had into that one kiss.

Loud pops sounded off from the other room. Gunshots. "Shit," Cruz leapt off of me grabbing his jeans and throwing them on, as I did the same. As we threw our shirts on, we both grabbed our guns. "Stay with Coop!" he ordered as he left the room.

More shots fired one after another. I could hear men yelling, a woman screaming. Coop began crying because of the noise which surprised me since he usually slept through just about anything. Setting my gun down, I picked him up, cradling him in my arms as I wiped the tears away. Grabbing the gun, I moved to the chair where I proceeded to rock him softly back and forth, just waiting.

The door flew open as Cruz charged in. "You two all right?" he panted out of breath.

"Yeah. What's going on?"

"Danny came to get Mindy." Shit. This was not going to end well. A brother did not come to the mother chapter opening fire. It was unheard of.

"Everyone okay?"

"Pops got a shoulder graze, but everyone's fine. Mindy's screaming 'cause we shot Danny in the legs. It's a fucking mess."

"Daddy!" Cooper screamed reaching out of my arms trying to get to Cruz.

"Come here, Buddy. Everything's just fine. Daddy's got ya." Cooper rested his head on Cruz's shoulder and wrapped his little arms around his neck.

"I'm gonna make sure Pops is okay." When I reached the main room, Ma was crying as she sat on the floor, and Pops was sitting beside her rubbing her back. On the floor across the room, was a screaming Danny with Mindy next to him, half screaming and half sobbing.

Rhys had his gun aimed at Danny's head, and Dagger had his aimed at Mindy's.

Walking up to Ma and Pops, I asked, "You okay?" I could see the blood coming through Pops' shirt, but he wasn't doing much to stop it.

"Yeah. I'm good," he said giving me a sad smile. His eyes showing wear from years of a hard life.

"Let me take a look, okay?" I asked him, grabbing some scissors from the bar. After taking his rag off, which had a slice in it from the bullet that would need to be sewn later; I cut his t-shirt off enough to see the wound. The slice was pretty deep, but the bullet didn't go all the way through. This would be an easy fix. He'd be sore, but fine.

"Buzz, grab me the first aid kit, please. Breaker get me some clean towels. Tug, I need a needle, and thread, and alcohol." I asked the Prospects, who immediately got to work getting the needed supplies. It was nice to have that relationship with them that they didn't think I was trying to be a bitch and order them around but that I just needed help. And they provided it every time.

After stitching Pops up, I gave him a couple shots of Jack before he took Ma to bed. The guys had put towels on Danny's wounds, and it looked as if the blood had stopped. "You want me to take a look?" I asked Dagger.

"Nah. He's fine. Doc will be here in about thirty. He won't bleed out before then." He turned to Danny, his words dripping with venom. "*If* he gets here on time."

Mindy decided her screaming rant was going to be over for the moment, long enough to talk. "I didn't mean for this to happen. I was just supposed to stay there till everything calmed down."

"You really are stupid. What the fuck did you expect to happen?" My annoyance was on overload.

"Princess, I can't go to Babs. She'll kill me," Mindy pleaded, and at least I now knew what the club's plan was, but would keep that to myself.

"What in the hell do you think these guys will do to you?" I waved my arm motioning to all the men in the room. "This isn't a fucking joke."

"You don't think I know that!" she yelled at me as I snapped.

"You stupid little bitch. Who the fuck do you think you are? Someone special? No. You're a fucking whore, and because you helped Babs, you locked me up for years. Maybe I should lock you in a fucking room with nothing for two years, so you know what it's like. Then I'll come in a couple times a week and beat the shit out of you just for the fun of it. And if you're really good, I'll go find some bitch who likes pussy and make you give it up to her over and over. Then I'll let the guys take turns with you, fucking every hole you have in your body." Mindy's eyes widened as she took in every word that I said. I exaggerated a bit with my scenario, but she didn't need to know that shit.

"You fucking want that bitch? 'Cause that's what could happen to you here. Death would be a picnic compared to what I have planned for you. And if you think for a minute that this pussy you have for an ol' man will save you, you're sadly mistaken. The fact his ass came in here shooting against his brothers is reason to remove those fucking patches off him."

Mindy didn't move. She sat there staring at me as if I was God going to give her absolution from all the shit she helped put into motion. She was sadly mistaken.

Looking at Mindy, I said, "You'll be cleaning up this blood all over my floor 'cause I sure as shit ain't doing it." Looking at Tug, I told him, "Can you get some shit for her to use please?"

"Absolutely."

Doc came in the doors, taking in the scene. "Princess, you didn't." He shook his head. Doc has known me since I was a baby and always thought of me as one of his kids. Even in a time like this, he found the humor.

"Well Doc, ya know. My gun just has a hell of time staying in its holster." I smirked.

As Doc got busy working on Danny, I watched as Mindy began cleaning her boyfriend's blood off the floor. Sitting at the bar nursing a Jack and smoking, I actually felt calm. Normal women probably wouldn't, but this was what I wanted to come back to. And here it was smack dab in front of me.

After Doc got Danny situated, he left the clubhouse. Walking up to Danny laying there, I had no remorse for the pain he was in. He shot up the club, my brothers, my dad, and all around *my* little guy.

I knew better than to open my mouth to a brother, so I focused on Mindy instead. I stared at her. "Bitch, I'm not fucking playing with you. These men may not kill women, but I sure as shit will in a heartbeat." With that, I turned to go find my boys.

CHAPTER NINE
Cruz

Two days and the bitch hasn't gotten anywhere. Babs was avoiding her like the plague, and the only reason I knew it was true was because we had Buzz tap her phone. We found out Buzz's skill by dumb luck talking about how we wished it were possible. Buzz chimed in explaining a bunch of techy shit and set it all up. He then set up all these cameras and video shit around the compound. We could now see who was coming in and out at all times even recording shit at the drop of a hat. Buzz was proving to be a great asset to the club.

Listening into the phone conversation was boring as shit. Mindy only got through that first time shooting the shit about old times. She actually sounded calmer than I thought she would be. But Babs wasn't biting. Bitch was a bit smarter than we gave her credit for.

Babs's man Rabbit still hasn't contacted Diamond,

which was pissing him off majorly. Respect in this community was all you have, and when that's slammed on, there's nothing left. This shit was going to start a war.

I'm actually surprised that Diamond has held off as long as he has. This laying low shit was weighing on all of us, but we still didn't know who has the paid hit on Princess. We've got some Intel coming in, hopefully this afternoon, and we're hoping for some answers.

Mel still hadn't signed the damn papers giving me full custody of Cooper. She hadn't stepped foot in the club, but had passed through Burnzie that *she won't have some biker princess raising her boy.* Little did she know that *biker princess* was more of a fucking mother to my boy than she'd ever been.

I wasn't going to be able to put Princess off of it much longer, though. She was riding my ass hard about Mel not getting close to Cooper. The more she asked, and the more I evaded, the more it pissed her off. And a pissed off Princess did not equal fun.

"Church! Ten minutes!" Pops yelled across the room. Each of us placed our phone in the old cigar box on the pool table before entering and taking our seats.

Diamond banged the gavel as he called the meeting to order. "First order of business. Princess. We're supposed to get the information from Deara today. Any packages delivered need to come to me immediately." We all nodded.

"Our run tomorrow. It needs to go smoothly. Dagger, Rhys, Becs, Cruz, Pops, and I will run it. G.T., Zed, Tug, Buzz, and Breaker will stay here with Ma, Princess, and

Cooper. It should be a day run, there and back, quick."
Everyone again nodded.

"Last order of business. Studio X." My ears perked up.
"Since the shooting, Liv's been running the show and
doing a great job. I know that Princess hasn't gotten back
in because of all this bullshit. I'm thinking we need to get
better security there."

"What do you mean?" asked Dagger. "We monitor the
place and do drive-bys all the time."

"No. I want Becs to start monitoring the books. I want
him there also monitoring Liv. Princess will be pissed
'cause she trusts Liv, and I want to, too, but I'm not taking
any chances. We need to get this shit sorted. All in favor."
We all raised our hands to vote yes. Diamond slammed
the gavel.

"Cruz. All Princess needs to know is that Becs is
helping Liv out. Nothing else, because you know Liv will
say something."

"Got it."

"Anything else?" Diamond asked, looking out over us.

"I got two extra runs lined up. It'll bring in about
three hundred thousand a pop, but I'll need G.T., Cruz,
Rhys, and Zed to come with me." Dagger spoke up. "It's
not a long haul, but the runs will take two days. One
there. One back."

"Who's the run for?" Diamond asked.

"Ransom." Diamond nodded. We'd run for this guy
many times before.

"When is it?" I asked.

"Right after this run." Shit. That'd mean I'd be gone
for three days. Dagger eyed me, "Problem?"

"Nah." I didn't want to be away from Princess and Cooper that long, but I'd deal.

Diamond threw down the gavel dismissing us.

"WHERE THE FUCK HAVE YOU BEEN?" I stared into the eyes of a very pissed off Princess and was relieved I wasn't on the receiving end of it this time.

G.T. had just walked out of church reaching for his phone. "Around."

"Bullshit you've been around. I'm here all the fucking time, and you're nowhere to be seen!" Princess barked, getting close to his face.

"I've got shit to do." G.T. wasn't getting off that easy, and he damn well knew it.

"I don't give a rat's ass what you have to do. I've been out, and you've seen me...what... two, three times. No, how the hell are you Harlow? Or you doing okay?" G.T. pulled out a smoke, rolling it in between his teeth. "No. You're fucking avoid me. So you tell me where the fuck you have been?" Princess's anger was shooting off the charts, and I sensed her fists wanting to make contact with G.T.

"I don't need another fucking mother. One's enough. Get out of my fucking business."

"Out of your fucking business? Are you kidding me with that bullshit?"

"All you are is a fucking ol' lady, and you'd be best to remember that shit before I lay you flat on the ground."

"Lay me flat, *Gage Thomas*." Princess threw off her leather jacket inviting him.

"What you think that I'm a pussy like this guy over here?" G.T. pointed at me as I began stalking towards him.

"Stop!" Princess yelled as she saw me coming. "This is a brother and sister matter. Five minutes in the ring. Let's see how big of a pussy you are."

"Fuck off. I'm not getting in the ring," G.T. snapped.

"Yeah. You'll be there." Princess turned walking back down the hallway to my room.

"What the fuck, Asshole?" I said getting close to his face. "Why the fuck are you gonna provoke her like that?"

"I didn't do shit. She needs to calm her shit down and remember that bitches don't run shit here. She thinks she fucking does, but I got news for her, that shit's stopping."

"And what? You're man enough to stop her?" I laughed knowing that there were only three men that could get through to Princess, and G.T. wasn't one of them. "Dumbass, she doesn't think she runs shit around here. You would know that if you got your head out of your ass."

"You'd be best to put your girl in check." G.T. crossed his arms over his chest, and the arrogance that came off of him had my hand clenching into a fist wanting to make contact with his jaw.

"That *girl* is your sister, your blood. You best remember that. Whatever you got up your ass right now, you'd better work that shit out in the ring, and get the fuck over it."

"Whatever." We both knew he wouldn't back down

from a challenge, be it his sister, or not. He wouldn't come up a pussy even if he did get his ass kicked.

THE FIGHT WENT on for much longer that we thought it would. Apparently these two had a lot of shit they needed to work out. Both G.T. and Princess were bloody from face cuts and a bit wobbly from all the chest kicks. They were both still standing, barely. Neither one of them were backing down, which was what I'd expected. They're too damn stubborn to give in.

"Daddy!" I heard Coop's small voice behind me as he ran up into my arms. Ma followed closely behind.

"What the hell is going on here?" she barked, causing Cooper to look into the ring. Cooper's body went ridged in my hold as if he were a statue. Looking at the shock and horror on his face, I didn't move quickly enough as he got his bearings, wiggling out of my grasp faster than a slippery eel.

Running after Coop, I called his name reaching for him, but he didn't slow down. "Mommy!" He yelled as he reached the ring with me right at his heels. "Mommy!" he yelled again making my mouth drop to the floor.

Princess stopped sparring with her brother, ripping the head guard off her head. She slipped under the rope of the ring to the floor kneeling in front of him staring into his eyes. "I'm okay, Baby." Her tone was soft and gentle.

"Hurt. Owie," Coop said looking at Princess's face.

"Get me a towel," she ordered to no one in particular. She wiped her face gently getting rid of some of the blood. "See, Buddy. I'm okay. Just a few scrapes."

"Why fighting, Mommy?" he asked her innocently. Princess looked up at me, her eyes showing me a small glimmer of a tear that wanted to escape with tons of unanswered questions swirling inside of them. She breathed in a deep breath trying to regain control.

"I was just practicing to be strong. One day I'll teach you." She brushed his hair away from his face lovingly.

"I be strong." He smiled.

"You are Buddy."

"Mommy?" Princess looked stunned as if she didn't know if she should answer. She looked to me asking for permission and I, of course, smiled, loving the fact that I was witness to this remarkable exchange.

"Yeah, Baby?"

"You need Band-Aid?" Princess laughed, wrapping her arms tightly around his little body.

"Yeah, Buddy. I sure do. Let's go find those Spiderman ones. I think that'll make it all better." Princess picked Coop up, carrying him to the clubhouse, the huge smile she sported, even with the cut up lip, was beautiful.

"You sore?" I asked, walking into the bedroom expecting to see Princess and Coop hanging out, but only found Princess.

"I'll be fine." Her face had been butterflied, and the

caked-on blood removed. She was beginning to sport some serious bruises, but her beauty still shined through.

"What the hell was that shit?"

"What shit? My brother or the fact your kid just called me mom?" She glared at me. I didn't feel the need to touch the mom comment, so I moved on.

"Your brother. What's going on?"

She blew out a deep breath, "Fuck if I know. He's been distant since I got out, and when he blew up on me, I couldn't hold back. Even in the fucking ring, he didn't talk to me, though." She shrugged.

"You two fight like that a lot?"

"We used to. He taught me how to fight and how to protect myself."

"While I'm gone, you need to work that shit out."

"Yes... Dad," her words dripped with sarcasm as she rolled her eyes. "You okay with Coop calling me mom?"

I walked over to the bed, sitting down on the edge. "It's more of a question of how you feel about it."

"Why do you do that? I ask you how you feel about something then you turn it back on me. I hate that shit."

Giving her a sexy smirk, I said, "I'm completely fine with it. You're my ol' lady and someday soon, my wife."

"Wife?" She sounded stunned. I didn't answer; I just let her sit on the idea for a few. If she didn't want to marry me, I'd throw her over my knee and spank her ass, and the fact that she hadn't confirmed yet that she was my ol' lady was not lost to me.

"We're leave in the morning," I said, pulling her out of whatever thoughts were racing through that head of hers as I wrapped my arms around her.

"Okay," she whispered.

"Be smart. You need anything you get the Prospects to handle it. You keep our boy safe."

Her eyes narrowed into mine. "Always."

"You know I wanted to fuck you, but you had to go get yourself beat the fuck up. Now I'm screwed."

Princess moved from her chair dropping to her knees in front of me. "Let me see if I can help."

CHAPTER TEN

Harlow

I woke up to the sound of crying scaring the shit out of me and jumped out of bed to Cooper's bed. "What's wrong buddy? Come here." I reached, grabbing him from the bed. He was sweating, burning up. Yelling out the bedroom door, "Ma!" I screeched as loud as I could.

I laid Cooper out on the bed as his screams were subsiding a bit now that his little body was waking up. "What's wrong, Buddy?"

"Icky," was all he said.

"You feel icky?" I said, rubbing his leg, not sure what I was supposed to do.

"Yeah..."

"Where at?"

"Don't know... icky." I guessed that was the best answer I was going to get.

"Okay, let's see what we can do. Lay here for a minute."

"No, go!" he yelled, as he clutched onto my arm.

"Okay, Baby, come with me." Carrying him into the main room of the clubhouse, two club mommas were laying naked on the pool table. I'm sure they were left-overs from last night, and I didn't want Coop to see, so I nudged Tug. "Can you get them out of here?" I asked, pointing to Cooper.

"Sure thing." He walked over, slapping them on the thighs. "Get the fuck out of here, now."

These women were all the same. They wanted the life and sucked dick to try and get there. But what they didn't understand was that would never get them a brother. They don't want whores for ol' ladies. My stomach churned. I knew now, that Cruz wouldn't do that. But it was always in the back of my mind.

They scurried off as I yelled, "Ma!"

Walking in, she yawned rubbing her eyes. "What's wrong?"

"It's Coop. He's sweating and hot. He woke up scream-ing. Ma, I don't know what to do." I heard the panic in my own voice, and it was very much warranted. Bullet holes I could patch up, but a sick child, not so much.

I handed him off to Ma as he tried to cling to me. "It's okay, Buddy, Ma just wants to see if she can help you feel better. I'm not going anywhere." This feeling inside of me was terrifying. It's as if I'd cut my own heart out of my chest so this little boy would feel no pain, ever. I periodi-cally thought about being a mom, but never put too much stock in it because of my no-brother rule and I'd never dared to go with a brother from another club. I saw that as disrespectful. It's amazing how everything changes.

Now, I couldn't imagine my life without this little guy. He's mine, just like his daddy.

AFTER ASSESSING that Cooper had the flu, we cuddled up on the couch down in the basement of the clubhouse. Ma brought down chicken noodle soup, which he didn't eat much of, and she made me pump liquids into him. We watched movie after movie, which normally I wouldn't mind, but how many times are we gonna watch this movie where the cars talk to each other; I was getting a little burned.

Cruz called, and I updated him on what was going on. He said he'd try to get back sooner, but I knew that wouldn't happen. A run was a run, and he had to finish it out. It was fine, though; I had everything under control; I thought.

On the second night, Cooper's fever broke, bringing back the fun kid I had grown to love. It's kinda crazy to admit, but I actually liked him being sick. He was a great snuggler, and I enjoyed every second of it, minus the back-to-back movies, but I dealt with it. I was glad he was better, and Cruz would be home soon.

He's called me mom and mommy repeatedly, and I never corrected him. I didn't want to. Every time I heard the word fall out of his mouth, my heart grew warmer.

I haven't had a chance to talk to G.T. yet. I wanted to, but the timing hasn't worked. I need to talk to him; something's up and he's damn well gonna tell me. What it is, I have no fucking clue, but I've only been out a short time, surely I haven't pissed him off that much already.

The envelope came today from Deara, and Diamond snatched it up before I could get my hands on it. I'd loved to have known what was inside, because holding this little boy in my arms makes me want to get this shit taken care of fast. He doesn't need this in his life. Innocence like this doesn't need to be tainted with stupid bullshit.

But Diamond was keeping everything from me, and I knew there was no use asking, because he wouldn't budge and tell me.

THE THIRD DAY, Ma wanted to spend some time with Cooper, and I couldn't blame her, but spending time alone with Tug, Rocky, Breaker, and Buzz wasn't doing it for me. They weren't too happy, but I needed to get away for a bit.

Riding to Studio X was utterly relaxing. I loved being back on Sting, feeling his rumble between my thighs and the cool breeze flowing through my hair. Breaker and Buzz were elected to come with me, which didn't bother me. They stayed out of my business and just hung in the background. I liked that. I needed that. It seemed that my every move was monitored by someone, and having any bit of freedom was amazing.

X was just starting to come alive when we stepped inside. Mostly men filled the tables as they drank in earnest. "Pour Some Sugar on Me" started blaring through the loudspeakers as the curtain opened. All eyes were on Blaze, the voluptuous brunette with huge-ass tits and a curvaceous body. Her small triangles of clothes left little to the imagination and watching the men in the room adjust their pants made me grin. She was one hell of a smart girl, who was only dancing to get through school. She was also my number one entertainment. I'd known her for years.

As Blaze worked the pole up and down, her clothes slowly fell away from her body, captivating everyone's attention. Looking at the B.Boys, they were fully entranced by Blaze, their mouths hanging open.

"Hey boys, I'm gonna go find Liv. Enjoy the show." Patting them on the back, I headed towards the office. Opening the door, Liv was behind the desk working on the computer. As she looked up, she glared at me. "What?" I asked, wondering where the hell that came from.

"You have Becs checking up on me?" Her voice was angry as she pushed back the chair, standing there crossing her arms.

"What the hell are you talking about?" Confusion set in as I thought back to everything that had happened and Becs having anything to do with it didn't register.

"Becs... he's been coming in here going over the books."

Initially, anger surged through me, wondering what

the hell was going on. "What the fuck are you talking about? I didn't know anything about this."

"You live with them." She looked at me dismissively. "You knew and didn't even bother to call me and give me a heads up? Becs has been into everything."

"Liv, seriously. I didn't know. First, what exactly do you mean by doing the books?"

"The books... all the money that comes in and goes out, everything that I'm supposed to be doing." She pointed at the desk to emphasize her words.

"Maybe just to help you out?"

"Come on. I've been doing this for two years. You come home and all the sudden I'm not capable? Bullshit." Her words were lacing with ferocity.

Thinking back over the last few weeks, I got it. "It's not you. It's me. They're trying to protect me."

"They're protecting you from me?" she asked, as if it were the most asinine thing in the world.

"Pretty much. Liv, I can't give you all the details. The guys are just handling shit the only way they know how, by taking over and controlling. Don't take offense to it, and Becs isn't a bad guy."

"I didn't say he was bad, he's just into everything, and it's driving me nuts."

"Is he treating you and the girls good?"

She sighed, "Yeah."

"Once all this shit blows over, it'll get better and back to normal. I'll actually be able to be here, and Becs'll be gone."

Blowing out a deep breath, she said, "Fine. Since you're here, we gotta talk about something." She sat down, and I followed sitting in the chair across from her. "Coke and heroin."

My eyes popped to hers. Since I started X, there has been a policy of no hard drugs used by the girls. I understood that some needed a little relaxation before getting on stage, so a little weed would fly, but no coke, heroine, meth, etcetera. "What about it?"

"Some girls are using, and I can handle that. The problem is dealing." She laced her fingers together pressing them to the desk. "Word has it that Stella and Moxie have gotten themselves in a mess, and the only way to get out of it is to deal, which they've been doing here at X."

"What have you done?" Outraged didn't even cut it. Guns I can totally handle, blood, fights, but my guy cheating and drugs in my studio were a huge no for me. When I started it, I didn't want a bunch of druggie girls not being able to keep their shit together. If they wanted to use, they didn't work at Studio X.

"This just came out the last couple of days. I haven't done anything, yet. I need to catch them in the act."

"Bullshit. You cut them. Get them the fuck out of here, now. I'm going to their lockers and flushing the shit, and then they get the hell out and never come back. They don't take the stage."

"But what about them?"

"What about them? They were told they didn't bring drugs to X, end of discussion. This is not how shit works here." Liv had a soft heart that I had been trying to harden before I left. Seems I wasn't able to break that in her... yet. "I'm handling this."

Getting up, I walked back to the dressing room, immediately going to Stella's locker. Picking up my cell, I called Buzz or Breaker, one of them. "I need bolt cutters, bring them to the dressing room, please."

Within a few minutes, I was busting through the lock going through all of Stella's shit, throwing out heels, bras, and thongs as I went. In the very back of the locker, was a metal box. Pulling it out, I tried to open it, finding it was locked. "B.Boys, can you get me a wire hanger and a small screwdriver, please."

Busting through the lock and throwing open the case, I was not shocked to see that approximately twenty-five small bags of white powder with several bills filled the bottom of the box. "Taste this, please." I opened one of the bags putting my pinky inside. Taking the tip, I placed it in one of the B.Boys mouths. "So?"

"Coke," he said with no hesitation.

It's what I assumed. Going through Moxie's things, proved the same thing. I decided while I was at it; I'd check the rest of the girls shit, too. Their contract has a clause in it that they can be searched at any time. I was invoking that right. There were condoms and vibrators, but no drugs.

Looking at the B.Boys, "Buzz go find Stella and Moxie, please. Get them in here, now." The man on the right nodded and took off.

The other man asked hesitantly, "What are you gonna do?"

"Kick their fucking asses out." My voice was void of emotion. I needed to separate business from emotion.

Moxie and Stella came into the room, trying to

wrench their arms away from Buzz, who wasn't letting go. "So, ladies. Something you want to tell me?" Their eyes both snapped to me as their faces paled and looked like they were going to be sick. I couldn't help feel a bit smug at their reaction, but I wouldn't show it.

Neither of them spoke, but they stopped fighting Buzz, who now had let their arms go. "Found some stuff in your locker. Care to tell me about it." I stood at the dressing table and put the two identical boxes in front of me, strumming my fingers on them rhythmically. "See... funny thing is. I found something in here that, while in my studio, is not allowed." Moxie gulped loudly while Stella stood there motionless. "Dealing in the studio is gonna stop. You need to get your shit, and get out."

Stella spooked out of her trance. "We have to sell, if we don't, he'll kill us."

"Who?"

"Rabbit," Son-of-a-fucking-bitch. I was sick of hearing that man's name.

"You've got to be fucking kidding me." Something wasn't right. Shit. "Call Tug, have him bring the cage, please. These two are coming with us," I told the B.Boys.

"We can't go with you. We have to be on stage." Stella placed her hand on her hip as if that position would threaten me in any way.

"If you think you are ever going out on my stage again, you're living in a fucking dreamland. We're going to the club, and we're gonna work this shit out."

RELAYING the information to Diamond and Pops, I actually felt unbelievably lucky to have these men in my corner. We're not a traditional family, but we stood by each other no matter what. And I was glad to have them on my side. They said they'd talk to the girls. Pops wanted me to put the girls on lockdown, which meant locking them in the one room with no windows and the lock on the outside.

Diamond said he'd call a church as soon as the guys got back to figure this shit out. Until then, he wanted Studio X fully swept for any kind of drugs. That was Rocky and the B.Boys' job.

Calling Liv and telling her that more of my guys were gonna be in went a lot smoother than I thought. She said the other girls were suspicious when all their shit was gone through, but it seemed that only Blaze knew what the two were up to. The rest were in the dark. This meant that the girls were selling to the men who watched them, not the dancers, which relieved a small part of me.

Curling up in bed, I wrapped my arms around Cooper, who was sound asleep. I knew I should put him in his crib, but I just couldn't. This time I needed the snuggle.

CHAPTER ELEVEN
Cruz

FUCK. FUCK. FUCK. BULLETS WENT WHIZZING BY MY HEAD one after another. This fucking deal didn't go as planned, at all. It was supposed to be a simple fucking drop and out, but some other fuckers showed up. I didn't recognize a single one, and no one had rags on.

As soon as we grabbed the cash, shots rang out, and we all jumped for cover, including Ransom's crew. He obviously didn't have a fucking clue what was going on either since he was fighting for his damn life, as well. I threw the duffle, with the cash, over my shoulder, keeping it tight against me. We kept firing back. All our guys were getting into position as best they could. We only had two automatics; the rest were 9mm.

Dagger and I were in the middle with G.T and Rhys on the right and Rhys on the right and Zed on the left. With one nod from Dagger, we all open-fired rapidly including Ransom and his crew. Rhys and Zed had the automatics, and they cleaned house pretty quickly.

Several of the fuckers took off running, we were able to nail a few of them, but one got off on foot. After making sure shit was clear, G.T and I took off after him our guns drawn as we ran. The fucker turned his arm sending off a few shots, but his aim was piss poor. Leaping into the air, I tackled him down to the ground with G.T. right on my tail.

G.T. kicked the guy's gun away from his hand as I hit and punched the living shit out of him, his face turning red with blood. "Brother!" G.T. called, but fury was in my blood; I wanted this fucker to be taken out by my hands. "Brother!" he barked. "We need this one alive to tell us who the hell these fuckers are." Coming up with some sort of control, I pulled back, looking at the battered man at my feet. I felt nothing but hatred for him.

Standing up, I moved away from the man on the ground, needing some air. "You got him?" I asked G.T. as the others were starting to approach.

"Yeah..." Walking off, I tried bringing myself down, but the high was too much. Anytime I fought and I mean really fought, for something, like the safety of those I loved, the adrenaline pulsed through me taking me a bit to settle down.

After coming back, the asshole was tied to a tree, hanging by his arms, his blood falling to the ground. It looked like the guys did a hell of a job on him. "Get anything."

"Only thing this guy knows is his boss, Mr. Snider over there." Dagger pointed to the dead man on the ground. "Got a call offering two hundred thousand to take us all out."

"Anything else?"

"Nah. If he knew anything, we'd know. He's just a piss-ant sent to do a job." Dagger nodded as G.T. put a bullet in the guy's head.

"What the fuck was that shit boys?" Ransom's anger was palpable as his crew stood beside him guns in hand.

"Man. I don't know what the fuck that was. Better question is how the hell they knew we were here?" Dagger turned on Ransom.

"If you think for one fucking second we said a goddamned word you're out of your fucking mind."

"Fuck!" Dagger grunted kicking the dead body at his feet. "What the fuck is going on here!"

"Don't know. Get Mr. Snider's phone, and trace all calls. Chances are he used a different one for the calls, but get it back to Buzz and have him work his magic," I said standing in a sea of dead bodies. "We need to set this place ablaze and get rid of shit. Ransom we'll figure this shit out." He nodded as his crew climbed on their rides and rode quickly away.

This cleanup was too much to do individually; it would take way too long, and I wanted to get home to my boy and my girl. The old warehouse was off the beaten path, so we could keep the fire contained enough not to draw any attention until everything was gone. Question remained, who the hell wanted us all dead?

RIDING BACK TO SUMNER, I just wanted to hold my son and my girl. They were the reason I breathed. I loved the club and my brothers. I'd do anything to protect all of them. Dagger had placed a call to Diamond and Pops before we left, so they knew what was going down.

Dagger seemed a little off after the call, but that was just Dagger. After six hours of riding, we pulled into the clubhouse which was dark and peaceful.

Walking into the clubhouse, Pops sat at the bar, nursing a Jack and Coke, while Buzz was continually wiped it down. "It's late old man, whatcha doing up?"

When the other guys all followed me in, Pops announced, "Church at eight a.m. Get some sleep." He dismissed us, or so I thought. "Cruz, stay here."

Nodding to the guys as they went to their rooms, Buzz followed behind them with G.T. on his heals explaining what we needed done with the phone. "What's going on?"

"I know you had a shit run, but you gotta hear this before you go in and see my girl." The hair on the back of my neck stood to attention. Several possibilities began racing through my head and none of them good.

"What's wrong?" I asked as I sidled up to the bar next to him reaching over for a beer.

Every word out of Pops' mouth chimed in my head as he retold the events that had taken place. I was concerned, but pride also seeped in knowing that

Princess went to the brothers and didn't try to handle it herself. "What do they have to say?"

"Stella's not talking, but I'm sure she would with the right persuasion. Moxie is. She says that about a year ago she was feeling pretty down and out. Her guy left her, blah, blah, blah. Anyway, Rabbit's crew just showed up, offering her a pick me up. She was in such a shitty place she took it. She got addicted, ran up a huge debt, and the only way to get out was to sell, which she's been doing for eight months."

"They set her up, knowing Princess would be out soon."

Pops nodded. "Moxie doesn't know any of that. She just wanted to be high, but that's my thought."

"So, Babs has drugs in Studio X, gives an anonymous tip to the cops, they raid the place, find the drugs, and with Princess's prior, nail her to the wall, and if she's got her piece on her, that's more trouble." Pops stared at his drink. "So it's the sure fire set up to put her back in. What's the plan?"

"It's getting deep. You ready for this son?"

"If it means protecting my family, ab-so-fucking-lutely."

Pops slapped my back. "Don't be late for church." He got up, making his way down the hall to his room. After locking the shit up tightly, I needed to see my family.

Unlocking and opening the door, I could see the small bathroom light was on as it cast a soft glow in the room. Princess's back was turned towards me. Walking over to Coop's bed, my heart sunk when Cooper wasn't inside. Searching quickly, my eyes landed on the bed next to Princess. Coop lay curled up in a ball with Princess's arm wrapped around him tightly. Both were sound asleep.

Moving closer, I reached down to scoop Cooper up and put him in his crib. Before I could get him fully up, a gun was placed at my head while a groggy Princess got her bearings. "Get away from my boy!" she barked, her eyes hazy from sleep.

"Baby, it's me," I said softly as recognition instantly hit her. She lowered the gun and placed it back under the pillow.

"Sorry. I've been a little jumpy," she said, rubbing her eyes looking down at Coop. "I just wanted to hold him."

"Baby, you don't need to be sorry for that." Scooping Cooper up, I placed him in his bed quietly shutting the door behind me. "I missed you, Baby," I said, kneeling besides the bed.

"I missed you, too."

"How's Cooper?"

She smiled. "He's perfect." She paused. "I think he's back to his normal self, only a little sluggish, but he's okay."

"You did great with him."

Her eyes locked with mine. "Cruz, I didn't know the first thing to do. Ma had to teach me, quickly."

"And I bet you sucked it up and did what had to be done." I had the utmost confidence in my girl. I watched her stitch up bullet wounds. I knew the flu wouldn't get her down.

"Yeah. He's a great little boy, Cruz."

"You know he loves you."

She smiled the widest smile. "Yeah. I know. I love him, too."

"Wanna tell me about tonight?"

She sighed, but went into every last detail of the events that happened. "I think Babs is trying to set me up again." God, my girl, was fucking smart.

"You do?"

Princess rolled on her side, placing her elbow on the bed, her head resting in her hand. "You can't tell me it's a coincidence that Babs's man is my girl's dealer. And then on top of doing drugs, getting them to run drugs through *my* studio. I think Babs knew I was getting out and wanted to set me up again."

I stared at the smart, beautiful woman before me. There were no words that could describe the way I felt about her. Love didn't seem to be enough. Soul mate seemed to pussy-ish to say. But something. Some deeper connection was happening with us. My heart constricted.

"You think that's what's going on?" she asked me, point blank. I couldn't divulge any club business, even if she was spot on in her assessment.

"Could be." She eyed me, and I knew she wanted to ask if I knew something, but she refrained. I loved that she knew better than to question it. "I'm gonna take a quick shower." Getting up, I stripped my leathers. Feeling the hot water wash away the dirt and blood helped me relax a little. There was no way I could tell Princess what happened at the drop off. All that shit had to stay locked inside. I'd talk about it tomorrow morning at church.

Crawling into bed, my naked body was still wet, and all I wanted was to feel Princess's skin. But what I felt were clothes, and I remembered she was lying with Coop. "Take it off, Baby," I nuzzled in her ear. She didn't hesitate. "I need you," I said, pressing my lips to hers, feeling the shudder run through her body.

She instantly fell into the kiss, giving back as much as she was taking. Rolling on top of her, my body pressed her tightly into the mattress as she spread her legs wide for me, welcoming me into her body. Kissing down her neck, I sucked on each of her beautiful tits rolling her nipples between my teeth, loving the moans escaping her lips. I needed the taste of her pussy on my lips, but I also needed her lips around my cock.

Falling to the bed, I said, "Baby climb up here and sit on my face." Princess scrambled up, facing the headboard. "Turn around." She did exactly as instructed without hesitation. As she lowered on my mouth, I began my assault maneuvering my tongue in and out of her hot pussy. God, I loved this taste. Using my arm, I pressed the small of her back lowering her down to my cock.

It didn't take her, but a second, to know exactly what I needed. As her tongue brushed up and down my dick, I was in my own slice of heaven. That place that I'll never really get to, but while here, would enjoy every second of it. Her warm mouth wrapped around my dick as she began fucking me hard going up and down like the little vixen she was. She didn't use her hands; they were propped at her sides holding her up, which made the feeling even more intense.

As my dick touched the back of her throat, she swallowed and hummed repeatedly. I was ready to lose it. I began sucking her clit hard and pumping my fingers in and out of her warm body, hitting that magic spot inside the top of her wall.

Princess's pussy clamped on to my fingers tight as her screams were muffled by my dick crammed in her mouth. As she kept sucking, I felt my balls tighten, and the bottom of my spine begin to pulsate. Stream after stream came pouring out of me as my orgasm ripped through my body. Princess swallowed every last drop, licking my dick clean before falling to the side of me on the bed. But I wasn't done with her yet.

Sitting up, I grabbed her legs and spun her around on the bed. Her laugh was beautiful. "What are you doing?" she asked, still trying to catch her breath.

"Any damn thing I want." My lips collided with hers, tasting myself, my dick instantly became hard again as she began rocking her hips back and forth on my dick. Rolling on top of her, I grabbed her arms, pinning them above her head. Her immediate surrender made me smile. My girl was perfect.

Sliding my dick inside of her, I loved how tight and wet she was for me every damn time. Using one arm to keep hers pressed down, the other came to her knee lifting it high to her chest. I wanted her as deep as I could get her. If I could climb inside of her, I sure as hell would. Thrust after thrust, I felt her pulsating beneath me as her body arched off of the bed. Harder and harder I pounded, claiming this woman again and again as mine. As she screamed my name, I came with a roar, sweat pouring off my body. Falling on top of Princess, I crushed her into the bed with my weight, but she didn't complain.

As I released her arms, she wrapped them tightly

around my body, brushing her hand up and down my back. "I love you," she said quietly.

"Me too." My words were muffled by the blankets, and exhaustion seeped through my body. With the last bit of energy, I rolled off of her, pulling her back to my front, falling fast asleep.

"SHE KNOWS," were the words that I uttered during our discussion of Princess and the plot to get her back in jail during church.

"What do you mean she knows?" Diamond accused.

"I didn't fucking tell her. She's smart. She put two and two together last night. Said she thinks the drugs were put there to get her sent back to jail." In no way did I want the brothers thinking I said a word to Princess. I love her, but I gave my word to keep club business separate.

"Damn," uttered Pops. "I should have known she'd catch on quick." He rubbed his hand over his head. "What'd you tell her?"

"All I said was 'could be.' I didn't say shit." I began strumming my fingers on the table.

"We're not confirming it to her. She obviously knows what's going on, so we don't need to." I nodded my head to Diamond.

"Next order of business is Danny." We all knew what he had done, so there was no reason to relive it. "All in favor of removing his patch ..."

The entire table voted yes. "Pass. We'll have the issue

with his back ink. It'll need to be removed. He'll have one week to do it on his own." Diamond's gavel slammed down. I knew in the back of my mind; Dagger would be more than likely the one removing it in about eight days, either by fire or knives.

Diamond nodded to Pops as he spoke. "Mindy's not getting anywhere with Babs. I say we cut her loose and keep tracking her phone."

The vote went down as a yes. There was no reason to keep this bitch around Princess any more than possible. And if she wasn't giving us information, she was of no use to us.

"The intel from Deara this time wasn't anything. But the note inside said they'd work on it. So we wait on that."

Our heads nodded.

"The drop." Diamond cut looking at Dagger since he was the one who set it up.

"Yeah, Boss. I don't know what the fuck happened. Talked to Ransom, he didn't know shit but wants in on the retaliation. Three of his guys were killed."

"Any idea who the fuck started this shit? Like we don't have e-fucking-nuf going on as is." Diamond said running his hands through this hair.

"No." G.T. chimed in. "Buzz did a track on the phone and got nothing. It was a pre-pay, and we got nothing from the guy there."

"Shit," Diamond clipped. "We need on this now. 200k to take you guys out... some shits going down."

"We're on it." Rhys said at his side. "We'll find out what the fucks going on."

Diamond nodded then cut through, "Next... Studio X. Princess brought in Stella and Moxie last night. They're hooked on blow and selling it at X." All eyes shot to Diamond. "Stella's not talking. Moxie is." Diamond replayed Moxie's words. The entire room muttered, "Shit."

"I've got 'em locked up for now. We're thinking this is Babs's way of getting Princess back in and for longer."

Speaking up for the first time, I said, "I think we should let Princess persuade her."

Diamond nodded. "Agree. Those in favor." Everyone said yes. "Cruz you're with her when she goes in, and don't let it get too far."

"Anyone else here realize that most of church has revolved around Princess?" Zed cut in.

"So?" I asked.

"Maybe you need to keep a tighter leash on her," he accused me as I clutched my hands turning my knuckles white. But I didn't need to say anything as Pops did it for me.

"You know damn well that this isn't Princess's fault. She hasn't done shit to warrant it, except get out of prison."

The tension became thick in the room, and Diamond could feel it, too. "Enough. She did nothing wrong." He slammed the gavel dismissing us.

"I NEED you to come with me," I said to Princess, as she was playing with Cooper at the table when we came out of church. She looked up and smiled.

"Ma. Can you watch Coop, please?" she asked as she stood up. "I'll be right back, Buddy." Her lips touched the top of Coop's head as her hand rubbed the top of his hair.

Leading her down the hall, I said, "I need you to go in and make Stella talk."

Her eyes grew wide with the recognition of what I just asked of her, as she nodded her head. "She's not talking to Diamond and Pops?"

"No. We need your help."

"Not a problem." Walking her to the door, I unlocked and opened it to find Stella pacing the room and Moxie lying on the bed.

I knocked Moxie's thigh to get her attention. "Up. Let's go." Moxie rolled groggily, but did as she was told. "Tug, come watch her."

"Got it," he said as he took Moxie from the room, as I shut the door. Grabbing a chair, I placed it in front of the door and sat in it, blocking the exit.

"What is this?" Stella asked.

Princess smiled and looked towards me. I nodded the 'go ahead.' I loved that she asked for permission. It literally made my dick hard.

"Sit," Princess barked and pointed at the bed.

"I think I'll stand," Princess smiled. She was in her element. With a roundhouse kick, she knocked Stella down; she hit the floor, hard. Stella sat there stunned for a moment.

"Guess now you'll be sitting on the floor." Princess laughed.

"What the fuck is this?" Stella barked, not showing any fear what so ever. Princess must have heard it, too, because the first few punches had Stella grabbing her face and chest as she groaned.

"First, you don't get to ask questions. I do. Second, you knew not to bring blow into my studio especially to sell it. It pisses me off." Princess picked Stella up off the floor, placing her in a chair exactly like the one I was sitting in. She then began walking around it like a tiger stalking her prey. It was fucking hot.

Stella's breathing began to pick up as the sweat on her brow began to form. Princess's hand slapped hard across Stella's cheek, causing her head to snap to the side.

"Now tell me why you started using." Stella looked at me as I crossed my arms over my chest letting her know I wouldn't be doing shit to stop Princess. This was her show.

Blowing out a deep breath, the blood from her lip was trickling down her face. "My man left said he couldn't handle his girl stripping in front of other men. He was pissed about the private dances, so he left."

"That's all that started it?"

"That and money being tight."

"How did you come across Rabbit and his crew?" I couldn't help but feel pride in my girl. She was damn good at this.

When Stella didn't answer, Princess punched her in the jaw hard enough to hear bone crack. Stella yelled out in pain as Princess began walking around her again.

Stella didn't move from the chair, but grabbed her jaw holding it. "Answer!" Princess yelled.

"It wasn't him at first. It was someone named Turbo from his crew. He came on to me at the studio. I went to a hotel with him that night. He offered the blow; I did it, and then couldn't stop." Stella hung her head.

Princess grabbed her hair, pulling Stella's eyes up to hers. "Then what?"

"Same as Moxie. Started running up a tab. I was fucking the crew to pay; then Rabbit said I had to bring in cash, or he'd kill me."

"Keep going." Princess pulled on her hair, then released it, standing in front of her with her arms crossed, pushing up those beautiful tits of hers.

"I didn't sell to the girls, only a few of the regular guys. One of Rabbit's crew came to collect the cash and give me more blow. I would do some and sell the rest."

"You ever meet anyone else in the crew."

"Yeah, I fucked six of the guys and saw some of the women hanging around."

"You ever fuck Rabbit?" The bitch stared at Princess.

"Fuck no. That bitch he has would have gutted me." Smiling, I was so damn proud of my girl.

"Tell me about this bitch." When she didn't talk, Princess held up her hand to strike.

"Stop, I'll tell ya." Princess backed off and listened. "Her name was Babs. She seemed to be running the show over there, more than the men. I didn't think that's how MCs worked." Fuck no, that's not how they worked. What the hell?

"She never hit me, but ordered the guys to do it. She

threatened to have Rabbit and his crew rape and kill me. She told me that if I didn't start bringing more clients to the studio and selling more, I'd be done."

"So you did what she said?"

"The bitch was going to have the guys kill me, and I knew she wasn't shitting. Her eyes were dead and cold. There was no emotion in them what-so-ever."

"Babs say anything else?"

Stella began sobbing, no doubt from the pain Princess's fists were leaving. "She asked about you. Wanted to know exact dates when you were getting out. I didn't want to tell her, but she had one of the guys put a gun to my head. I didn't have a choice."

"What all did you tell her?" Princess asked as she stepped closer to her.

"I only told her the date you were getting out. That was all I knew."

"When are you supposed to meet for the next exchange?" Princess asked, seeming unfazed.

"Tomorrow. 7 p.m. at the studio."

"Who are you meeting, and how much cash is expected?"

"I never know who's gonna be there. Could be a crew member or Rabbit. Fifteen hundred."

"You're selling fifteen hundred dollars of blow in my studio a week?" Princess's anger rose. She grabbed Stella, pulling her to stand up. Then she attacked. Blow after blow, she pounded this woman into the ground. When Stella fell to her knees, Princess was seething.

"That's enough," I barked out. Princess looked at me and nodded, walking over to stand beside me.

"Wh... at's gonna happen to me?" Stella asked.

"We'll let you know." Wrapping my arm around Princess, I led her out the door. "Tug, put the other one in, give her a first aid kit and lock 'em up." Tug nodded as he got to work.

I walked Princess to my room, locking the door behind us. "I need to use the bathroom." Her voice was very distant.

"You okay?"

She gave me a small grin. "Yeah. I'm gonna take a shower." She turned, shutting the door behind her.

Leaving the room, I went and told Diamond and Pops everything that Stella said. They were in agreement that we should set these men up tomorrow night, and we decided we'd talk about it at the next church.

Coming back to the room, I found Princess curled up under the blankets, her back facing the door. Her body was shuddering making me think she was crying. Stripping my clothes off, I crawled into bed beside her. She instantly wrapped her naked body around mine, clinging to me for dear life.

As I rubbed her back, she began to relax into me. "Talk to me," I said softly.

"I don't get it. How the hell can she be so pissed off at me that she wants to destroy me? Something's missing. I need that puzzle piece, and I have no clue how the hell to get it."

"I'm not sure, Baby, but we'll figure it out."

"I need you," she whispered into my chest, her warm breath grazing me.

"I'm right here, Baby." Princess opened her legs as I

slid my dick deep inside of her. This wasn't some quick fuck. This was slow and sensual as I rocked my hips in and out of her. Wiping the tears from her face, I leaned down, kissing her lips. As we came together, she wrapped her arms around me tight, pressing my body into hers.

After rolling off to the side, I stared down at Princess as I propped up on my elbow. "You know, I love you." My other hand brushed the hairs that lined her beautiful face.

"I know. I love you, too." Her smile was the most beautiful thing on this planet. I loved being the one to put it on her face.

"I need to ask you something." She nodded. "You my ol' lady?"

Her smiled widened, "Yeah, Baby. I am." I kissed her hard.

"Good, I have something for you."

CHAPTER TWELVE
Harlow

WATCHING CRUZ'S FINE ASS WALK ACROSS THE ROOM, MY body hummed. I loved this man. I loved his loyalty. I loved his honor with the club. I loved how he was such a wonderful dad. I loved how he loved me.

Cruz opened the top drawer of his dresser, pulling out a black leather rag. My heart began pounding in my chest, and it felt hard to breathe. This was it. The one thing I said I'd never do, and now it's the one thing that I want more than anything.

As he walked back to the bed, I sat up, letting the sheet fall down exposing myself to him. "I had this made for you. Been waiting for you to say it, and since you did, I want you to wear it."

I tried to hold back the tears, but my vision was becoming blurry. In my world, this was the same as a wedding proposal. This was everything. Cruz held up the vest turning it around to the back. I couldn't stop the tear that rolled down my cheek as I quickly batted it away.

The back had the top rocker with Ravage written on it, and below that was a large patch that said 'Property of Cruz.' I knew that once I put this rag on; I would need to keep myself in order, not letting any of my actions reflect badly on Cruz. I'd been doing my best this last week, but now best wasn't good enough. I'd need to do better.

Looking up into Cruz's eyes, I felt the love pouring out of them. "I'd love to," I said quietly.

"Turn around, Baby." As I did, I felt the cool leather touch the skin on my back sending tingles throughout my body. Moving my arm out, he placed the rag up one arm and then the other, wrapping it around my body like a glove. "Stand up. Let me see."

Moving off the bed, I stood in front of him naked, except for the rag, as I slowly turned around giving him a wonderful view of every part of me. "Damn, Baby," he growled, turning my insides to liquid.

Cruz didn't give me time to think as he grabbed my ass, hoisting me up in the air, my legs instinctively wrapping around him. Cruz slipped one arm and then the other underneath my knees opening me up to him. As his dick slid inside, he began pumping into me like a piston of an engine as it revved up. Before I could get my bearings, I came hard, but Cruz wasn't done. His hips continued pushing as I set off again.

I felt my grasp on his neck beginning to break, so I clutched him much tighter. Over and over, he kept sending me into oblivion. When he released inside of me,

I held onto him for dear life, never wanting to let this man go.

My entire body was like Jell-O as he laid me down on the bed. I didn't think I'd be able to move again. Cruz looked down at me lying on my back with his vest on my body. I could feel the pride coming off of him, and I knew I'd never want to disappoint him. I couldn't. Yawning, my eyes began to droop. "Baby, take a nap, and then me and you are going for a ride."

I nodded as I curled into a ball, falling into a fast, sated sleep.

WALKING into the main part of the clubhouse, I felt like all eyes were on me, well... because they were. Cruz had his arm wrapped around my shoulders leading me through. When the whistles and hollers began, I felt the blush creep into my cheeks, not from embarrassment, but from happiness. No one at that moment could wipe the smile plastered across my face off.

"Let's see!" Zed's ol' lady, Legs, came up to me grinning. As I turned slowly, the noises behind me got louder. "It's beautiful, girl. I'm so happy for you."

Turning back around, I wrapped Legs in my arms, hugging her tightly. "Thank you." Legs got her name because she's barely five foot tall, a short little thing. That's how names work around here. Names come about depending on the person. You're short we name you,

Legs. You laugh a lot and are the life of the party; they name you Bubbles.

She pulled away. "We're going to Bimbo's tonight. You guys wanna come?" I stood there shocked. I'd never been invited out with them before. Being the club's kid, I didn't do those things. Parties, yes, but actually going out with the brothers and sisters? That was new... and thrilling.

"I need to talk to Cruz first." She smiled knowingly. Bubbles, Becs' ol' lady, and Flash, Dagger's ol' lady, came up and hugged me, as well. All of these women I've known most of my life, but this was different. It was a different kind of hug. This was a sister's hug.

"Of course. We're going around eight." Nodding, I walked over to Cruz. He smiled down at me, wrapping his arm around me as he pulled me tight into his chest, and he kissed me on the top of my head.

"They invited us to Bimbo's tonight if you want to go," I said into his chest smelling the leather and smoke.

"Sure, Babe. Come on, we got some place to be."

Excitement flooded through me. This would be the first time I rode as Cruz's ol' lady.

As the wind whipped all around us, I enjoyed having my arms wrapped around Cruz. Between the smell of him and the rumble between my thighs, I was getting way too turned on.

Being on the back of someone's bike was something I was still getting used to. After an hour and a half of riding, we stopped to eat and climbed right back on. We were lucky that Ma said she'd watch Cooper all night, so we were really free for a while. But my mind kept reverting to the shit going down in my life, and every time

I closed my eyes, I couldn't shake the feeling that something bad was going to happen.

As we pulled into a park, Cruz killed the bike. Climbing off, we moved over to the picnic benches as I laid my head on his shoulder. "Everything okay, Babe?"

"Sorry. My mind just keeps running. I try to turn it off, but it doesn't help."

He wrapped his arm around me as squeezed me tightly to him. "We'll get it all figured out."

"What about Mel?" Cruz's body stiffened at the name, but I didn't say a word. "She hasn't signed yet. She can't have my boy."

"I was giving her the benefit of the doubt. I don't know why, but I was. Now ..." He trailed off squeezing me as he kissed the top of my head. "I'll take care of it."

"What about Babs?"

"That's club business, Babe." I nodded, knowing there was no more he could say. I respected that even though I wanted to know.

"I'd like to go back to Studio X full time again. You okay with that?" Asking him wasn't as hard as I thought it would be. It just came natural.

"Yeah, Baby. You have to have a Prospect with you all the time, though." I smiled.

"Becs is there a lot." He stiffened. "It's okay, Baby. I know you're just looking out for me. I smoothed it over with Liv. But having him there will help. I'd just need someone to ride with me to and from."

"Have one of the Prospects." Nodding, I relaxed into him. I hoped that going back to the studio would allow me to get my mind off of things. Maybe if I did that, I'd be able to see a clearer connection with all of this. "What about Cooper?" he asked.

"I'll see if Ma can watch him at the shop, and more than likely I won't be going in till noon, so I'll be with him until then."

"I'll be around a bit, too. We've got some runs coming up that will take me away for three or four days at a time, but I'll do my best."

"It's hard being a 24/7 dad, huh?" I said, nudging.

"I didn't know what to expect. I just always thought he'd be better with Mel. She's supposed to love him and take care of him. But over the last year, it's been going downhill." He held his head down.

"When did you find out she was hitting him?" I wasn't sure I wanted the answer to that question, but it just fell out of my mouth. Part of me needed to know.

"A few weeks before you got out, I noticed something was up, but didn't put my finger on it until about a week before you got out. Then when I saw her grab Coop in the clubhouse, I knew she couldn't be around him anymore."

"And having me around helped?"

"Of course. It just showed me the mom that Coop needed." He squeezed tightly.

My heart warmed, not only that Cruz thought I could be the mom that Coop needed but at the prospect of being that person in Coop's life. I'd never really thought of being a mom. I wasn't the type to plan out my future or have these expectations. As far as I was concerned, a quick lay, my studio, and the club was all I needed. It's a bit mind-boggling how much my life has changed.

I go from prison and alone to an ol' man and a kid in a short period of time, and I wouldn't change a damn thing.

"You sure you wanna go tonight?"

"Absolutely. It'll be good for you to get to know the ol' ladies."

"You know I've known Legs, Bubbles, and Flash for a long time, but this just feels different."

"It's cause you're an ol' lady, now. It'll be fine."

I smiled up at him as he leaned down, kissing me on the lips. I pulled his head tightly against mine, kissing him with everything I had. Before I knew what I was doing, I was straddling him on the picnic table, rocking my body up and down on his hard cock. "The ride get you all worked up, Baby?" he asked against my lips.

"What'd you think?" My hips had a mind of their own as they thrust and thrust. I was so close to coming.

"Take your pants off," he barked roughly.

Looking around, I had a moment of panic. Here we were out in public for anyone to drive by and see us. My body froze.

"I'm not telling you again. Take them off." I stared at him feeling my inner thoughts suffocating me. I wanted to make him happy, and I wanted to fuck him. Fuck it.

Hopping off of him, I stripped out of my leathers and boots. Standing before him, the hunger in his eyes took my breath away. He slowly stood enough to unzip his pants and pull his hard cock out. Licking my lips, I wanted him. The sun was bouncing off our skin making the flush I already felt ten times hotter.

"Get up here and ride me baby," he said pulling my

body to him. Not thinking twice, I climbed on, sinking him inside of me in one deep push. Up and down, I rode him as hard as I could in the position we were in. The table bumped my leg repeatedly, but I didn't utter a single complaint.

Reaching down, I cupped Cruz's face pulling him to me as I kissed him hard. He broke off the kiss, and I really started my movements using my legs to squat up and down quickly.

Throwing my head back, I felt the waves wanting to wash over me. I couldn't hold back. I needed to come. "You there, Baby?" I asked him.

"Since when do you ask me that?"

"I just wanna come with you Baby," I said, grabbing onto his shoulders for more stability.

"Faster," he growled. Doing as he says, I felt his dick growing more inside of me. I knew it was coming, and I was there ready for him. "Now." We came together, rasping each other's names.

With Cruz still fully seated inside me, we tried to catch our breath. With the sun beating down on my naked ass, it pulled me back to the reality of where we were. My head darted up scanning the park. "Relax, Babe." Pulling out, he smirked. "Get dressed."

Rushing, I threw my leathers and boots back on, and fixed my braid. Relaxed now, I was ready to ride.

PULLING up to Bimbo's bar, I couldn't help a slight nervous flutter in my stomach. This would be my first test as an ol' lady. Could I keep my temper in check? Could I fit in with these women who have been doing this for years? Could I be a good ol' lady?

I wanted to. I really wanted to and make Cruz happy.

Walking into the bar, all eyes were on us. I felt them, but kept ahold of Cruz's hand, following behind him closely. I knew I could defend myself, but this was different. I knew all eyes were on me because I was his ol' lady.

Cruz led us right over to Zed, Legs, Becs, Bubbles, Dagger, and Flash, who were all sitting around a large table drinking and laughing. As soon as we approached, every single person stood, each one hugging and kissing our cheeks one at a time. The hugs from the women were tight and ultimately warm. The hugs and kisses from the guys were also warm, but each of them whispered in my ear.

Zed, "So glad you're here." Becs, "About time you became a patched sister." Dagger, "You must be what Cruz has been waiting for." It made me want to cry my eyes out, but I refrained.

After sitting, the waitress came by taking drink orders. I knew I'd only have one or two because there was no way I'd risk being drunk on the back of Cruz's bike. It's hard enough driving with another person on the back of your ride, add a drunk woman who's isn't thinking straight... not a good combination. Not only that, it would embarrass the shit out of him and me.

Having Cruz next to me, his arm wrapped around the

back of my chair with his brothers and sisters was exhilarating. I guessed this was what happiness felt like.

"Brothers, let's walk," Zed said, lifting his chin, leaving me with the three other ol' ladies. Looking around at the table seeing the women I've known my whole life, I couldn't help but see them in a different light. They were my *Ma's friends*. Now they are mine, my sisters. Considering I have no sisters and Casey was never around anymore and doesn't answer my phone calls, I was excited and nervous all wrapped into one.

Legs smiled, patting my hand, "Hey, girl. You doing okay?"

"Yeah, why?"

"You seem off. Not yourself."

Blowing out a deep breath, "It's just I've known you all my whole life, and this is... different."

"It's nothing for you to be scared or nervous about. You'll just get to see us. Not the moms who run after their kids, but the real us. I think you'll like what ya see." Legs laughed, the others following suit.

"I know I'll like you, I just don't know if you'll like me."

"Oh nonsense, girl." Bubbles spoke. "We love that you're feisty and speak your mind. You do that with us, just not with the brothers." She winked. Now that I'm an ol' lady, I knew that my mouth was a direct reflection of Cruz, and I'd need to keep myself together.

"We're all a bit crazy in our own ways. You'll learn soon enough, Princess," Flash said, pushing her long blonde hair to her back. Her green eyes were covered in a smoky eye shadow, making them pop in a very sultry way.

"Shots!" Bubbles yelled.

"Thanks, girls. But I'm taking it easy." I'd gotten drunk many times in front of these women, but always at the clubhouse where I could crash in Pops' room, never in public.

"Hell no! You drink. This is a celebration." The waitress placed a shot down for each of us. "To our new, patched sister!" They raised their glasses as I followed their lead. Downing the liquid, I could feel the burn all the way down, and after about the fifth shot, I was feeling pretty damn good and loosening up.

My stomach actually hurt from laughing so much with these women, and they were right. This was an entirely different side of them, and one that I really really liked. All my nerves and worries melted away as the night went on. These women treated me like, well, one of them. They didn't handle me with kid gloves or hold back; that's what made me fall in love with them for a second time in an entirely different way.

We watched the men shooting pool and doing whatever it was they were doing. Every once in a while, I'd get a chin lift from Cruz, just letting me know he saw me. The night was going better than I could have hoped.

These women were fun. They were more fun than I'd had in a long time, and that included my time before prison. It was actually remarkable that not one of them asked me about it. Part of me thought it would be the topic of conversation with them, the idiot who got set up by some bitch. No one made fun of me in any way, though, and that, totally put me at ease. I'm sure they'll ask at some point, but not tonight, and I could kiss each one of them for it.

"Heads up, ladies," Legs said, looking at the men across the room. My eyes shot in that direction while three young women, wearing barely any clothes, approached our men. Two of them were smart; they actually walked away when Becs and Dagger turned them down. The third wasn't as smart. I watched before my very eyes as Cruz nodded his head the direction she came, my guess, asking her to go. But the dumb bitch didn't get the hint. Her hands began roaming his arm as he stepped out of her grasp.

Fury boiled inside of me. I wanted to cut this bitch up.

"Let's go," Flash said quickly. But I was a bit apprehensive. I knew that if I went up there, I'd be beating the shit out of this bitch, and I didn't want to embarrass my brothers or sisters.

Flash saw my apprehension. "You let that bitch keep pawing your man, it will happen every fucking time you come here. It's your job to end it." With her encouraging words, I knew what needed to be done. Sliding out of my chair, we walked towards them. My fists clenched so hard my nails dug into my palm. I was gonna try to be civil first.

"Excuse me," I said, tapping the woman on the shoulder. She turned around scowling at me.

"What?" she barked as I brought my hands in front of me, holding them together... or more like holding them, so I didn't punch the living shit out of her.

"You need to back off." She eyed me up and down

looking at the leather on my body, but not deterred. She even glanced at the women standing behind me, and it didn't faze her. Stupid bitch.

"Fuck off," she said as she turned back around, her hand going directly to Cruz's arm. Looking up in his eyes, I tried to make him see the fiery rage that was burning inside of me. With a lift of his chin, I grabbed the bitch by the back of her hair, pulling her far away from Cruz. My sisters formed a circle around me, but stood back letting me have the control.

"Fuck off, huh, bitch?" I threw her down on the floor as she fell with a crash in those stupid heels. "Stand up!" I yelled. She got to her feet with a wobble.

"What the fuck is your problem?" she barked.

"You wanna know what my problem is? You're touching my ol' man. He told you to get the fuck off... and your dumbass didn't listen. Then I asked you the same thing, and you didn't listen. So now this ..." I swung, my fist connecting with her pretty little face, sending blood flying.

"You bitch." God, this woman, clearly fell off the stupid wagon.

Picking up my leg, I kicked her directly in the stomach, then took my right hand and pummeled her face twice, being sure the cut was nice and big. "Bitch, huh? No, I'm his ol' lady, and this shit don't fly with me." After two more punches, I felt a strong hand on my shoulder. I could feel Cruz's body become flush against mine. I stood there watching the idiot crawl over to her friends, chicken shits that never helped her once. At least I knew my sisters had my back.

"Let me see your hands," Cruz said as I turned to face him, not knowing if he'd be pissed I caused a huge scene. His smile made my knees week. The pride in his eyes was so bright for me. I held up my hands as he touched them gently. Without them being taped up, they took a good hit. I had several scrapes and blood, and of course, the bruising, but nothing that wouldn't heal.

Cruz let my hands go after inspecting them as his lips came down hard on mine. My arms instantly wrapped around his neck, pulling him tightly to me. As he pulled away, he whispered, "Thanks, Babe." Then he smiled in his sexy way. "Let's get you a drink, Slugger."

Rolling my eyes, I followed him back to the table as he ordered me a shot of Jack.

"Damn, girl," Legs said, sitting down. "Your Ma always said you could fight, but I've never seen you in action. Damn, you kicked ass."

Smiling, I felt the burn of the liquor slide down my throat.

THE NIGHT TURNED out to be a huge hit. And even though I was a bit tipsy, Cruz proved he could handle my ass just fine on the back of his bike. Another one of my worries smashed to smithereens.

Pulling up to the clubhouse, people were floating all around, which surprised me considering we were out with four of the brothers. Guess the others decided to have a party. Women were in abundance throughout the club, most of whom were eyeing Cruz like he was their next target. I felt the daggers darting out of my eyes at each one, making them turn away from my man.

Cruz never once let go of my hand, except when he hugged the brothers from the Davis chapter as he walked by them. I felt completely out of place here, for some reason.

As Cruz moved us to his room, he locked the door behind him. "You stay in here with the door locked. I'm gonna go get Cooper and bring him in." I nodded my head as he left the room.

Stripping out of my clothes and putting my tight yoga pants and an 'I Support the Ravage MC' t-shirt on, I grabbed a bottle of water out of Cruz's small fridge. Downing the bottle quickly, I went in search of some medicine to kick the headache forming in my head.

When the door opened, Cooper came flying in the room right into my arms. "I thought you'd be asleep, Buddy."

"Ma watched movies."

"Ahh... and she let you stay up, huh?" Coop nodded his head.

"I gotta go, Babe. Stay in here with the door locked. Be back in a bit." With a peck on the lips and a ruffle of Coop's hair, he left us.

"Wanna snuggle up with me, Buddy?" My eyes were beginning to droop. It'd been a long day, and if I couldn't cuddle up with Cruz, I had the other man in my life.

"Mommy. I hungry," Coop said, rubbing his tummy.

"We'll sleep, and then we'll have breakfast in the morning."

"No... Mommy... my tummy's making noise." I smiled at the way he explained his feelings.

"Grumbling, Buddy. Your tummy is grumbling." Walking over to the small shelf where we kept a few snack foods, I began naming things off to him, but he wanted none of them. "Then what do you want?"

"Peanut bubber and dwelly." He smiled excitedly.

"I don't have any, Buddy. Let's pick something else."

Cooper began crying, hard. Panic flooded me as I tried to figure out what to do. We haven't really had moments yet where I told him no, or he couldn't have something. We've been just learning together as we go. I'm guessing this was the first taste.

"Come here, Buddy."

"No... me want peanut bubber!" he yelled in my face.

"All right... all right. I'll go to the kitchen and get you one. Sit here and watch that rabbit show you like. I'll be right back."

Exiting the room and locking it, I instantly felt that I was doing something wrong, and I should turn around, but looking back at the door, I knew there was a little boy on the other side of it that I needed to take care of.

Pulling myself together, I threw my shoulders back walking past the main room and into the kitchen. I quickly made Cooper's sandwich, grabbing some chips and a soda for myself. Picking everything up from the counter, I screamed when a hand came and rested around my waist.

"Stop," I said after the shock wore off.

"Why would I do that?" a deep voice I didn't recognize said.

"Because I'm Cruz's ol' lady," I said with force as I turned to face a man I'd never met before. He must have been a new patch member since going in the joint.

"Ol' ladies aren't here tonight, and you don't have his patch," he said, moving his hand up my body to my tits groping them. I moved out of his grasp flying to the other side of the room.

"I am his ol' lady. I'm on lockdown here. I had to get my boy something to eat," I said, quickly seeing the patches on the man's rag. He was a full-out member. Shit.

"Bitch. You need to stop spreading lies about my brother." His voice became angry as he stepped close to me. "You know what we do with dirty whores who lie around here."

"I'm not lying. Go get him. He'll tell you," I pleaded, not knowing what was going to happen, and knowing that since he was a fully patched member, I'd needed to keep myself together.

"Bitch. Don't fucking tell me what to do. Who the hell do you think you are?" The back of his hand came across my cheek hard, but I didn't move. I stood there looking him straight in the eye.

"I'm Cruz's ol' lady," I said, deadpanned.

"Yeah, we'll see. I'll call him in here, and when he tells me you're full of fucking shit, we're gonna take turns fucking every single hole of your body."

It took every bit of my strength not to rip his balls off and feed them to him. I wanted to punch, kick, and kill this fucker in front of me. But at the sound of hearing he was going to get Cruz, I was relieved.

"Don't fucking move," he barked at me, and I didn't move a muscle.

"Princess!" Cruz's voice boomed in the room. I turned to the voice, feeling relieved. "What the fuck are you doing out here? And without your fucking rag?" he growled at me angrily.

I stood there, stunned, my stomach sinking to the floor. I didn't even think of putting the rag on. I just thought of getting my boy some food.

"I'm sorry," I whispered.

"Sorry? I told you to stay in my fucking room!" he bellowed as the other man came in, crossing his arms over his chest.

"This one yours?" he asked Cruz.

"Yeah. My ol' lady."

"Shit brother. That's Princess? I didn't know. She didn't have your patch on."

"No, she doesn't. Can you leave us, bro?" Suddenly I felt like I wanted the psycho in the same room with us, so Cruz didn't kill me where I stood.

I'd never once felt scared with Cruz, but I was feeling it now. I thought I should explain. "Cooper wanted a peanut butter and jelly sandwich. I just came to get him one."

"I told you to keep your ass in that room. And then you come out without your rag on. That means your fair game to all the brothers. You want that? You want them all to take turns fucking you?"

"No."

"Damn straight, no. I told you that pussy is mine. You are mine. Go back to the room. Now."

Grabbing the sandwich only, I raced to the room, locking it behind me.

"Yea... Mommy. Tank you!" Cooper began gobbling it up as he watched his rabbits' cartoon.

"Coop, I'm gonna go take a shower. Be out in a minute. Stay right there." He nodded his head, his mouth too full to respond.

Sitting on the toilet, I buried my head in my hands, letting the tears free fall from my eyes. My first day as an ol' lady and I've already fucked up. I embarrassed Cruz and myself in front of a brother, the one thing I didn't want to do. I should have had the rag on, I should have known better.

Stripping out of my clothes, I washed away the tears, wanting to get them all out before going out to Cooper.

Coop was lying on the floor, his mostly eaten sandwich lying on the plate in front of him. His eyes were drooping almost to closing.

"Come on, Buddy." Instead of putting him in his bed, I brought him in with me. Wrapping my arms around him, I listened to his slow breathing. I wanted more than anything to fall asleep. Call me a chicken or a pussy... I didn't give a shit. I didn't want to face Cruz. Not after this debacle.

As I watched the clock flash red numbers one at a time as each minute passed, my body wouldn't relax enough to sleep, but when the door opened, I closed my eyes hoping he would think I was out.

The rustling of clothes was behind me along with the thump of boots hitting the floor. Keeping my eyes closed, I felt the dip on the side of the bed where Coop was laying, and then the removal of him. I evened out my breathing, knowing that he was going to be back any minute.

The bed dipped as his warm body slid beneath the sheets. "I know you're awake, Princess." I didn't move, hoping he was wrong. "Come on, if you were asleep you'd have had a gun to my face when I moved Coop." Letting out a sigh, I slowly opened my eyes, waiting for him to talk.

"You have to wear your rags. Whenever you're in the clubhouse, you've got to wear them. It's the only thing that's gonna protect you." He rolled over on his side, his voice calm and collected, nothing like earlier in the kitchen. With his anger gone, I relaxed a bit and listened. "That guy was Butch. He's from the Davis chapter and didn't have a clue who you were. If he would have, I'd have kicked his ass for hitting on my girl." Letting out a deep breath, he continued, "I know you were taking care of our boy, but you gotta wear your rags."

"I'm sorry," I whispered, not wanting to say much.

"I'm sorry too, Baby. I just lost it." Cruz pulled me into him, wrapping his arms around me tightly. With my head nuzzled in his chest, I breathed him in, comforted by his gentle touch.

"I'll wear it. I promise." After lying there for quite some time, I spoke. "Cruz?"

"Yeah?"

"I was scared. I was afraid of what I'd have to do," I whispered, feeling the need to let him know how I felt about the whole thing. I didn't say a word about the man slapping me. I didn't need to add more shit to the already burning inferno. But if it had gone further, I would have protected myself, brother or not.

"I know Baby. I know." He rubbed my back, slowly lulling me into another restless sleep.

"BABE, GOTTA RIDE." Cruz called out from the main room. I walked out with Coop in my arms and my rags on. Coop wiggled out to get to his daddy. "I'll be back. Love you." Cruz kissed him on the cheek as he squeezed him tight.

Looking deep in his eyes, there were many things I wanted to say. Like, be careful, stay safe, don't get shot, but I kept it to myself. I knew exactly where he was going thanks to Stella, and I couldn't say that I liked it. But it was club business, it just so happened to have me smack in the fucking middle of it. It pissed me off that I was putting the brothers in danger, and then on top of it; I didn't know why the hell this was happening.

Cruz gave strict instructions for me to stay away from Studio X tonight, and I was completely fine with that. I didn't want to be in the way or have anyone worrying about me as it was going down. I wanted to be here safe with my boy.

But I didn't like it. I didn't like sending him into something where he could be killed. I couldn't imagine my life without him in it. It would kill me. Even though I knew it was part of the life, it didn't mean that I had to like it.

Cruz wrapped his other arm around me, "I'll be fine,

Baby. Love you." He kissed me deeply with Coop still in his arms.

As he pulled away, he told Coop, "I love you, too." Cruz handed me Coop, walking out of the clubhouse.

Ma's firm arms were there to wrap around us. "He'll be fine."

I smiled weakly at her knowing she's been around long enough to know what the hell goes on, too. This time, I wished I didn't.

MA TOOK Cooper up to the shop for a while to give him a change of scenery and me a break. Even though he's been a wonderful distraction from what's been going on, I needed an adult time out. Walking around the compound, I loved seeing all the banners and paintings that graced the inside of the walls. Most had the Ravage MC symbols of flaming skulls, and others had Harleys.

As I glanced at the shop, I saw Casey bent over an engine, hard at work. It was killing me that we had not seen much of each other since I'd gotten out. I didn't understand it. It's like she was avoiding me at all costs. She knew I had been staying here, and even though she came to work here every day, she never came in to say hi.

Walking up behind her, my voice startled her as she jumped. "Hey, girl."

"Shit. You scared me," she said, moving away from the engine wiping her hands on the nearby shop rag, not making eye contact.

"Where you been, Casey?"

"Mostly here." Her avoidance pissed me off.

"What the hell is going on?" She shrugged her shoulders. "Bullshit. Talk now." My temper began flaring, wanting to know what the fuck was going on.

"There's nothing to talk about. Just trying to get these rides done," she said, waving her hand over the car in front of us.

"What the fuck is the deal? I get out of prison, get shot at, take on an ol' man and kid, and you're nowhere to be found. That's not like you, Casey. You need to tell me."

Casey looked around the garage seeing that we were the only two in the building. When her eyes met mine, I could see the pain in them deep, hard, and hurtful pain. I also saw the confliction she felt. She wanted to, but she didn't. I stood there waiting to see which one would win in the end.

"I fucked him," her voice void as she spoke.

"Who?"

"G.T." Shock and exasperation flooded my body. Wasn't this the same woman that was questioning me a few weeks ago about sleeping with Cruz?

"You fucked my brother?" I questioned as she nodded. "Just once?" She shook her head no. "How long?"

"A couple months. I just ended it about two weeks ago."

Normally I wouldn't think anything of this, but we'd always said that we'd never fuck brothers. I fell off the bandwagon, but I never thought Casey would. "Why did you end it?"

Her eyes grew cold in an instant. "Because I will not be one of his whores that he can fuck when he wants to. He fucks everything around here. I couldn't do it, couldn't watch it."

I understood all too well. I've seen G.T. with many women and some images I'd like to bleach out of my eyeballs, but that won't happen. He wasn't shy about his dick being in any hole he could find, and the ladies lined up for miles for it. They loved it. And so did he.

"So you've been avoiding me or my brother?"

"Both."

"Why?"

"I didn't want you to be pissed at me, and I couldn't show up in that clubhouse when he was there. I didn't want the other guys thinking they could fuck me, too. It's not gonna happen. I'm done with bikers."

"What are you gonna do?"

"I'm moving away." I stared at her as if she grew another eyeball as my stomach plummeted to the ground.

"What?" My world came to a stop as everything left me empty and bereft.

"I'm going away to Cherry Vale to college. I wanna get my degree in business so I can start my own shop and build something for me. I have cash saved up from working here, and from Dad."

"When are you going?" I asked, wanting to crawl into a hole. I'd been without her for two years, and now she was moving away. How could this be happening?

"I'm leaving at the end of the week."

"What! You can't leave in four days!" I yelled, my

hands flying in the air. What the hell was this woman thinking! She can't just fucking leave here.

"I have to. I got a job there at a shop, while I'm taking classes. They wanted me as soon as possible."

"You're going just to get away from G.T," I didn't hide my anger. I was pissed as shit.

Casey walked up in front of me, placing her hands on my cheeks. "Low, you know better than anyone that even though I'm a past member's daughter, it means nothing. And add the fact that I fucked G.T. with no commitment... that puts me in the whore category. I've been around long enough to know; it's not a place I want to be. This is all I know. This shop. These men. I need to get away and start a life somewhere away from here." The gentleness in her voice made me want to cry, not that I would.

"What about us?" I asked quietly.

"I love you. You know that. But you have a family now, and you need to be with them." She let out a deep sigh as she moved to the side of the car. "This is where you belong. It's where you've always belonged. You were born to be an ol' lady. I'm not; I need to move on. I know I've been a shitty friend, and I'm sorry for that. We'll keep in touch I promise."

Something deep inside told me that I wouldn't be seeing my best friend again. This journey would take her away from everything, including me. And I couldn't be selfish and beg her to stay, even though I wanted her to, more than my next breath.

"I'll miss you," I said hanging my head down.

"I'll miss you, too, but it's for the best. You know it."

"I don't know shit. But if this is what you want, I'll support you." Loud pops started going off near the office of the shop. "Get down and stay here!" I yelled as I began taking off towards the sound of them. Grabbing my gun out of the back of my jeans, I ducked low to see what was going on.

Ma was lying on the floor holding her arm with blood pouring out, as Mel stood over her aiming the gun at her head. My eyes were unable to meet hers. Cooper was crying like a mad man as Mel yelled "Shut the fuck up!" at him, sending my blood boiling. Then I heard the words I had been dreading. "I'm taking my boy!"

Coming around the corner as quietly as I could, I moved to the side of the door. Peeking around the corner, Mel's back was to me. Just as I got a clear shot of her, Cooper yelled, "Mommy!" At that moment, everything went chaotic. Something hot hit me hard from the back, a gunshot, as Mel pointed the gun at me in front.

"You fucking bitch." My shoulder was on fire from the shots. Somewhere from behind, something hard hit my head causing me to fall to my knees. Mel kicked my gun out of my hand as my grip loosened from being a bit disoriented from the blow, and I fell to my stomach, the pain in my head a bit more than I could bear. I held my stare with my little guy. As blow after blow came from the back to my head, I struggled to remain conscious. It's baffling that I could go blow for blow with the guys, but a couple of unexpected blows to the back of my head could wipe me the fuck out.

"Coo... per..." I called out to him, trying to reach him, but my body wouldn't listen to me. The pain in my head and shoulder taking over. Cooper came barreling towards me and just as he was about to reach me, Mel scooped him up. "No..."

Mel kicked me hard in the face, which normally wouldn't affect me, but with everything else it made me see stars. I wanted to get up to my knees, but I couldn't. I was stuck where I was. Lying flat on the shop floor, my eyes were going in and out of focus. The last thing I saw was Mel carrying Cooper off, and there wasn't a damn thing I could do about it.

CHAPTER THIRTEEN
Cruz

As we sat back in the trees waiting for this asshole to show up, I replayed last night in my head. If Butch had tried fucking her, I would've killed him. Whether she was wearing the rag or not, she fucking told him she was my ol' lady. Sure, bitches lie, but my girl wasn't. I was just damn happy that it didn't come to that point.

This waiting shit was for the birds. Becs was inside the office like he always was. He's sending texts every so often, but nothing has happened. Dagger was hidden in the dressing room with Stella close by. Rhys, Diamond, G.T, Pops, and I were scattered outside. We needed to get the outside threat gone first, then move in.

The sound of bikes in the distance had us getting our pieces ready. The plan was to do this cleanly and just capture the fuckers. Hopefully it goes as we planned.

Three bikes pulled up wearing the Bobcat Demon

patch, none of whom I recognized. One of the men stayed outside as their watch, while the other two went inside. Nodding at each other, we snuck up behind the fucker watching the bikes. I pointed my gun directly at his head; he immediately grabbed for his piece. "Don't," I ordered, his arm instantly stopping.

"What the fuck do you want?" he said as I ripped his pieces off his body, handing them to Rhys. After he was secure, I handed the man off to Rhys.

"You'll find out soon enough fucker." Nodding, Rhys, took the asshole to the waiting cage we had parked on the side of the building.

"Let's go." Placing our pieces back in our jeans, we slowly made our way through the building. Women were dancing, their tits bouncing everywhere, oblivious to what was about to go down in back.

Weaving through to the dressing room, Stella was on her knees with one of the assholes dicks sliding in and out of her throat. "Hurry up, Bitch. We don't got much time, and I need mine," the other asshole said as he smacked her ass, hard, making gagging noises come out of Stella. Seeing Dagger out of the corner of my eye, I nodded. With G.T. and Pops on my sides, we moved in quickly. G.T.'s gun at one of the fuckers and mine at the one getting head, they immediately reached for their pieces as Dagger stepped out of the shadows.

"Don't fucking move pricks," his low voice grumbled as he stepped into the light, pointing his gun at them.

Stella fell back to the floor as the guy whose dick was just in her mouth kicked her hard in the stomach. "You fucking bitch. You're dead," he growled. The butt of my gun slammed into the fucker's skull with a loud crack as he fell to his knees.

"Don't move," I growled, aiming at his skull as we swept for their guns quickly. "Stella, get out of here, now."

"Guys," G.T. said from the side. "Drugs and cash."

"Grab it," Diamond cut in from behind us. "Get these two fuckers in the cage, and get 'em up to the barn. Meet there in fifteen."

THE BARN WAS an old building the Ravage MC acquired about ten years ago. It was located in the center of a hundred acre farm where no one could hear anything. The road into the barn was rough, making us unable to take our bikes down the path. Parking them in a small shed at the edge of the property, we hopped on the four-wheelers while the cage followed between us.

The barn was very stark. We stored supplies there and used it for the occasional informational gathering. The floor was dirt, and the wooden beams had seen better days, but it served its purpose.

Rhys and Dagger unloaded our special guests and brought them to the center of the dirt floor. "Give us your rags," G.T. ordered.

"Fuck you!" they barked in unison. I smiled. This was gonna be fun.

Each of us took turns pounding their faces leaving them utterly bloody, but still able to talk. Diamond grabbed the discarded rags as the men groaned. "Looks like you had to take them off, anyway. At least you did it with honor," Diamond said laughing.

"Why you guys targeting girls at X?" Pops barked. None of the men said anything, causing us to give a few hits. "Tell us!"

"Rabbit told us to." No shit there.

"Why?" Pops was obviously leading this interrogation. When no words were spoken, a few hits to the skull changed their minds.

"She's going after Babs," the one on the far right said. We then knew he was the weak link.

"Tie those two up Rhys," Diamond said as Rhys got to work. "So, what has Babs said?"

His eyes widened as we stood around him, just itching to start fighting. When he hesitated, Diamond ordered, "Tie his hands and attach them to the beam up top." G.T. and I did as instructed, leaving the man hanging with his feet about a foot off the ground. He moved and shook, trying to loosen the rope, but we knew it wasn't any use. Hitting him in the stomach detoured his movements. "Now try this again. What has Babs said?"

"Princess is after her. We gotta take her out." Shit we already knew.

"What happens if Princess takes her out?" When he didn't respond, Diamond nodded at Dagger who reached for his knife. He began twirling it in his hand back and forth through his fingers like a well-oiled machine. He placed the knife on the man's t-shirt slowly and meticulously cut it cleanly away from his body. Taking the blade, Dagger began running it up and down his sternum never cutting the flesh. The man trembled beneath the blade.

"You either tell us, or he's gonna gut you and we'll watch you bleed out."

The asshole didn't hesitate. "Then there's a bounty on Princess's head for 50k." I stood there for a moment. Didn't the Intel say that it was a million?

"You sure that's the amount?"

"Y... es" I didn't believe him. I could tell that Diamond didn't either by the scowl on his face.

Diamond growled, "Dagger."

Dagger began carving into the man's chest and stomach, deep enough to cut, but not deep enough to release any internal organs. With each cut, the man's screams became louder. The other two men sat on their knees watching, but with the gags in their mouths, all that could be heard were weird grumbles.

"What's the fucking amount?" Diamond grumbled loud.

"50k I swear... please..." The asshole cried.

"Who's putting out the hit?"

"Rabbit..." he moaned.

"Is he the only one that can put it out?"

"Ye... s"

I still thought Babs was working with someone. "How did you guys know the girls were having a hard time and needed the drugs?"

"Don't know... never told us." Dagger put a few more blows to his ribs as he grunted. "Don't know... assumed Babs."

When my cell rang, I pulled it out quickly going to push ignore, but when I saw Ma's number, I looked up at Pops, who nodded at me.

Walking outside, I answered. "Hey Ma, how's it going?"

"Cruz, get to the hospital. Mel... she shot Princess and knocked her in the head, pretty hard. She's hurt really bad, and Mel took Cooper." My entire world was frozen by the words she just spoke. I couldn't form a single word. "Cruz!" she yelled, snapping out.

"Mel has Cooper." I repeated back to her. "Is he hurt?"

"No. He was fine when she took him." That was a relief, but didn't mean it would last.

"Princess, is she okay?"

"I don't know. The docs have her in surgery. She took a shot to the shoulder, but it's her head that's the worst. God, Cruz... it's not good, Cruz. It's not good." Hearing Ma's sobs, I kicked into high gear.

"I'll be there as soon as I can." I closed my phone, charging back into the barn. "Diamond, Pops!" Their eyes turned towards me as they began to walk.

"Princess has been shot and Cooper's been taken by Mel. We gotta go... now!"

Diamond barked, "End it." And three shots rang out. "Dagger and Rhys, get this cleaned up. We gotta get to the hospital; Princess has been shot." We hopped on the four-wheelers, racing to our bikes.

ONCE WE GOT to our bikes, I asked Zed and Becs to call Tug, Buzz, and Breaker and search Mel's house, work, parent's house, and anywhere else they knew to look. I'd be joining them soon, but first I needed to make sure Princess was okay.

Rushing down the hospital halls with Pops, G.T. and Diamond on my tail, I felt dread... utter and complete dread. I couldn't lose her. I wouldn't survive. And Coop, God knows where he was with that bitch. I swore when I fucking found her, and I would find her, I would end her. Fuck that no hitting women rule that bitch was dead.

Asking every person in a damn white coat where the hell Princess was pissing me off. Every worker there was scared and petrified us big bad bikers were in their hospital. If they didn't tell me where she was soon, I was gonna give them a reason to be fucking scared, real quick.

Finally, an older lady with graying hair and round as can be, directed us to a waiting room where Ma was propped in the corner with her hands covering her face. G.T. ran up to her. "Ma! What's going on?"

Ma looked up, her eyes red and puffy. "G.T.!" she yelled as she jumped up, wrapping him in her arms, hugging him tight and sobbing. Her knees gave out, and G.T. picked her up and set her gently in the chair.

"You okay, Ma?" Pops asked, looking at the bandage and blood on her shirt.

"Just a graze, not even enough for stitches." Pops wrapped his arms around her, kissing her on the forehead.

"How is she?" I said, panicked and not hiding it one bit. It's amazing how my world could spiral down so quickly.

"I'm so sorry, Cruz." Ma wept. "She's in surgery. The blows to the head were what knocked her down. The bullet didn't do much, but I haven't got an update yet. I'm just waiting."

"What happened?" As Ma replayed the entire scene, my gut ached, and my fury boiled. "Who else was there besides Mel?"

"That's what I don't know, Cruz. I didn't see them."

"Did Mel say where she was going with Coop?"

"No. The only thing she said was 'I'm taking my boy.' I'm so sorry. After the bump on the head, I got dizzy and couldn't get myself together to help either of them." She sobbed harder. "I'm so sorry, I let down my babies."

Pops pulled Ma into his chest as she sobbed uncontrollably. I was stuck between a rock and a hard place. I wanted to stay here and see how Princess was doing, but I needed to go out and find my boy. Thank God, my brothers were doing it, because I would lose my shit if they weren't by my side right now.

That damn clock ticked and ticked and ticked. I felt like eternity that we waited. Ol' ladies came in along with other chapter members. When Dagger and Rhys came in, I jumped up immediately. "Any sign of my boy?"

"Not at the house, her work, or parent's house. We even checked the local hotels showing a picture of Coop... nothing. But one of the nearby gas attendants swears he saw the little boy come in and use the bathroom with a woman matching Mel's description. He then saw them get into the back of a green, four-door Honda. He even gave us the plates from one of their security cameras. I had Buzz go back to the club and run them. That's the strongest lead we've got so far."

"Fuck!" I yelled; I ran my hands through my hair,

pulling it tight. I never felt this out of control in my life. I felt, so God damn helpless. I couldn't help Princess; she was in the doctor's hands, and I have no fucking clue where that bitch took my boy. Dammit.

Dagger wrapped his arms around me, hugging me tight, "We'll find him. Don't worry. Becs, Zed, Tug, and Breaker are waiting for the word on the car. And the guys here," he motioned to the room full of men from the other chapters, "have all agreed to ride as soon as the location comes in. We will find him."

"The family of Harlow Gavelson," a man with green scrubs called as he emerged from the door his eyes scanning the room carefully.

"Over here," I barked. As he looked at the men and women, he gulped loudly. No doubt seeing us all together was intimidating. Good. He'd better make sure she walks out of this alive.

As he stepped closer, the beads of sweat beginning to form on his temples suggested his nervousness. "I'm her ol' man. What's going on?" I said as I stepped in front of him crossing my arms.

He cleared his throat repeatedly seemingly trying to get the nerves under control. "Sir, she suffered a minor shot to the shoulder that was easily repaired. It didn't hit anything major. Unfortunately, the hits repeatedly to the back of her head caused a serious concussion. Right now, we expect a full recovery. She's under anesthesia, but in about an hour, you'll be able to talk to her. She may be confused a bit. I'll let you know when she's in her room."

"Thanks, Doc," I said, holding out my hand. He sucked it up, reaching out, shaking it back. After he left, I was surrounded by brothers and sisters with hugs and pats on the back. Even though I was relieved, I wouldn't be all right till I saw her and talked to her, knowing that she was here and okay.

The waiting took forever. Minutes kept ticking away. With not being able to see Princess and not hearing back from Buzz, I was wearing a damn hole in the hospital's linoleum floor. My mind kept focusing on my boy, wondering where the fuck Mel could have taken him. She doesn't love him. She doesn't want him. When he was first born, she tried several times to give him to me, but my ass didn't want the full responsibility. Now I'm kicking myself hard. Why the fuck does she want him now?

Diamond stood in my pacing path his boots being the first thing I saw. As I looked up, his eyes were masked. "Buzz got a lead on the car. It's about three hours out."

"Fuck," I shook my head lacing my fingers through my hair. Do I stay here with my girl or go find my boy?

I didn't have time to make that decision when the same gray-haired nurse that helped us out earlier came into the room. "Family of Harlow Gavelson?" I took off to the door with Ma right behind me.

"Yeah."

"You can go in and see her now. She's still a bit out of it, but she's slowly coming to. Only one at a time for now."

Turning to Diamond, I pleaded, "Please go. Text me the address, and I'll be there soon."

Ma patted me on the shoulder as I left rushing to Princess's room. The walls were sterile white. She had machines on both sides of her body beeping and making other strange noises. My girl laid on her back with tubes and wires coming out of every part of her body. She didn't move. She laid there... lifeless.

My stomach dropped to my knees at the thought of losing her. Grabbing a chair, I pulled it alongside the bed, grabbing her hand, holding it for dear life. It was warm which was a comforting feeling. I wasn't sure how long I stayed like that. Time evaded me. When Princess started making noises, I looked at her face. Deep lines crossed her forehead as her head began to move slowly side to side.

"Baby. It's okay. You're gonna be okay." I whispered gently into her ear.

Princess's eyes began to flutter open as she blinked repeatedly trying to adjust to the bright hospital lights. She stared at the ceiling as I talked calmly to her. "Princess. You're okay. I'm here."

"No... don't touch me..." she groaned as her eyes rolled in the back of her head, and her lids shut, scaring the shit out of me. I instantly yelled for the nurse and jumped her as she walked in the room. "Her eyes rolled back. And she's not moving." I was unable to hide the panic laced in my voice.

"It's okay. She's just coming out of the meds. Give her some time."

I didn't have time. I had to get to my boy. I texted Diamond, saying that I'd need to stay a bit longer, that as soon as I could, I'd be on my way. He instantly texted back saying my brothers would find my boy. A small sliver of relief came over me, knowing they were the ones out looking for Coop.

Waiting... waiting... waiting. That damn chair was uncomfortable as shit. Over the course of two hours, Ma, Pops and the ol' ladies all came in one at a time. It was a revolving damn door, but it kept the time moving. Ma tried to get me to leave and take a break, but there was no way in hell that was happening. The fucking cops had so many questions that, even if I could answer, I wouldn't. I felt closer and closer to falling off the edge with each passing minute. The cops got to Ma in the waiting room, but Pops was there to handle it.

Casey came briefly and held Princess's hand as she sobbed, saying she was sorry. When I asked her for what, she said that she shouldn't have listened to Princess. Apparently, my girl told her best friend to stay put instead of coming with her. It was the right thing to do, even if Casey didn't see it now.

Staring at the TV, I couldn't even tell you what the hell was on. It was just there for the noise. I couldn't stand the sound of these fucking machines beeping on and on. Each one told me that Princess hadn't woken up yet. Docs kept saying she would, but as more time passed my anxiety kept increasing rapidly.

Suddenly the moans from the bed were a bit louder than before, I moved over to Princess's body. Her eyes were a wrinkled mess, and her arms start moving a little. I began saying the same soothing words as before, "Princess. It's okay. You're all right."

Her eyes fluttered open as she continued blinking. When her eyes settled on me, she just stared, not saying a word. After about fifteen minutes of my reassuring words, Princess's eyes changed, as if something in them clicked and she'd actually woken up.

"Cooper," she croaked out, her voice sounding nothing like her own. At that moment, she gained strength, and she started pulling at her arms. When she saw the wires, she tugged at them and pulled some of them out. The machines going crazy with noises.

"Princess. Stop!" I said forcefully, but she didn't listen. She kept tugging as I reached over, grabbing her hands, pinning them down to the bed. "Stop!"

"I can't. I... I have to find Cooper... she's got him." The pain in Princess's eyes was breaking my heart. I knew she loved him as much as I did. I just wasn't ready for her reaction when she woke up.

"Baby. I know. We're on it. We'll find him." I said still gripping her hands to the bed.

"I'm so sorry, Baby. I'm so sorry." Her words came out in choked sobs as I released her hands, rubbing her matted hair away from her face. She rolled over to her side pulling her knees to her chest as if she were trying to hide.

"It's okay. We'll find him." I tried to reassure her.

"I couldn't stop her... I couldn't do anything. I lay there and watched her take him. I watched her take him!" She screamed the last part, her face covered in tears.

"You were protecting our boy. It's not your fault. We will find him."

"Has she called?"

"No, Baby. But we will find him."

"Cruz. You need to go find him. Now!" Her voice

became more and more determined by each word she said.

"I will. I will." The nurses began rushing in because of all the bells and whistles going off.

"Ms. Gavelson. You need to relax." The nurse said as she began sticking all the wires back onto Princess's body.

"I can't!" she barked at the nurse, who pulled out a very large syringe.

"What the hell are you doing?" I asked, about ready to throw this bitch on the ground if she thought about sticking it in Princess.

"Sir, it's a sedative. She just got out of surgery and needs to heal. She can't be agitated or upset. It will just let her go to sleep for a while."

"Cruz... no don't let them give it to me. I gotta go find our boy!" Princess pleaded, but I nodded to the nurse. As much as it killed me, it would be the best thing for her to rest.

NOTHING... fucking nothing. Before I was able to hop on my Harley and meet up with the guys, Diamond called. He said there was no car. It had taken off about an hour before they got there. They were now on the road going the direction the hotel manager said it went, but nothing was coming up. At least we had the car and license plate number.

Every chapter was now looking for this car and my boy. Diamond called every president demanding help, and they all began the search. I kept holding out hope. I should be out looking for my boy, but he's more than four hours away, and by the time I got there... it would be another four hours. I'd always be lagging behind. It was best to let those who were closer ride.

One piece of information from the hotel clerk was interesting though. He said that Mel was traveling with another woman. I thought back to the people in Mel's life. Calling Buzz, I had him run traces on every one of the bitch's friends that I could think. I needed to find out which one was helping her ass.

"YOU HAVEN'T FOUND HIM YET," Princess groaned as she turned towards me. It's been two days and nothing. Not a single person has seen the car or them. My guess was they had somewhere to go and hid the car. Maybe the bitch was smarter than I gave her credit for or the woman that was with her was the smart one.

Princess had a pretty severe concussion, so they wanted to keep her at the hospital for those two days. They were talking about releasing her. Too bad her fucking mind was not right. She blamed herself repeatedly for Coop being taken. She didn't seem to understand that when you get shot and hit in the head repeatedly, it kinda puts you out of commission. But better than anyone, I felt her pain and guilt.

"We will."

"You keep fucking saying that, but he's nowhere! How

does he just drop off the planet?" She clenched her fists. Anger was raging through her like a momma lion about to attack her prey. And damn if I didn't find that sexy as shit, wish the timing was better, though.

"We're working on it." She glared at me. I knew she was sick as shit of hearing those words, but it was all I could give her; I didn't have anything to share.

"Working on it. How?"

"We will find him."

"Dammit! I just want to know how you're finding my boy. I don't want to know club business. I just want my son found!" She swung her legs over the bed, standing up. She moved into the bathroom slamming the door behind her.

Fuck. I couldn't tell her everything we found. Her state of mind was making it hard for her to trust me. I knew deep down she did. Once she got off all these fucking meds she would come back to her damn senses. I just had to wait it out.

Diamond came in the room as I sat there trying to figure out what I was gonna do. "You all right, son?"

"Not really." I said shaking my head.

"We'll find him. Got every brother in the country looking for him. It's only a matter of time." I wasn't giving up hope, but the more time that passed, the worse things looked.

Princess stormed out of the bathroom. "You here to tell me how you're not finding my boy, too?" she accused him.

"Princess," Diamond warned.

"What? Seems everyone can go find him but me.

Then, the ones I trust to find him won't tell me shit!" she barked.

Diamond's eyes grew furious, and I knew that he was going to blow. "Princess. Enough! You hear me? Enough!" he growled. Princess's eyes widened and lowered as she fell hard on her knees to the floor, the machine at her side falling within a crash.

She was sobbing uncontrollably as I rushed over to her. My strong woman was breaking before my eyes, and at this point, I didn't know how to fix it. Sitting on the floor, I pulled her onto my lap wrapping my arms around her, held her tight. "I'm so sorry." She cried in my shirt.

When the nurses came in and took sight of the scene, they quickly picked up the machine that fell, but said that Princess didn't need it anymore and took it away.

"Come on, Baby. Let me put you in bed." She nodded her head as I scooped her up in my arms, laying her on the bed. I crawled up with her holding her tight until she fell into a deep sleep.

CHAPTER FOURTEEN
Harlow

MY INSIDES WERE NUMB; MY HEART ONLY BEATING TO PUMP blood throughout my body. It had no other function. The bullet wound and head have healed, but that wasn't what hurt. My boy had been missing for two weeks. Two weeks and nothing. Not a word from Mel, and not a trace of the fucking car.

I laid in bed curled up in a ball. It's where I've been since I got out of the hospital. I didn't look at anyone or talk. The only time I did was to ask Cruz about our boy. I totally closed him out. His comfort no longer working. At this point, he could be fucking every whore in this place, and I wouldn't give two shits. My heart was hollow. Empty.

My shoulder hurt like a bitch. Doc came in the other day and said I needed to keep moving it around, or it would lock, but I didn't listen. The throbbing actually

244 | RYAN MICHELE

helped me feel something. The pain was just a reminder that I should have saved Cooper, that it was all my fault.

When I first started this mothering gig, I never expected the pain to cut so deep. I never thought that something could hurt this much. I was dead inside, and I might as well have been in reality. I didn't want anything to do with food, and I only took a shower when Cruz forced me. I didn't want anything to do with anything, except my boy.

When my cell rang, I groaned reaching for it on the night stand. I've only answered when it says Cruz or Pops. When a number popped up with a different area code, I tossed it to the side of the bed burrowing my head in the pillows. The phone rang again, and seeing the same number, I reluctantly picked up.

"Yeah," I said not wanting to talk to whoever was on the other end of the line.

"Well, well, well. She lives." The voice on the other end was one I didn't think I'd ever hear again.

"Mel?"

"Ding... ding... we have a winner." Her sarcasm was not lost to me.

Sitting up quickly, "Where's Cooper?" Fury mixed with panic flushed my body intently.

"Listen to you, pretending to be all protective of *my* son." Anger won as it boiled uncontrollably. I tried to hold my shit together. She wanted something, and I needed to find out what it was.

"Is he hurt?" I asked not beating around the bush.

"I'd never hurt my boy," she clipped, but I knew that was a lie since I saw her grab him right before my eyes.

My stomach dropped; she'd better not have laid a fucking hand on him.

"Can I talk to him?" I heard the pleading in my voice even though I wasn't trying to show it, but damn if I didn't want to hear the little guy's voice.

"I tell you what. Give me what I want, and I'll give the little shit to you." I'm gonna rip this fucking bitch to pieces one limb at a fucking time. Once my hands got on her, she was fucking dead.

"I want a hundred thousand cash, small bills. You get on that little bike of yours and head north on I-95. In two hours, I'll call you back. Don't bring the guys, or I'll kill Cooper." Mel recited her demands as if she practiced them over and over again, but I didn't give a shit.

"Don't you fucking hurt him," I growled.

"Oh, there you go again. Look I just want the cash, then you can have him back. Done. Talk to you in two hours." Mel hung up the phone sharply.

Throwing on my jeans, t-shirt, boots, and rag, I ran out into the clubhouse to find Cruz. I knew by the loud music there was a party going on, but fuck if I cared. Seeing the blonde whore trying to straddle Cruz's legs while he was talking to the guys, set me off. I knew I said I wouldn't give two shits who he fucked, but I lied. Grabbing the bitch by her stringy hair, I yanked her further away from my man. "Get the fuck away." Cruz stared at my rags.

"Back to the living." As the anger flooded through me, I needed to release it. Grabbing the blonde bitch on the floor, I gave her a few punches to the face. Making me feel a little better, but not much. "I take that as a yes."

"Mel called," I barked at him as everyone in the club-house froze.

"Out! Everyone who's not patched in, get out, fucking now!" Cruz growled as he stood up barreling towards me. The brothers proceeded to get everyone out of the club-house and locked it up tight. "What'd she say?"

"I've got two hours to get a 100k. Need to start riding north on I-95, and she's gonna call me for the drop off. Said no brothers."

"Fuck her if she thinks I'm staying away."

"I know Cruz, but she said she'd kill him." The color drained from his face at my words. "We need to play this smart." I needed the brother's help, and there was no way that I'd go coldcocked doing this shit on my own. Too much was at stake.

"That fucking bitch. I will end her."

"Not if I get to her first. Can we get that much cash in small bills?" I questioned him.

"Got it. Diamond?" He looked over at Diamond, who nodded snapping his finger at Becs, who ran off.

"I know you don't want me in this, but I have to be. I'm the one she wants to come. If you guys go, it has to be inconspicuous." Ol' lady or not, I was the one she wanted.

"I know Baby. Let's go get our boy." Cruz pulled me tight to his chest as I breathed for the first time in weeks.

"If you fucked someone while I was down and out, and I find out, I'll cut your dick off," I whispered.

"I knew you would, and I didn't." I nodded my head, trusting him. It was time to find our boy.

TWO HOURS LATER, I was on Sting with a backpack of cash strapped to me, riding. The night air was cool, so I wore my full out lid to block the wind from my face and all my leathers. I rode the speed limit making sure not to fuck up along the route. With my gun in my back holster and two in my boot holsters, I didn't want to get pulled over and waste time.

If this bitch thought for one second that she was getting away with this, she was sadly mistaken.

The guys were following behind in a couple of cages. A few had their rides parked inside the bigger one, but we wanted to be as quiet as possible. Having several pipes humming would be a dead giveaway.

I could see the cages a few cars back. They were doing good at keeping their distance, not that I thought Mel had the power to have me tailed the entire way. About an hour into the trip, I pulled over checking my phone and sure enough there was a missed call with no voicemail. Calling it back quickly, "Mel."

"I figured you'd be calling soon. You got any guys with ya?"

Keeping my voice as void as I could, "No."

"How'd you get the money?" Bitch was smarter than I thought.

"Pulled money out of Studio X," I lied.

"Good. Keep going up I-95 to exit 107. About four

miles down the road will be a hotel off to the left with some flashing pink sign. Come to room 18."

"Got it," I snapped.

"You'd better not be fucking with me about the brothers."

"I'm not. What do you think I am stupid? I want my boy," she laughed. That fucking bitch. I couldn't wait to beat the living shit out of her.

"Good. Get here quickly," she said in a nauseatingly sweet voice as she hung up. Calling Cruz fast, I relayed all the info. He said he had brothers from another chapter making their way towards us and that he'd call them and have them get into position.

Riding into the parking lot of the hotel, it was eerily quiet. Only a few cars lined the rooms, but for the most part it was a dive hotel that probably sold the room by the hour. Watching my mirrors, I saw the guys parking. I didn't know where they were gonna be, just knew they were around.

I knocked on room 18 as the door slowly crept open as if the latch was broken and hadn't caught the closed door completely. Mel sat in the far corner of the room holding a gun pointed directly at me, but the room was empty. "Where's Coop?" I asked quickly.

"Not here," she said smugly.

"Where is he?" I growled, my anger reaching new heights as I clenched my fists.

"With a friend. See this is how this is gonna work. I have someone that really wants to see you. Guess you pissed her off pretty good. Whatever. She wants you. So, I'm delivering."

"You fucking set me up?"

She laughed. "And you fell for it, you stupid bitch." She waved the gun. "Come in and set the bag on the bed. Along with your guns." Taking off the book bag, I placed it and one of the guns I had in my boot on the bed. "Where are the others?" I reached slowly to my back pulling out my baby, putting her on the bed, too. "Any more?"

"No."

"Lift it all up so I can see." I slowly lifted my shirt getting closer to her in the process, but not enough for her to notice. "Good. Now lie down on the bed face down and touch your hands to your ankles."

Really this bitch was seriously stupid, she thought she could tie me and hold the gun at the same time? I laid exactly as she told me, waiting, biding my time. "You know Princess. Cruz sure is a great fuck." Anger surged through my body. "He'd lick my pussy, making me scream over and over for him." With my head turned to the side, I watched the bitch grab the brown rope from a bag on the table. As she stepped closer, she barked, "Don't fucking move."

I felt her hands trying to tie the rope and took it as my chance. Darting my leg out as quickly as possible, I kicked the bitch backwards as she smacked her body hard into the wall. Flipping over, I grabbed the gun from my boot aiming it at her hand that held the gun, shooting. Her gun fell out of her hand as the hole I just shot into it poured out blood. The door was kicked open as Cruz, and some of the brothers came barreling in with guns drawn.

"Where is he?" Cruz yelled.

"Not here. This bitch says he's with a friend. He was never here." I smacked the bitch across the face with the butt of my gun. Her screams were annoying the shit out of me. But I needed her alive to tell me where Coop was. "I need some stuff to stop her bleeding. She has information."

Cruz barked, "Get her some towels," to Becs, who rushed over to the bathroom bringing them quickly.

I leaned down into Mel's face, "Don't worry, Bitch. I'll let you bleed out soon enough." I wrapped the towels around her hand not wanting her to die just yet. "Tell me who's got my boy."

"I'm not telling you shit!" she yelled.

"Cruz, can you please hand me the backpack?" I asked as it was thrown to my feet. "Thanks."

I pulled Mel up to sit in the chair next to her as I grabbed the rope that she was going to tie me with, wrapping it around her arms and legs and tying her to the chair. "Wh... what are you gonna do?"

"Oh. Not so tough now, huh? Well, since your 'not gonna tell me shit' then I guess I'll have to make ya." Grabbing the bag, I pulled out a small pouch in the front pocket. As I rolled it out on the nightstand, Mel's eyes widened. "Cruz. I have to do this." I stared into his eyes. I really needed his approval on this. As he nodded, I smiled. I could kiss him right now.

"Princess, you sure you want to?" G.T. asked as I glared at him. I hadn't spoken to him about Casey, but that was a topic of discussion for another time.

"Dead sure." Grabbing the scissors, I cut the shirt and

bra off of Mel's body. "Look at those tits boys. Nice huh? You know Cruz, before you got here Mel was telling me how you'd eat her pussy and make her scream. I'm not gonna eat that rank pussy, but I do promise to make you scream." I smiled sardonically.

"Boys, clear the rooms around us." Cruz said as the guys nodded leaving the room quickly. The only ones who stayed were Cruz and G.T.

"Let's start with these." I said holding out the pliers. "Hmmm... should I do your teeth or your nails," I said walking around to her chair. "You know they'll both make you scream, but if I start on the teeth, I may not stop. You know once upon a time; I wanted to be a dentist. Hmm..." I smiled to myself as the color left her face. "Oh shit, let's just start here." Taking the pliers, I grasped one of her nipples twisting it hard as she screamed, and blood trickled down.

"Now. Tell me who has my boy!" I was turning into a crazy bitch, but I didn't care.

"I told you. I was supposed to give you to Babs. She's supposed to call me in forty-five minutes with the location." I smacked her across the face as I heard Cruz yell "Bitch!"

"Yeah. I forgot to tell ya, Baby. That's what she was doing with me, and the stupid bitch thought I wouldn't put up a fight." Removing the pliers, I reached the other nipple giving it the same treatment, as she screamed repeatedly. I pulled back, not wanting her to pass out just yet.

"Tell me who you were with when you came and got Cooper."

"I can't. She'll kill me," she said, shaking her head back and forth.

"What the fuck do you think I'm gonna do with ya?" I said, smacking her across the face again, her head snapping to the side quickly.

She hesitated as tears rolled down her face. I didn't feel the least bit sorry for this bitch. "It wasn't supposed to go like this."

"Oh yeah, and how was it supposed to go?" I asked, trying to pry as much information out of her as I could, and if this where the dumb bitch wanted to start, so be it.

Sucking in a deep breath, she explained, "I was to get the money and give you to Babs. Then she was gonna give Cooper back to me, and I'd give him to Cruz, cause I didn't want him. I was gonna disappear."

"Too fucking bad that didn't work out for ya, huh?" I barked. "Who was with you at the shop? Who shot me?"

She sobbed. "Babs's girlfriend."

I felt as if I got sucker-punched, and Cruz must have, too. "Girlfriend?" he asked her as we looked at each other with the same puzzled look.

"Yeah. She was helping Babs get Princess."

"And who is this girlfriend?" Cruz's voice turned utterly menacing, and Mel heard it too as her eyes widened to him. He popped his knuckles back and forth.

"Liv."

My world stopped for a moment as fireballs seemed to have fallen from the sky, pounding the ground around me, but I couldn't move. Cruz stepped in speaking the words I so badly wanted to leave my mouth. "Liv from Studio X?"

Mel shook her head yes. "Is that who has Cooper?" He asked as she shook her head again.

Fuck. Fuck. Fuck! I looked at Cruz, pleading with him with my eyes. My mind tried to revert to the helplessness I felt just a few hours ago before the call, but I tried to fight it. I needed to stay strong, but there's only so much a person could take.

Cruz saw the pain in my eyes as his eyes softened to mine. Sitting down on the edge of the bed, I clutched the gun in my hand, wondering what the hell we were gonna do next. I didn't need to think; Cruz was able to do it for me.

"Here's what you're gonna do, Mel, and if you give any part of it away at any time, I will blow your fucking brains away." She didn't move as I listened with her. "When Babs or Liv calls, you play it off as if you have Princess tied up and ready for them. You get the drop off location and time. Then you're gonna drive with a gun pointed at the back of your fucking head to the location with Princess in the backseat." I stared at Cruz wondering how the hell this was all gonna play out. It always sounded good in theory, but in reality—not so much.

"I don't like it," G.T. clipped in.

"I don't give a fuck what you like," Cruz said, turning to him.

"You're gonna put my sister in the line of fire? Not gonna happen."

"G.T.," I said finally finding my voice. "We need to get to Babs so we can get to Cooper. It is what it is. I can take care of myself."

"Since when does an ol' lady get involved with club business?"

Cruz didn't hesitate, "When that business involves her and her family."

"Shit," G.T. leaned against the door. "You sure about this Princess?"

"If it means getting my boy back, I'm ready." My voice sounded steadier than I really felt.

"I'm gonna need to rough you up a bit. There's no way that Babs is gonna think this bitch overtook you. She already looks like she was in a fight, gotta give you some marks, Babe."

I nodded.

AS FAR AS WE KNEW, Babs bought the bait. We even added me yelling some choice words through the phone muffled by a small towel to emulate being gagged. I gave Mel my leather gloves after padding her hand up with a towel, she bitched and complained that it hurt, but I didn't give a shit. It was stupid of me to cut her fucking shirt, but luckily she had a bag of clothes in her trunk to change into.

Laying in the backseat of Mel's car, I held on tight to my gun. If anything went wrong, I'd shoot to kill in a heartbeat. Babs wanted Mel to bring me to an old warehouse about ten miles off the beaten path. Already giving the location to the brothers, Cruz said he'd have all the guys in place. I had a towel to tie around my mouth, and when we got closer I was to put the gun at my back and slip my hands in the loose knot that Cruz made for me.

We just needed to see Cooper, and then the guys could come in. I just needed to buy a little bit of time. "Don't do anything stupid, Mel, or the guys will find you and kill you in a heartbeat. You follow what we tell you; you'll walk away alive." I was full of shit, but she didn't know that. For some reason, she trusted me; maybe thinking she was smart was a dumb idea.

"Will I get the money?" I rolled my eyes. What the fuck?

"Yeah, Mel. You can take the money and start off somewhere new, but don't contact Cooper again." I threw in the last part to edge the knife home, but it didn't faze her.

"Got it."

"You'd better not set her off, Mel. I mean it."

"I won't. I swear."

As the car came to a stop, I placed the towel back inside my mouth, put the gun away, and laced my hands behind my back slipping it into the knots. I even squeezed out a few fake tears to add to the blood from my cut cheek, courtesy of Cruz.

The door flung open as Babs stood their laughing. "I didn't think you'd pull it off, Mel. I thought she would have killed you by now."

"Nah, I kept the gun on her and made her get rid of hers." Mel's cocky attitude was working well.

"Looks like you two got into it," Babs said skeptically more than likely knowing I could take Mel in a fight hands down.

"She tried to get the gun away, but I hit her in the back where Liv shot her. She went down for the count." Well played Mel, well played.

Babs seemed to have bought her replay of events as she began to look around. "Brothers around?"

"Nope. She wanted the boy so damn bad; she came alone."

Babs laughed hard. "For an ol' lady, you sure are a moron." Babs pulled my arm having me climb out of the car. My mind wandered to how she knew I was already an ol' lady. She must have better Intel on me than I thought, but just as that thought came into play, Liv popped into my head. Liv must have been feeding her information. I wondered for how long.

As we entered the big building, the smell of mold and musk invaded my nose. With my head snapping alert, I searched around as far as I could see to find Cooper, but when I didn't see him anywhere, my stomach dropped.

Babs threw me into an old chair in the middle of the room as I continued to search every dark corner around.

"Can I have my boy so I can go?" Mel asked like she was pissed off having to wait.

"Sure. Go through those doors. He's right there." Mel walked to the doors opening them wide. Two shots rang out through a silencer, as Mel fell to the ground, dead. "She really is a few bricks shy of a full load." Babs walked over to Mel and began pulling her by the arms, dragging her to the end of the room. My eyes stayed focused on the door where Mel was supposed to go through. "Clear!" Babs yelled as Liv walked through the door holding Cooper.

"Mommy!" he yelled, my eyes softening to him. But when my eyes landed on Liv, her once beautiful face was void of emotion. It was as if the person looking at me was someone I'd never met, let alone let run my studio or trust.

Babs started laughing. "That will be the last time he calls you that. See Liv, and I are gonna take him as our own. You'll never see him again. Well that and you'll be dead. But I don't want to scare the poor boy."

"Surprise," Liv said with a deadpan. "You think I was gonna let you come back and take everything that I worked so hard for these past two years. Bitch. If you'd have just stayed the fuck away, none of this would have happened."

This bitch was fucking crazy. I didn't take jack shit from her. It wasn't hers to begin with.

With my mouth still loosely gagged, I stared Babs down. She must have seen the questions rising from my eyes. Babs began talking, as she walked around the chair I was sitting in, gun pointed at me. I kept my eyes trained on my boy, but I was aware of where she was at all times.

"You remember Luke?" I stared in confusion racking my brain with the name, but nothing came to mind. She laughed. "Yeah. I didn't think you would since you whore yourself out all around town so bound and determined not to fuck a brother... yet you fuck anything outside making you exactly that. Including my man." Her man? What the fuck is she playing at?

"I can see by your wrinkled up little forehead that you're trying to piece the puzzle together. So let me help you." The butt of her gun slammed down on the shoulder that was shot a couple weeks ago, sending shooting pains throughout my arm, but I didn't move or make a sound. Inside I wanted to scream like bloody hell, it was healed, but still tender.

"Luke was a bartender at Damon's." My mind instantly knew who she was talking about. The brown-haired, brown-eyed hunk of a man I fucked in the back room of the bar a very long ago. He was barely a blip on my radar. How the hell did I know he was her man? It was a onetime gig. "I see you remember him. He's hard to forget." Her fist collided with my stomach, but I remained impassive. Cooper, on the other hand, began to squirm. I just needed to wait for the right time, so Babs was in front of me instead of behind.

"See, he was actually my fiancé when you decided to fuck him. And you want to know how I know it happened?" She continued pacing, rage seeping out of her. "Because he fucking told me. He said he didn't want my pussy anymore... that you're 'vice grip' pussy was what he wanted," she barked out. How the fuck could he want me after one time in my fucking pussy. Seriously?

But she wasn't done. "Said he knew a buddy of his that was a hang around for the Ravage MC. Said since you were the Princess over there, he was gonna join. I couldn't let that happen." I stared at her. "He had to be dealt with."

The pieces of the puzzle started falling into place, but they seemed minuscule in the grand scheme of things. I fucked her fiancé; she wanted to get back at me, so she created this elaborate scheme to do so. This chick was fucked in the head, more than I initially thought.

She walked around to the side of the room and clutched her gun in her hand. I took this as an opportunity to loosen the rope from my wrists.

As she walked towards Cooper, I halted, watching. "See, Liv here." She ran her hand over Liv's face lovingly, making me want to puke. "She and I had common ground. Hatred for you. Although her hatred is purely professional, it's still there."

As she walked towards me, I slowly grabbed my piece; I was done with this dog and pony show. In one swift move, I aimed and shot Babs right between the eyes as she dropped into a heap on the floor.

Liv screamed as Cruz, and the brothers came barreling through the doors from every direction. I aimed my gun directly at Liv. "Give me my boy."

"Fuck you. I'll kill him before you have him," she snarled, clutching the gun that just shot Mel.

Cruz didn't waste any time. Shots rang out as Cooper fell to the hard ground screaming. I ran grabbing him tightly pulling him away from everything that was about to happen.

"Mommy!" he cried, grabbing on to me tightly. I clutched him hard, not wanting to let go of him, ever.

"It's all right, Baby. Mommy's got you. You're safe." I rocked him back and forth as his tears poured into my shirt. I heard shuffling and Liv's screams but ignored them clinging onto my boy.

"Babe?" Cruz knelt down to the ground in front of us, wrapping his arms tightly around us. "He okay?"

"I haven't looked him over yet, but he feels it."

"How about you?"

"Better now. She gone?"

"No," he said kissing Cooper's head and standing up.

"What?" I yelled shocked. "Why the fuck not?" I picked Coop up off the floor and stared at the woman lying on the ground in a puddle of blood. From the rise and fall of her chest, I knew she was alive. The few shots on her legs were not life threatening.

"Club business," he clipped as I glared at him. Normally I'd let that shit slide, but this time, it was taking everything in my power to hold it together.

Liv laughed, lying on the ground in her puddle of blood and dirt. "What the fuck are you laughing about?" I asked as Coop's head buried into my neck.

"You killed Babs, now someone will kill you." G.T. slammed his fist hard into her jaw. I could hear the bones cracking at the contact.

"Wh... what's she talking about Cruz?" My voice was unsteady. I thought this shit would be over, but it was becoming to be far from it.

Cruz looked across the room at the brothers who all nodded to him. "Babs put a hit on you if you killed her. Right now the only one that can place it is Rabbit. So we need to get to him before he finds out. We're gonna use Liv here. She, after all, has been fucking his ol' lady."

Liv's body went still, all the cockiness from her little confession gone at those words. "You can't tell Rabbit. He knows nothing about me." Her voice shook.

"That's what I was banking on," Cruz said as he nodded to Dagger and G.T. They tied her arms and legs and gagged her, dragging her off.

"Cruz, what's gonna happen?" I knew that in our

world having a price tag on my head meant everyone would be after me. Everyone would want the chunk of the money. I'd be a sitting duck just waiting to die.

"I take care of you. Trust me." I nodded my head because if anything was certain, it was that I trusted this man.

"Thank you," I whispered to him.

"For what?"

"For getting my boy back," I said, squeezing his little body into mine.

"Babe, you did this. You brought him home. I'm just here for back up." I smiled up at him knowing he was only partially right.

"Can we go home?"

Cruz looked over at Diamond, who nodded to us. "Yeah, Babe. Let's go."

CHAPTER FIFTEEN
Harlow

LYING IN BED NEXT TO CRUZ, I THOUGHT OVER THE WEEK I'd had. The whirlwind of emotions was tearing me up. Tension around the club was through the roof with everyone on edge about the meeting with Rabbit tomorrow night. Cruz has been in meetings non-stop, and I haven't been privileged to the information. Part of me wanted to know badly what the hell was going on, but the other part wanted to distance myself as far away from it as possible.

I made it my life's mission to keep Cooper in my sight at all times. I kept him attached to my hip, not letting anyone watch him. I knew that Ma didn't intend on him getting taken, and she'd have done anything to protect him if she could have, but I just couldn't risk it.

Trusting someone else with him was incredibly hard. Just the thought of someone else watching him kicked up my anxiety. I hadn't been back to X, and as far as I knew Becs was running the joint.

I didn't even have the urge to go there right now, or leave the clubhouse for that matter.

Shutting my mind off tonight was proving to be more difficult than I thought. Even having a couple of shots before bed hasn't relieved the uncertainty of tomorrow. The horrible part of not knowing what was gonna happen was... I didn't know what to do to help. They didn't want me to. Cruz was on edge, but he's been doing everything he can to be calm and collected for Cooper and me.

He's doing a great job at it, considering at times I wondered if he was affected at all.

After about an hour of lying there, I couldn't take it anymore. Sliding slowly out of Cruz's grasp, I needed another drink. The clock on the nightstand read 1:37 a.m. and I knew someone would be up in the clubhouse, and there were no parties going on.

Walking into the main room of the clubhouse, the place was dead silent, my plan was ruined. I guess 1:30 a.m. on a Monday morning was not party-central. Grabbing a bottle of Jack, I headed down to the kids' media room in the basement. It was quiet with all the families being gone, and it was peaceful.

Walking slowly down the hall, I made my way to the movie room, thinking some Vin Diesel would be a good pick-me-up. Passing through, rough moans began to invade my ears. As I passed the last bedroom door, the voices became more intense. Rolling my eyes, I kept moving along. Hearing this was nothing new in the club, it was actually quite normal.

"You like that pretty little asshole fucked. Don't you?" The voice. The voice made me stop dead in my tracks as I listened unmoving. "You dirty little whore." A loud slap followed by a woman's moan and the slapping of skin had memories that I buried deep down coming to life right before my eyes. Making my feet move, I peeked inside of the door needing to see the face behind the voice.

Looking through the small crack, my body shuddered as my hands clenched tightly. Rocky was pounding away on the blonde that tried to give Cruz a lap dance a while back. This couldn't be. It couldn't.

"You fucking little whore. Doing this for daddy, huh?" My breath left me so fast it was as if I was a balloon, and someone just popped me with a needle. I was suffocating inside my body, but not wanting to make a sound for fear he would hear me. My mind raced faster than I could catch up. It was him. It truly was him. *Was it?*

I needed to get out of here. Needed to get away... get away from him. He couldn't be here. Rocky... no. It just couldn't be. Racing as fast as I could, I ran back up to the main clubhouse and locked myself in the bathroom.

Bracing my hands on the counter, my head hung as if my neck decided to take a vacation. This just couldn't be. It couldn't. First off, the brothers would have checked Rocky's background. There's no way they would let someone like him Prospect for the club. They couldn't know. It's the only explanation.

His words kept ringing through my head over and over

again. *"You fucking little whore. Doing this for daddy, huh?"* He said those exact words to me over and over again, night after night. A memory I wanted to stay locked up forever was dredged up like vomit in my mouth. I focused on the mirror in front of me as my own eyes stared into each other. *Whore.* That's what I am. That's what I did in there for this club... to protect this club. Between him and Babs, the one thing I never wanted to be was being proven, I truly felt like a whore.

The wheels in my head turned quickly. I needed to protect this club again, but I needed to make a hundred percent sure it was him. In prison, he was the guard who provided me with the supplies to take care of some of the women giving the club troubles. But he always wanted payment, regularly. But Rocky, didn't look like him... it's the voice. The voice was his; I knew it.

I'd thought from the beginning that something was off with that man. I just never imagined this could be it. His body was so much different, while about the same height, the officer in prison was pudgy with a belly that protruded. Rocky was lean and muscular. The officer had green eyes, while Rocky had brown. The officer had no facial hair, while Rocky was covered with a beard and mustache, not to mention he had long hair while the officer had short.

As far as looks were concerned, nothing was similar, and I hoped to God I was wrong about that voice. I needed to make sure. I needed to know. My mind began formulating a plan, and thank God Casey decided to stay two extra weeks after everything went down to be here for us... for me. I was gonna need her help if I was gonna pull this off.

THE REST OF THE NIGHT, I laid next to Cruz trying to control my breathing, not wanting to wake him. Today was such a big day for our family. I didn't want to fuck with any of the brothers' heads. They needed all their shit together, and this would fuck them up. The good thing was that Cruz mistook my uneasiness for nerves about what he was going to go do. While I was coming up with all kinds of scenarios of what could happen, I needed to screw my head on straight and get my end together.

For the first time in a week, I asked Ma to watch Cooper. It scared the shit out of me, not having Ma watching him, per se, but having anyone watch him that wasn't me. I gave Ma another gun and told her to shoot first and think later. I wouldn't lose my boy again.

After a quick text to Casey telling her, I needed her help and to be at the club at three o'clock, I pulled myself together before the guys left. Earlier this morning I asked Cruz, who was staying back with us, and when he said Buzz and Rocky, I was relieved. I needed Rocky here. I needed answers.

"Babe, you sure you're okay?" Cruz asked while lacing up his heavy boots.

Walking over to the chair, he was sitting in, I kneeled down in front of him. "Yeah. Just be careful, okay?"

"Always. I'll be home in a couple of hours and all this shit will be over." I wanted to believe him. I really did, but what I was about to do... if I was wrong, the brothers would have my ass on a stick. I'd be dead, but I needed to know for the club and myself.

Leaning up, I wrapped my arms around his neck threading my fingers through the back of his hair. Staring into his beautiful blue eyes, my lips fell to his. He instinctively pulled me closer, deepening the kiss. I hoped this wouldn't be the last time I did this, because if I were wrong about Rocky, it just might be. That fear almost held me back from doing what needed to be done, but I couldn't let it. If it were true, the guys needed to know.

"I'll be back soon." Nodding, we both stood.

"Daddy!" Cooper yelled from his room. Cruz smiled, shaking his head. After lots of hugs and rough manly kisses, Cruz handed Coop off to me as he left.

Liv had been staying here in the same room that Stella and Moxie were privileged to a while back. I never went to see her and stayed very clear of the room as it was very tempting to go in and beat the living shit out of her, but I didn't. I wanted to at times... but didn't, only because Cruz said no. They needed her; in turn I actually needed her.

After a half hour, the sound of revved-up Harleys filled the room. I listened as they left the clubhouse. Gathering Coop, I handed him off to Ma, who eyed me as if she knew I was up to something, but didn't say a word. I left in search of my target.

He was here; I just needed to find him. I grabbed my bag that looked like an oversized purse because I needed to make sure everything I packed was with me and well hidden. Walking through the clubhouse, Buzz was behind the bar cleaning it up as two of the club mamas were mopping the floors. "Hey, Buzz. You see Rocky?"

"I think he's out at the shop." Perfect. I'd planned on doing this in the basement of the clubhouse, but the shop would be even better. Off the backroom, where Sting was kept for so long, was a small room about eight by eight with mainly storage inside. Sending out a quick text to Casey, I made my way out into the sunlight.

Walking into the shop, the first man I came across was Greg, the man I had hurt the first day I was here. Even though I've apologized to him, I still felt a bit bad. Poor guy was just protecting my bike. Walking up to him, I said, "Hey, Greg." He smiled broadly.

"Hey, Princess. What's going on?" he asked while wiping his hands on the shop towels next to him.

"Just out for one of my walks. Hey. I'm gonna go look for a couple of things for Sting in the back. I'm thinking of tuning him up." I wiggled my eyebrows suggestively.

"You and that man of yours." He smirked. "Sure thing. Go on back and get what ya need."

"Thanks. Hey, you seen Rocky?"

"Yeah, in the office."

"Could you ask him to come back? I need to talk to him about something."

"Sure thing, Princess."

"Thanks!" I smiled my most sultry smile at the guy. Flirting always worked around this place. One thing a man couldn't deny was pussy.

Making my way to the back room, I took in all my surroundings. Three men were working in the shop, but seemed to have their heads stuck in their work. It looked as if Rocky was the only one inside the office, at least from what I could see through the mini-blinds.

"Hey, Bitch!" Casey called from behind me as she waved to all the guys. I was so gonna miss her.

"Hey, Babe. Come to help me look for parts?" I winked taking in the oversized purse she was carrying, as well. Men never seem to give a second thought to the purses, man, what they didn't know.

"Absolutely." Since giving Casey a quick rundown early this morning about why we were going to be doing what we were about to do, I felt calm with her by my side. I had to give her a hell of a reason, or she wouldn't want any part of it. It was too dangerous, and I couldn't help that feeling lingering in the back of my head saying, *what if I'm wrong.*

Shaking myself out of those thoughts, we headed towards the back. Casey instantly went to work, clearing a small space in the center of the room and placing a chair in the center. I knew if I were gonna do this, it would have to be fast and methodical... no mistakes. The guys have already been gone for an hour, and if everything went okay, Cruz said he'd be back in two. I needed to get to work.

"You ready?" My eyes focused on hers. She may not have become the gun-toting girl that I did, but she still had her father in her, and when he came out to play, it was game on.

"Let's see who this fucker is." Nodding, I made sure my guns were loaded. I gave Casey a taser and stuck mine in my side holster. It was made to look just like a gun and was gonna be my tool of choice for this inquisition. We were as ready as we were gonna be.

I wasn't as nervous as I was last night. Having that extra time to think and not react helped keep my head on straight. Now if this shit was confirmed, I couldn't say it'll stay that way. I was playing that one by ear.

Going out into the connecting room, we began looking for *parts* for Sting, always keeping our eyes attached to the door. When it slowly creaked open, I glanced over at Casey who nodded.

"Hey, Rocky. Can you help me find some plugs for Sting?" He grunted, but hearing his boot steps getting closer, I turned and smiled at him. His eyes were still the same brown as they've been every other time, but this time I imagined them green, and as I did, an elusive chill ran down my spine. I didn't let it show, instead; I gave him a very vibrant smile. "Thanks."

Casey walked up on the other side of Rocky as he turned to look at her, appraising her up and down. That was just what I suspected he'd do, with her long legs and painted-on jeans; no one could resist her. "Hey, Rocky, you know Casey, right?" He nodded his head.

"Hey, Rocky." Casey's voice was a soft purr, very seductive and inviting. This woman rocked.

Rocky kept his head turned towards Casey as I began to creep a bit closer. Casey amped it up by moving closer to Rocky, giving him the fuck-me eyes that men fell for every time. Rocky was no different. Taking the taser out of my holster slowly, I placed it behind my back waiting for the perfect time. Casey leaned in close to whisper in his ear. Keeping herself far enough away, to avoid the shock she knew would be coming. Reaching around, I placed the taser on Rocky's neck, hitting the trigger hard, he fell to the ground shaking and mumbling some garbled up shit that I couldn't understand. Tasers only gave you a short period of time, and we had a lot of work to do.

"Now. Come on." Casey grabbed one of Rocky's arms while I grabbed the other, dragging him into the room. Picking the big lug up, I dug in Casey's purse finding the rope and duct tape. At first I thought of using the rope to bind him, but then thought better of it, duct tape would work just nicely, and it's harder to break out of.

Quickly, I taped his hands behind his back and then taped them through the slats on the chair. Moving his knees up the side of the chair, I taped them to the back chair poles. There was no way he could stand and swing the chair at either of us if he got the chance. I then taped his thighs and torso just for good measure.

Casey searched through her bag, finding an old sock. "Perfect for now. I'll get it all done; then we'll have to take this out to do the rest." Taping the sock into Rocky's mouth, he began to come back from the shock.

"Hey there, big guy. Remember me?" I asked as his eyes grew wide, and he began shaking his head. "Well, I think I know you from somewhere, so I've gotta check some things out."

He tried to move in the chair, but realized if he did the only place it would get him was the floor, and for me that'd be just as good as where he was. Reaching into my purse, I grabbed the battery-operated shaver and flipped it on. Rocky began squirming. "What's wrong? Have something to hide under all that hair?"

He shook his head repeatedly, but his body was tensing up, as he was trying to move his arms out of the binding. I would hit him a few times in the face, but just wanted to make sure I was correct before I completely fucked myself. Gripping his head, I held on tight to the top of it as my buzzer cut his hair. Rocky tried moving to get away from the cutters, but didn't put up too much effort.

I began swiping through his hair, cutting every last bit off, giving him a military short haircut. This looked more like the officer. Next I moved to the beard and mustache.

I moved the cutters closer to his face as his eyes got wide, and he started thrashing around. This was no good. "Casey, tase him." After she did, I cut the length of it off. Casey went and grabbed the razor, water bottle, and soap out of her purse. After the first few strokes, my heart was beating out of my chest. My hands became sweaty, and my eyes saw red. I shaved around his gag; there was no need to take it off. I ripped the tape when needed to go around, placing it back, but kept the gag in place.

With him still out from the taser, I opened his eyelid placing my finger on the colored part of his eyeball. When my finger moved to the side, it revealed a brown contact that I slid out of place. I did the same to the other. The green eyes I dreaded stared back at me.

Stepping back, Officer Macaffe sat in front of me. The one man I never wanted to see or think about again. The only man inside that I fucked, repeatedly, and not by choice, the one man that could truly call me a whore.

As he began shaking his head getting whatever fog out from the taser, I stared him down.

"This him?" Casey asked, already knowing the answer.

"This is Officer Macaffe. He and I got really cozy in the joint. Didn't we?" He didn't say a word as his head dropped down to his chest. "I'd let you talk, but I don't give a flying fuck what you have to say."

Grabbing the gun from my back holster, I slammed the butt of it into the side of his face repeatedly giving him a few kicks to the ribs as Casey held the chair. It was like she knew what I was doing before I did it. I loved how that worked.

It wasn't enough, though. I wanted him to know what it felt like. What it was like to have something rammed in your ass over and over again.

He was gonna feel it.

CHAPTER SIXTEEN
Cruz

RABBIT AGREED TO MEET WITH US IN A LARGE COTTON FIELD just outside of Sumner. We cased out the spot earlier in the day and didn't find anywhere where men could hide. With the cotton, just getting picked, even staying low they would be exposed. We had Tug and Breaker in the cages fully armed with autos and everything else we might need, and of course, Liv.

As we rolled up, we parked our bikes methodically in a row, with Diamond's first. How the old man still hung with everyone like he was thirty was beyond me, but he made me damn proud to be at this side.

Rabbit's crew stood next to him, guns in their hands at their sides. We expected this to be heavy, but were hoping for the best, and with the amount of firepower we all had, we hoped smoothly. When Diamond talked to

Rabbit on the phone, he didn't want to meet, but in pure Diamond fashion, he worked it out.

"Princess killed my girl, and you killed three of my men," Rabbit stated matter-of-factly while Diamond stood in front of him, each of us flanking his sides, guns in hand.

"No, she didn't. Your ol' lady was a cheat. As for your men, they were selling blow in our business, you knew that was a no-go."

"Bullshit!" Rabbit's hand on his gun was starting to pulsate. He wanted to shoot.

Diamond held his hands up in front of him as he was the only one of us who didn't have a gun in his hand. "Gonna pull an envelope out of my rag." When Rabbit nodded flippantly, Diamond pulled out the manila envelope that was delivered earlier this morning by Deara's connections. She really came through for us.

Diamond pulled out pictures of Babs and Liv fucking like animals in Liv's apartment. He showed Rabbit picture after picture as his jaw ticked. "So you see, Rabbit, your girl was a lying slut. Playing you. And lucky for you, we have the bitch who shot your ol' lady."

Just as we suspected, Rabbit's eyes flared at the betrayal. Without the pictures though, this would have never worked.

"What about my men?" He glared, becoming twitchier with his gun.

"That was circumstance. You knew not to sell blow at Studio X, my establishment." Diamond said casually.

"Fuck. I should take out three of yours." Rabbit's eyes

were focused on the cage in front of him. "Give her to me," he demanded.

Diamond wasn't just going to hand Liv over; we had our own demands. "If we do, Princess is free and clear, no hits on her, and everyone leaves her the fuck alone. Also, no retaliation for the clean kills of your men."

"Fuck," He thought a bit longer than expected. "Deal, I ain't got no beef with your girl. That was all Babs that fucking little whore. But my men were good men." Rabbit paused. "Fine. Hand her over." Diamond stepped forward holding out his hand, which Rabbit took in turn, shaking the deal closed. I couldn't help but feel a little relieved. This was easier than I expected.

"Pull her out!" Diamond called to Tug and Breaker. As they dragged her body out of the cage, her eyes widened, and she started thrashing against the men. She knew exactly who Rabbit was. Too bad for her he didn't give a fucking shit who she was. With the gag in her mouth, we only heard muffled pleas as her head shook profusely.

The thing was; there was no way we could let her go with them alive. If he didn't kill her immediately, we'd have to take her out. Her mouth was too much of a problem that we didn't need. If she were to confirm that Princess did, in fact, kill Babs, we didn't know for sure what way Rabbit would sway, even with the betrayal.

Tug and Breaker threw Liv at Rabbit's feet as she landed on her knees. The loud crack of his gun slamming into the side of her face echoed throughout the field, as did her whimpers. We couldn't leave just yet, even though

278 | RYAN MICHELE

we all wanted to. We needed to make sure the final deed would be done, and her lips were sealed forever.

Turning my head, I didn't want to watch this shit. I didn't care for Liv and wanted her fucking dead, but these assholes were nuts and pissed. That could really fuck with a man's head.

After what seemed like forever, a single gunshot rang out over the vast field. Turning to see Liv dead and lying on the ground with a bullet in her head, I was finally able to breathe. Princess would now be safe, and we could go on with our lives.

THE RIDE back to the clubhouse was peaceful and calm. I wouldn't change a fucking thing about my relationship with Princess. It was fast, but that's how I live. I see something. I take it. You never know when it will be taken away from you if you wait.

I couldn't wait to get home and lie in bed with her. She doesn't know this yet, but she's not going back to that fucking apartment, ever. She's with Coop and me forever.

Pulling up to the clubhouse, the shop was moving more than normal as Buzz started making his way to the bikes. He acted almost nervous as he came up to the side of my bike.

"What?"

"Hm... well..."

"Spit it the fuck out!" I yelled my anger peaking as the guys began listening intently as they took their lids off.

"Well. Princess, Casey, and Rocky went into the back room of the shop a while ago and some of the guys said they heard moaning." My body began pulsating as my head felt like it was going to explode. There was no fucking way Princess would cheat, especially after the shit she gave me. Not to mention, I'd fucking kill her. Ripping the lid off my head, I climbed off my bike and jogged into the building. My long strides were not getting me to that fucking room quick enough.

Boot steps behind me began pounding, as well. G.T. heard the name Casey and was one step behind me. Turning the knob on the door, it was locked. I pounded. "Princess open the fucking door."

"In a minute!" she yelled sounding out of breath. Fuck this shit. Taking my boot I slammed open the door pulling out my gun in front of me. As the brothers and I poured into the room making it so much smaller than it really was, I took in the sight before my eyes. I was stunned into shock.

A man whom I assume was Rocky without all his hair was tied up, hands behind his back, knees up in the fetal position, bound by his torso. A sock gag was wrapped around his face while he lay their butt-ass naked. Blood covered the floor, mixed in with hair and various objects like a broomstick, bottle, and a large dildo. His face was a mangled mess with blood coming out from every angle of his body.

"What the fuck is going on here!" Diamond boomed as I stood there staring at everything. When Princess turned around, she met my eyes, but it wasn't her inside of them. This woman was cold, determined, and down-right angry; there was no warmth at all. Detached.

When Princess didn't say a word, I looked at Casey, who crossed her arms over her chest and stared at a very pissed off G.T. as Diamond continued, "Princess, who the fuck do you think you are doing this to a potential brother?" Diamond pulled out his gun aiming it at Princess's head.

Princess's demeanor didn't change as she stood up from the crouching position she was in on the floor. When her eyes locked with mine again, the fire was burning heavily, and I knew she meant everything she did to Rocky, but why?

"Princess, why would you do this?" I asked her through gritted teeth. This would for sure exile her from the club, and there wouldn't be a fucking thing I could do about it.

"Because he's a traitor." Princess's voice was even-toned and hollow, as if she was coming out of a trance or something.

"What?" I clipped, with Diamond right behind me still aiming his gun at Princess who didn't flinch away from the gun.

"You gonna shoot me, Diamond?" This was so not the time for cockiness, but leave it to Princess to say it.

"Tell me right now what the fuck is going on here," he demanded, not pulling the gun away instead cocking it ready.

Princess began walking around the small space with her bloody hands behind her back. We were all specta-tors as she began, "Officer Macaffe here..."

"What the fuck!" Officer? I checked this guy out seven ways to Sunday and had Buzz track him. How the hell could he be a cop? No fucking way.

Princess turned to me, her eyes void. "See the Officer and I got cozy in prison. He's an ass man... as you can plainly see." Looking down at his bloody form, blood was oozing from his ass. What the fuck did she do to him? "In order to get the tools I needed to take care of some of those bitches you boys needed dealt with, this fucker here said I needed to fuck him regularly, or he'd stop giving me the shit."

I saw red... blood thirsty all-consuming red blurred my vision as my hands began to shake. Turning to the brothers, they didn't acknowledge what had just been said, but having them there in unity helped. As my fist connected with the drywall, it didn't relieve my anger.

"How do you know it's him?" G.T. asked, seeming to be the only one thinking at the moment.

Princess continued to pace. "Didn't, not until last night when I heard him fucking the blonde club momma." Princess eyed me then continued. "He said, *'You fucking little whore. Doing this for daddy, huh?'* That's how I knew it was him, but I couldn't tell you guys until I knew one hundred percent."

"Is that what all the hair is from?" G.T. began to step towards Princess.

"Don't," she barked at him as G.T. stopped in his tracks. "I had to shave him to know. I also took out the brown contacts; he has green eyes. It's him."

"Princess... I... I'm so sorry." Pops voice came across,

but Princess didn't seem to register it, but the despair in his words hung in the room like a gray cloud.

I couldn't see shit because his eyes were swollen shut. Princess bent down, reaching into her bag and pulling out a crumpled piece of paper handing it to me as she stared into my eyes. "I knew if I did this, and I was wrong, I'd be out. As much as I didn't want to be right, I am."

Opening the paper, a picture of an officer stared back at me, looking nothing like the Rocky that we know today. Shit. Shit. Shit. Handing the paper off to Diamond, he lowered his gun staring at the paper. "Holy fucking shit," he mumbled as he passed it around from person to person.

"You didn't know, right?" Princess asked with sadness laced in her voice.

"No, Baby. We didn't know," I said, taking a step towards her, and when she didn't oppose, I stood right in front of her, wrapping her in my arms. Her entire body began to sag as I tightened my grip to hold her up.

"I'm so sorry," she whispered in my chest as the tension from her body began to evaporate.

"You have nothing to be sorry for, Baby. Nothing." Kissing the top of her head, I felt the sobs begin to take over her body, but as quickly as they came... they were gone again.

Princess pulled away staring into my eyes, "Guess I turned out to be a club whore after all."

As I stared into the depths of her eyes, this was what was haunting her. I couldn't let her feel this way. "You are not a fucking whore, never have been, never fucking will be." I crushed my lips to hers, tasting and swallowing her tears. No more of that shit.

"Do I need to take care of this?" she asked, pulling away and motioning the room.

I chuckled this damn woman. "Nah. We got it." She nodded, grabbing random things around the room throwing them haphazardly into her bag as if she were just going through the motions. Casey began doing the same. "Princess, meet me in my room." She nodded as she walked out.

"Casey!" G.T. barked as she jumped and then stared at him.

"What?" Casey looked hurt, but what the hell could I tell.

"Come with me."

"No. I'm leaving G.T. I'm done with this shit." Casey continued picking things up, throwing them in her bag.

As she went past G.T., he grabbed her arm, "This isn't over," he growled at her.

"It is over. You won't see me again." Casey stood on her tiptoes, kissing G.T. on the cheek. "Bye G.T.," she mumbled, as she walked out of the room.

G.T. started to follow after her, but stopped when Diamond yelled, "Fuck!" as he kicked the man lying in front of us. Fucking shit. This was bad. "I thought you said you checked this asshole out!" His finger pointed in my face as I stood their stoically, not giving any emotion. "This is fucking on you!" he growled. "Shit!"

"Diamond," Pops warned. He was the only one that Diamond allowed to pull him back, and it wasn't all the time either. "Talk about this first." Diamond shook his head as if trying to clear his thoughts.

"You checked everything about him?" Pops asked me; his eyebrow raised; the guilt from this revelation etched in his face.

"Yes Sir, have all the copies in the file. Everything he told us came up on those papers. There was nothing linking him to the prison or to being a cop."

"Fuck! That means the fucking cops changed every-thing to get him inside. What the fuck does he know, and what has he reported back? Fuck!" he yelled, kicking this asshole in the ribs.

"Only one way to find out." Dagger nudged Rhys as he left the room. I knew he was going to get his kit. Let the fun begin.

CHAPTER SEVENTEEN
Harlow

MY BODY WAS DRAINED, NO ENERGY NO FEELING... NOTHING. Cruz has been gone for hours, and I didn't expect him back anytime soon. Casey talked Ma into keeping Cooper for me, and I knew that I would have a talk coming from Ma very soon.

Staring at the blonde beside me, Casey's eyes were slowly shutting as I felt mine doing the exact same thing. This time, I hoped the nightmares would disappear.

"BABE." The slight rocking of my body was arousing me from my sleep, sleep I so desperately needed. Opening my eyes, Cruz was peering down at me. "Babe as hot as it is to have two very hot-ass chicks in my bed, I only want one." Looking over, Casey was sound asleep, and the clock said 6:06 a.m.

"Got it," I croaked out as my voice decided it didn't want to wake up.

"Gonna take a shower, be out in a minute." He kissed the top of my head and moved to the bathroom.

Nudging Casey's body, she began to groan, "G.T. stop." Rolling my eyes, I moved her harder. One thing I didn't want to hear this morning was about her and G.T. fucking.

"Wake up, Casey." As her eyes slowly opened, she smiled.

"Morning beautiful." Casey rubbed her eyes appearing to clear the fog out of them.

"Hey, girl. Cruz is back. Gotta go." Casey rolled out of bed without a word. It's something else I loved about her. She knew this life and knew what was expected. I'd never have to explain anything to her.

Putting her shoes on, Casey's words killed me. "I leave tomorrow."

Closing my eyes, I held in everything... all the thoughts, feelings, anger, sorrow... Casey needed this, and I was gonna be strong. "I'm gonna miss you."

She turned in the bed hugging me, "I'm gonna miss you, too. You take care of yourself."

"Always."

The bathroom door swung open as Cruz stepped out wearing nothing but a towel around his hips. "Unless you both wanna fuck me, Casey, you gotta go." I glared at him as the sexy smirk made an appearance on his lips.

"Bye, girl," I said giving her one last squeeze as she walked out of the room.

"I heard she's leaving," Cruz said as he approached the bed.

"Yeah, going to school. Really, she's getting away from G.T."

"Yeah," he grunted. I wasn't shocked he knew. I expected it, and even though he never said anything to me, it didn't piss me off. Or maybe it's just been a hell of a night... or morning now.

"She's leaving tomorrow."

"Sorry, Babe."

"I just want her happy." Cruz threw the towel off his body, giving me an awesome view of his toned abs with the V ever so present, and his throbbing cock bouncing against his abdomen. I knew I would never get tired of seeing this fine specimen of a man.

"Speaking of happy. You're not going back to the apartment. You're moving in with Cooper and me. I'll have the Prospects pack your shit and move it over."

I nuzzled closer. "Okay." Cruz's body stilled.

"You're, not gonna put up a fight?"

"Nope, too tired," I said as I yawned.

"Not too tired, 'cause my dick needs you, right the fuck now."

Smiling I spread my legs open wide for him as he let out a low grumble moving in between them. Cruz slid inside my pussy; my body always seemed to be ready for him. Closing my eyes, I relished in the feel of his weight on top of me as his thrusts became more powerful and needy. My body rose higher and higher as we exploded together in the heat of passion.

"I love you," I whispered.

"Love you."

As I drifted off to sleep, Cruz's words filled my ears. "It's all over babe." His words lulling me into a deep, nightmare free sleep.

CHAPTER EIGHTEEN
Cruz

WHAT WE GOT OUT OF ROCKY, OR SHOULD I SAY, OFFICER Macaffe, blew my fucking mind. Cops knew more than we thought. They apparently had been tracking the runs we were doing and our connection to Rabbit long before any of this shit went down with Princess. She was just a means to their end.

Drugs. It all came down to drugs. Cops wanted Rabbit, not us at the time, but I guess that shit changed. They knew we ran through Rabbit's territory and were going to use Princess to get information, which really she had none of. They soon realized she wouldn't flip no matter what, even if she did know something.

It wasn't our local cops; it was the big time feds. Those fuckers were ruthless. When I asked if fucking Princess was part of the deal, Rocky actually had the fucking balls to tell me it was just for fun. Fucking prick. After a few stabs into his flesh, I still didn't feel better. Nothing about this situation was making me feel better.

And the fucked up part now was, we knew the cops were gonna come. One of their own was missing and wouldn't be found. We knew they'd sweep the club and try to take us in, but we made sure that nothing was around to connect us to Rocky. All evidence from that day burned up in smoke or was bleached away. It's only been a couple of weeks, since everything went down. I thought for sure the cops would have come to the clubhouse, and ripped it up by now, but nothing.

Now, we were just waiting.

After Diamond lifted the lockdown on Princess, I didn't waste any time getting my family into our home. I'd always spent more time in my club room than here, but now I can't seem to stay away. Princess just lights every damn room up when she enters. I couldn't get enough of her.

Cooper's the best boy a man could have. I kick myself in the ass for missing his day to day shit before, but now I wouldn't miss a single fucking second of it. Princess was the best thing that could have happened to that boy. After everything that happened with him, she's fiercely protective. I'd be surprised if she lets him go to school in a few years. I chuckled at the thought. She'll probably want to be behind him in class with her fucking hand on her gun.

Shaking my head at the thought, I moved over and wrapped my arm around Princess, who lay next to me as naked as the day she was born. Tracing her shoulder tattoo, my dick instantly became hard. There was no taming that boy down when it came to her.

As she rolled over, her eyes fluttered open. "Hey, Babe." I loved hearing her groggy sexy voice first thing in the morning.

"Hey." I captured her lips with mine, and as she tried to pull away, I held her close to me taking what I needed from her. As she melted into the kiss, I slowed down. "You doing okay, Babe?"

She'd been on edge, and I knew it was from the revelation of what she did to Rocky, but I didn't want to push that shit. Some things are better left in silence until she's ready.

"Yeah." She squeezed her arms around my body. "Can I ask you something?"

"Anything."

"I didn't want anyone to know what happened inside. But now that you do, you're cool with it?" Her voice came out cracked and strained.

"Fuck no, I'm not cool with it. That fucker should have never touched you." The rage I felt towards what happened to her never seemed to diminish. Just the thought of it made me want to bring that fucker back from the dead so I could kill him again.

"I know that. I mean. That I used my body to get what I needed."

"It wasn't your fucking fault." I pulled her away and stared into her eyes. "I want it erased from your fucking head. He won't ever touch you again. No man but me will ever touch you again."

She sighed, "Well you pretty much know everything about me now." I knew this was a segue into asking about the military, but it was something I just couldn't talk about. I couldn't tell her the fucked up shit they did over there just for the fun of it. At least when we had to do shit for the club there was a definite reason, a reason that meant something. Over there, they just did it for the fun of it.

There was no way I was gonna put those thoughts in her beautiful head. If anything, I wanted to scrub them out of mine. I just couldn't do it.

Instead, I rolled on top of her as she opened her legs wide for me. I loved that she was always ready for me no matter when I wanted her.

Sliding in deep, I stared into her beautiful eyes feeling all the love I felt for her reciprocated tenfold. As we came together, I held her close. I loved this woman with every part of my soul.

THREE MONTHS LATER

EVERYTHING'S BEEN PRETTY QUIET, surprisingly. Our church meetings always consisted of theories and getting inside information on our cop problem and the hit on us that took place when we did the run for Ransom. Our local chief of police didn't know shit, and we've been working on getting someone in on the feds' side. That's always easier said than done, but not impossible.

The police came in and questioned us about Rocky, so they called him. They stated they had an anonymous tip connecting Ravage to the man's disappearance. With no one in Ravage saying a word and the cops seeming to think we didn't know Rocky was a rat, they went away without another word. But we did a full sweep on everyone in the club, just to make sure. Even I got swept, which was fine. I'd rather everyone know I'm true then to have any questions about my loyalty. I didn't think for a second the cops were done with us. There was only a matter of time before someone else would try to get in and take us down. This time we'd be ready.

There had been nothing from the hit. It was as if it was a figment of our imagination. Every avenue we went down for answers fizzled. No leads, no information... nothing. And not another attempt to take us out. We'd thought at first it was because of the whole Princess situation, but conversations with Rabbit found that theory to be a dead end.

This meeting was the same as the others.

"Meeting with Rabbit at three," Diamond ordered as he slammed down the gavel. Rabbit had been talking to Diamond over these last few months, but this was the first meeting we've had with him since we handed over Liv and made our deal. Everything with Rabbit was on good terms as these conversations lead to more work and cash flow in the club. But we always had our guard up with him. There was still retribution for shooting up

Pops' house that would need to be dealt with, but we voted to keep it on the backburner for now.

Leaving church, I needed to take care of something. "G.T.," I barked as he grabbed his phone out of the box on the pool table.

"What?"

"We need to talk."

"*We* don't need to do shit," he growled at me. Ever since the fight with Princess, he hasn't talked to her. It's been fucking months now, and this shit needs to stop. She's had her moments when she lets this shit get to her and breaks down, but always puts herself back together. She's attempted several times to talk to him, but nothing. He won't respond or give her the time of day.

"*We* do. Now," I growled standing toe-to-toe with him. I'd had enough of this shit, and something had to give. My girl was hurting, and I was fucking done with it.

"Whatever." He walked over to the couches, and I followed closely behind. "Get out!" he barked at the two club mommas sitting at the end of the room. I watched as they scurried away. No doubt G.T. had been inside both of them.

"Why the fuck are you so pissed at Princess?" I said, plopping down next to him.

"That's none of your fucking business," he clipped as I tried to hold my anger in check.

"It is my business. And since you're not gonna tell me, I'll tell you what I think."

"I don't give a shit what you think."

"Too bad. Casey." His demeanor didn't change as he stared blankly at the wall in front of him. "It all revolves around her. You're actually pissed at your sister for getting out of the joint, because that's what ultimately sent your piece of ass away."

His head snapped as his eyes narrowed. "You fucking call her that again, and I'll pound your ass."

Throwing my head back, I laughed hard. Stupid fucker. "Like I said, it's not Princess's fault. It's your own. Get your fucking shit together."

Getting up from the couch, I didn't bother looking back at G.T. I had shit to do before the meeting.

Harlow

MOVING into Cruz's house went much better than I thought it would. Tug and the B.Boys worked their ass off moving shit from my apartment to here. I didn't keep much furniture, but a shit ton of clothes. I really wanted my clothes.

When I first entered the house, I instantly felt at peace, like something in the home grounded me, something I really hadn't felt before. Being on edge was just something that I lived with for so long that being at peace was only something I felt on Sting, never in a home.

The front door opened as I turned to see my handsome man coming in, his hair a mess, making my mouth water. God, I loved him.

Wrapping my arms around him, I smashed my lips to his. I needed to taste him. Never in a million years did I think I'd fall this hard for a brother, but now, I'm in it. Hard. "Well hello to you, too, Babe." His sexy voice always made my pussy cream. I take that back, everything this man did, made me want him in a way I never thought possible.

Those one-night stands were nothing compared to this.

Moving him to the couch, I pushed him down, so he was sitting as I climbed up on top of him, straddling him as I kissed him relentlessly. My hips began to move quickly as his cock hit my clit in just the right spot. "Take it off," he growled, and I wasted no time standing and stripping. Cruz flung his shirt off and unbuttoned his pants just enough to pull his hard erection out.

"Ride me," he said, stroking his cock up and down. Climbing on top, I positioned him at my entrance and slammed down on him hard. "Fuck," he groaned as I squeezed the inner muscles of my pussy over and over again, working him up. His hands went to my hips as he began forcing my body up and down at an intense pace. My eyes began to roll in the back of my head when he barked, "Eyes on mine." I instantly followed. Watching the passion I had for this man swell in his eyes was my undoing. I needed to come, squeezing him with everything I had. "Come now," he commanded, and I detonated, shattering into a million pieces around him. Cruz thrust three more times, grunted my name, and buried himself deep in my body.

"I love you, Babe."

"Love you, too." Happiness surrounded me like a bubble that I never wanted to escape.

CONTINUE READING FOR THE EPILOGUE...

EPILOGUE
Cruz

FUCK! FUCK! FUCK! THIS WAS NOT SUPPOSED TO FUCKING happen. I heard gunfire everywhere, so much that we had no fucking clue where it was all coming from. Fuck.

Firing back was getting us nowhere, and at this point we were getting backed into a fucking corner. This meeting with Rabbit was not supposed to fucking happen like this. Talk. That's all this was about. Yeah, fucking right. Tell that to the fucking bullet whizzing by my head.

When we arrived, Rabbit's crew was waiting for us. What we didn't expect was the T-Dart crew to be with him. T-Dart's had a thing for us from several years ago that I only heard about by word of mouth. It was said that T-Dart's leader, Zane and Diamond had a falling-out over some land, but that dispute was settled a long time ago with us acquiring the land. But with Zane having died about a year ago, his boy Paine took over the gavel. Paine was a mean motherfucker, who apparently didn't see this beef as settled any longer as the gun he had pointed at us was shooting bullets one after another.

Having ridden bikes here, the only blockage we had was the cage that Tug and Buzz followed us in, but it was about twenty feet away, and getting to it was becoming a challenge. Instead, we were using our bikes as a shield. Diamond, Pops, G.T., Dagger, Rhys, Zed, Becs, and I were all shooting to save each other lives. But the bullets kept coming.

"Get behind us, Diamond!" Dagger yelled over the gunfire. He must have realized, too, that this shit was going bad really quickly. But like always, Diamond stood with us, not wanting the protection that we needed him to have right now.

As the fire continued, we took a small opportunity to move to the cage, quickly. Everything from this moment happened in slow motion. More gunfire.

Diamond rushed to the cage as shots began hitting him. G.T. pushed him out of the way trying to block him. Shots continued as they stuck G.T. Running after him; Dagger covered me as I grabbed G.T. under his arms and pulled him behind the cage. Pops was on Diamond pulling him out of the line of fire. Suddenly the sound of automatics started ringing through the air as grunts and groans filled everything.

Pops was with Diamond while I looked over G.T. to see the wounds. He had a shot to his chest and one to his shoulder. So much fucking blood. Shit! Pulling off my cut and then my t-shirt, I covered the wound, putting as much pressure on it as I could, to stop the bleeding. The automatic was still going off, but there were no shots coming from the other guys. "What the fuck is going on?!" I yelled.

"Tug and Buzz!" Dagger shot out. "They're holding them off. I'm going in." Dagger jumped into the side door of the cage grabbing one of the autos inside and began shooting at everything that wasn't us.

"Pops! We gotta get out of here... G.T.'s bleeding bad!" Looking over at Pops, I could see his arms were wrapped around Diamond. "Pops!"

He looked over at me. "He's gone."

Vomit seeped into my mouth. Gone? What the fuck? "Everyone in the fucking cage! Now!" I barked as we all loaded quickly. "Fucking drive!"

Buzz jumped into the driver's seat, speeding down the road right after everyone piled in on top of each other. G.T. laid in my arms while Pops continued to hold Diamond. Dagger was on the phone with who I'd assume was Doc, so he'd be waiting for us. As the cage sped away, the shots ceased, and we somehow got the fuck out.

"Talk Pops," Zed said from the corner staring at the sight in front of us.

"He's gone. Diamond's dead." His voice was solemn and broken. "How's my boy?" He asked, looking at me.

"Bleeding a lot. Bullet hit something."

"Fuck!" Pops yelled. "Drive faster!" he barked at Buzz, who slammed on the gas.

Pulling up to the clubhouse, Dagger, and I carried a barely conscious G.T. in, laying him on the pool table. The gasps came from the bitches in the corner. "Get the

302 | RYAN MICHELE

fuck out!" I yelled as they scurried away. Doc was already there and waiting.

Pops and Zed carried in Diamond placing him on the couch. Doc went over to him first, feeling the side of his throat. "He's gone. Cover him up," he barked, rushing over to G.T. "What the fuck happened here? They shot his fucking artery."

Doc didn't expect us to answer but got straight to work on patching up G.T. As he barked shit he needed, Breaker was on the move.

"Lockdown this fucking place, now! Get your families here, now!" Pops barked out as he grabbed his phone and dialed, no doubt getting Ma here.

I did the same. "Princess, get Cooper and get to the clubhouse now!" I said as soon as she answered.

"What's going on?"

"I'll explain when you get here. Come now. Load the cage up with shit for us for a couple weeks. And move fast."

"Got it. Be there soon." I hung up, going back to G.T.'s side. He lay there completely out of it while Doc did whatever the hell he was doing.

"Go to my van, get the blue cooler. It's got blood," Doc barked to no one in particular, but Zed was closest to the door and took off.

After Doc stitched and pumped G.T. full of blood, he removed his gloves, snapping them as he did. "He needs rest and take these meds, but he should live." He reached in his bag pulling out a vial and needle. "This is morphine. He needs it every four hours for today. I'll be back tomorrow morning and see what he needs from there."

"I'll do it," I said knowing that Princess would be more than likely the one that would be at his side whether he liked it or not.

"Fine. Put him in his bed and don't let him move except to get up and piss. He'll be coming to at any time." Doc turned to Pops. "What do you want to do with Diamond?"

"Know a guy at the cemetery. We'll get him fixed up." Doc nodded and headed out the door.

Fuck! I knew what this meant. We were at war.

CONTINUE with the Ravage MC family in Seduce Me available now!

ABOUT RYAN

Ryan Michele is the *Wall Street Journal* and *USA Today* **Bestselling author** of over 40 romantic suspense novels. She found her passion bringing fictional characters to life, being in an imaginative world where anything is possible. Her knack for the **unexpected twists and turns** will have you on the edge of your seat with each page. She is best known for **her alpha, bad boy bikers and strong, independent heroines who refuse to back down.** When she's not writing, you can find her on her swing, watching the water ripple in the pond and daydreaming about her next book.

Join my Reader Group: https://www.facebook.com/ groups/RyansSultrySinners/
Sign Up for my https://www.subscribepage.com/ 918BackmatterSignUps

facebook.com/AuthorRyanMichele

twitter.com/Ryan_Michele

instagram.com/author_ryan_michele

BB bookbub.com/authors/ryan-michele

ACKNOWLEDGEMENTS

Thank you to everyone who took the time to read Princess and Cruz's story. I absolutely loved writing them and hope you loved Cruz and Princess as much as I do.

Thank you to the following women who took time out of their lives to help me with this book: Lori, Jade, Becky, Sarah, Megan, Melissa, Dawn and Shey. This book is what it is because of all of your feedback and help. I couldn't have done it without you.

Lori. I don't even know where to start. Thank you doesn't seem to be enough, but I'll start there—Thank you. Not only for your help, but for the countless hours just chatting, learning and talking about books. I am utterly grateful for you—Thank you.

Jo. Thank you.

Editor: Chelsea Kuhel
Editor: Laura Hampton
Cover Artist: Cassy Roop, Pink Ink Designs

Thank you for reading!

Ryan
Michel

.